the incredible

HADLEY HILL

TAI STITH

OWL ROOM
press

Body text set in Baskerville

Cover text set in Scandiebox One, Polly Rounded, and Avenir

Copyright © 2017 Owl Room Press

ISBN-13: 978-0-692-95930-5

For I, N, L, and D:
My partners in adventure and mystery.

ACKNOWLEDGMENTS

Much gratitude to Michelle, Kat, and Mindy. Thank you for your attention to detail, creative insights, and dedication to making this a much better book!

PART ONE

chapter one

The wheat fields skimmed by, broken only by the occasional barn and lone grove of oak trees. Ari Cartwright gazed out the window. Sunlight shone through, highlighting some light blonde streaks in her otherwise medium brown hair. Freckles dappled her cheeks and the bridge of her nose, barely contrasting from her olive skin. She glanced in the side mirror on the passenger side of the car. She shielded her deep brown irises from the early summer sun as she looked out the window on the other side of the car. More fields. More livestock. More country.

Ari was accustomed to skyscrapers and suburbs for as far as the eye could see. The view from the car window was different altogether.

"How much farther?" Ari's forehead propped against the window.

"Well, from the looks of it, we're getting pretty close. Getting excited?" She could tell her father was trying to sound cheerful.

Excited was the last word Ari would use to describe herself at this moment. She had just finished up ninth grade and missed her friends, missed her old apartment, and longed for just about everything familiar about the life she had previously known. Her dad had just taken a new job, hundreds of miles and a state away, and she was beginning to feel very overwhelmed by it all.

A green interstate sign announced the upcoming town of Rivers. An off-ramp and a few intersections later, Ari and her father had gone through the entire town of Rivers and had turned off on a little-traveled road that ascended from the valley floor.

"Is the house up here somewhere?" she asked.

"I think we're on the right road, Ari." her dad said, rustling the

1

map. "We're looking for Hadley Lane; that's our stop."

She watched the road signs, which were becoming few and far between. There were more and more trees now, and the road kept climbing higher. An old hand-painted sign was hiding behind an evergreen branch. "Hadley Hill," it whispered with faded brushstrokes.

"Wait—Dad, I think that's it."

They made a right-hand turn, crossed a single set of railroad tracks, and started up the road. After a stand of evergreens, the trees suddenly cleared to reveal an old but dignified two-story farmhouse. It was newly painted white, with an oak tree shading the front yard. On the wraparound deck, a porch swing swayed in the summer breeze. This was so completely different, so much *bigger* than where she lived before.

"Here we are! Ari, this is our new house! It's even bigger than how it looked online. Wow..." His voice drifted off a moment and they sat in awed silence. Finally, her dad turned off the engine. "Ready to check it out?"

They made their way up the front steps and Ari's dad used his key to unlock the grand front door. It squeaked open to reveal an empty foyer. Sounds echoed off the shiny wood floors and bare walls. The house was cold and silent and the walls were stark white. Ari slowly went upstairs as her dad surveyed the downstairs.

The upper floor consisted of four bedrooms: one master bedroom, two rooms on the right side of the hallway, and one at the very end of the hallway. Ari was able to choose her room for the first time in her life. *Maybe moving isn't all bad*, she thought. She walked toward the door of the first room. It opened with an ominous creak. Ari peeked her head inside. *Too small for my bedroom*, she thought. On down the hallway she went, checking each room to see which one suited her best. Her mom and younger sister Lily would move into the house at the end of the summer, and it was up to Ari and her dad to set up the house as best they could before September. Finally she came to the last door at the end.

"*Ooohhh*," she breathed as she opened the door. Despite its bareness, the room was magnificent. Two rectangular windows flanked an arched window, complete with its own window seat. Sunlight poured in from all the windows and reflected on the polished wood floors. "I found my room!" she yelled to no one in particular. Dropping her backpack on the floor, Ari crossed the room and sat in the window seat. From here, it seemed like she could see the whole hilltop and the valley below. To the north, there was the back of a large pasture, which included the backyard. It looked like, long ago, the backyard and gardens had been quite beautiful, but now were in sad disrepair. At the edge of their pasture, the oak and fir trees took over and continued to the valley floor.

The only house she could see nearby was the top of another farmhouse sticking out above the oak trees, probably at the end of Hadley Lane. She wondered who lived there.

"So, this one looks nice. You're claiming it?" Her dad appeared in the doorway.

"It's just right," Ari said decidedly.

"Great, I'll start bringing your boxes up. I think the moving truck is here. Why don't you be in charge of unpacking?"

"Alright," Ari followed her dad downstairs. Within moments, she was hauling her boxes up to her new room. Opening the first one, she carefully peeled away sheets of newspaper that protected a bundle of photo frames. The first photo she unwrapped was of her mom, standing in the kitchen of their San Francisco apartment.

A pang of sadness hit Ari. The home she'd known for her entire life was being packed up and emptied out over the course of the summer. The day before Ari and her dad began driving up to their new home, Ari had caught her mom in tears, standing in a doorway.

Her mom had been scrubbing away at the doorframe where

she'd marked Ari and Lily's heights. The markings where Ari had stood at one year old, two years, three years...all gone with the swipe of a sponge. Of course, her mom had photographed the pen markings before cleaning them off, but it didn't hurt any less as her mom wiped them clean. Ari had hugged her mom and held back tears of her own.

"The move will be good, Ari," her mom had assured her, despite her tears. "This promotion is something your dad and I have been hoping for, for a long time." Her mom had paused. "We just didn't anticipate the move to be...so far away. We thought we'd still be in California, at least."

In the silence of the empty room, Ari studied the photo of her mom. It had only been a few days since she'd seen her last, but her mom was as close a friend to her as any of the other friends Ari had left in San Francisco.

Ari set the photo on the window seat, since none of her furniture had been moved in yet. She was about to unwrap another photo frame when she heard a noise outside. She looked out the window. Everything looked the same as before—*wait!* Ari thought she saw something moving through the oaks at the edge of the pasture. She looked closer to see if it would reappear, but it didn't. Without thinking too much of it, Ari went back to her unpacking.

chapter two

It took Ari several days before most of her belongings were in place. Ari's dad put her in charge of figuring out where all the furniture would be arranged. Never in her life had she been able to decide the layout of a house, and part of her found it thrilling, while the rest of her pined for her former home. Ari tried her hardest to focus on the task of making the old, but dignified, farmhouse into a home for herself and her Dad.

She was beginning to get a sense for her environment, for the house, and the town below them. She still missed her friends and her mom and Lily so much, but with the massive amount of possessions they had to move and organize, the days went quickly. The first Saturday after they arrived, she ventured out into the backyard for a quick break.

She could see that long ago, the garden had been beautifully designed. Once-white trellises were now faded with peeling paint. Almost hidden stone borders curved around the lawn with graceful lines. An overgrown rose garden still bloomed with rambling abandon. A solitary greenhouse, paneled in frosted glass with a verdigris frame, occupied the far corner of the yard. A cobblestone path visited each section of the garden, from the steps of the house's wraparound deck to the arched trellis with a bench underneath, to the old marble birdbath, all the way out to the edge of the oak grove.

Ari smiled as she thought about her mom's affinity for plants. Unfortunately, living in the city hadn't allowed many opportunities for true gardening. Her mom had to settle for dozens of seedlings in terra cotta pots on the roof of their flat.

A vision flashed through Ari's mind. What if she could give new life to this once-cared for garden? What if she could have it done before her mom moved in? She smiled as she considered the surprise of a lifetime for her mother. She figured it didn't matter that she had no experience growing things. She was always up for trying new challenges.

"Dad!" she yelled, running towards the back deck. "Dad! I want to fix up the backyard for mom, before she moves up here, you know? Now she'll have all this space and wouldn't it be awesome if it was all beautiful for her?" Ari breathlessly landed on the back deck. Her dad looked up in surprise. "Can you imagine how happy she'd be if she had an amazing garden?"

"That sounds like a great idea. I'm glad you've got a plan, Ari. I was starting to worry you'd die of boredom out here," Ari's dad gave her a sad smile. "I know how hard it must be for you, missing all your friends and half your family." Ari nodded in agreement. She then looked back to the garden. A flash of white caught her eye. Something was definitely moving through the oak trees at the edge of their pasture!

"Dad! Did you see that? I thought I saw something! Did *you* see something in the trees, Dad?

"See what, now?" Her dad shielded his eyes and looked to where Ari was pointing. "What did you see?"

"I don't know. I mean, it was white, I think." Ari shook her head but didn't stop watching the trees.

"Sorry, hon, I guess I didn't see it. It could've been a neighbor's cow, for all we know. Heck, we should probably go next door sometime and introduce ourselves."

Ari couldn't see the closest neighbor's house from where she stood, but she had gazed upon the top story of their house from her room above. She hadn't seen any people, just a light or two go on at night. She hadn't even heard any other noises. That was another thing she was having a hard time adjusting to: the utter lack of urban noise that the countryside was famous for. In the few days she'd been there, she'd felt nearly suffocated in silence. It was almost like sensory deprivation. Where were the sounds of life? Voices, honking cars, rushing traffic and echoes off the glass-plated buildings: these were the sounds that brought her comfort. It was all she'd known.

6

Her dad was right. She needed a project to get her mind off the things she missed so much. She ran inside the house, got a pencil and notepad, and went outside. Gazing upon the garden, she started making a list of all the things they would need to get it back into shape.

They had hauled six huge bags of mulch from the car to the backyard before Ari collapsed on the porch. "Gahh. I'm done for a minute. Dad, do we have any juice? Or lemonade? Or anything cold?"

Ari and her dad had made a trip to the only hardware/garden/auto parts store in Rivers and had come back with a pretty good load of necessary tools and supplies to get started. "Yeah, you wait here." Her dad wiped his feet on the doormat. "I'm going to get us a huge pitcher of lemonade mixed up, then we can start weeding this mess. Sound good?"

She nodded and closed her eyes. She listened to the shrill hum of some bugs—whatever they were—and the chirping of nearby birds. A slight wind rustled everything in the garden. A heavy-sounding clank suddenly resounded from somewhere nearby. Ari's eyes snapped open.

She stepped off the porch and walked into the garden. Following the cobblestone path, she left the formal garden and started towards the pasture. The stones of the path had almost disintegrated in the pasture grass, but she had little trouble following it. At the end of the pasture, she came to the grove of oaks. Two substantial square stone columns stood sentinel on each side. Brass plaques, with one honeybee on each, adorned each column. She gazed into the woods. Dare she follow the path?

Ari looked back at the house, which was a good distance away; within shouting distance, definitely. But the oak grove seemed dense and endless. Ari paused. A brush of air startled her, then she nervously giggled. Boy, if her friends could see her now. Big city girl, terrified of the big, bad country. Ari snorted and stepped into the grove.

If it had been silent at her house, it was doubly silent here. The sky was obscured by the canopy of oak leaves. What confused her was the definition of the trail she was on. It had obviously been used recently; leaves were shuffled out of the way, and the dirt was packed. Had animals done this? Was it a deer trail? Ari didn't know. She stepped a few more feet into the trees, and abandoned the path for a moment. Ari examined at a nearby oak tree, and for the first time in her life, she thought she saw a real bird's nest, complete with small blue eggs.

"Ow!" Ari had been so intent on getting closer to the nest that she stubbed her toe on something in the ground. Looking down, she noticed a glint of metal. Bending, she brushed crispy, dried oak leaves from the ground below. Ari took a deep breath and blew off the rest of the leaves to reveal a circular shape. It was huge! Maybe three feet in diameter, it reminded her very much of manholes that dotted city streets. This was no manhole, however. Or if it was, it was certainly the most ornate manhole she had ever encountered. It protruded from the ground about an inch, which was how she had stubbed her toe. A delicate stylized design of leaves, vines, and tiny honeybees had been wrought in brass. And in the very center, an old-fashioned keyhole presented itself. "Woowww..." Ari shook her head. What was this thing?

"Ari? Aaaaribelllle!" Because of her venture she had totally forgotten about her dad and the lemonade. She so badly wanted to find out what this beautiful thing was, but she had to get back to the house. As she ran back, she contemplated telling her dad. *Maybe not until I find out what it is*, she thought to herself.

"Exploring, I see!" her dad chuckled and handed her an icy glass of lemonade. "Ready to start gardening?" He gave her a reassuring smile. "Your mom is going to love this, Ari. This is such a great idea."

"Thanks, Dad. Let's start." Ari picked up a weed puller and a bucket, and began working. She was itching to get back to the brass circle, but knew it had to wait.

*   *   *

Ari and her dad had worked late into the evening. With the long summer days, it gave them plenty of time to work outdoors, with light to spare at the end of the day.

Around sunset, Ari's dad went inside and started unpacking more things. She could hear kitchen utensils and dishes clanking around, with jazz playing in the background. Always jazz at night; that was her dad's trademark. Whatever he did in the evening was always accompanied by Miles Davis or Louis Armstrong or John Coltrane and the faint scent of pipe smoke. She smiled. It didn't seem so awfully quiet anymore and the house they had moved to was just beginning to feel like home. Knowing her dad was occupied at the moment, Ari figured she had just enough light left to take one more peek at the brass circle.

Running down the path, she paused as she entered the grove. It was much darker within the trees than out in the open. She was a little scared, but her curiosity overwhelmed her. She jogged back to the brass circle.

Ari ran her fingers across the vines. She could barely see the details now that the dusky horizon was losing light. She tried in vain to pry the circle open. It had a keyhole; she figured it must open somehow. She felt along the edge for a hinge. Just as she caught the edge of something with her hand, a sudden noise of crunching leaves sent her wheeling around. A boy was standing right behind her.

chapter four

"Aaaughhh!!" Ari jumped back and onto the brass circle, catching her breath. The circle made a deep, hollow thump as she landed. The boy jumped back as well, and was poised as if he was going to run away. "Wait!" Ari recovered quickly, then lowered her voice. "Wait. Who are you?" she hissed.

"I, uh, I live in the house at the other end of the trees." His voice wavered, as if he was still deciding whether to run away or not. Ari saw he had dark hair, and was lanky but muscled. He was taller than her, even as she was standing atop the brass circle. "I have to go," he said, and dashed through the woods before she could object. Ari got down off the circle. Her heart was still pounding from being startled. It was nearly pitch black in the grove now. She'd had enough surprises for one night; it was time to head home.

Ari got up early the next morning, excited and mystified about what she'd found the day before, and the boy she'd encountered in the oak grove. As always, though, there were things that needed to be done before she could explore.

"Ari, would you mind running down to the mailbox and putting these bills in for me? We haven't even been here a week and they're already pouring in. Hmmph." Her father chortled and smiled as she reached for the envelopes. "How'd you sleep last night?"

Ari just shook her head; she never slept well in new places before, and this new house was no exception. Especially with the intriguing events that had taken place, which she'd run through in her mind, several times over. And she'd heard some noises in the distance. People, or a person, yelling, or loudly talking, or perhaps both. Maybe she'd dreamed them; she couldn't be sure. She never knew which noises were normal in this new place.

Ari snatched the envelopes from his hand and dashed out the screen door. Their mailbox was at the bottom of their long driveway, which met up with the driveway of the house at the end of the grove, which she assumed to be the boy's house. Neither house could be seen from the mailboxes, but it wasn't too long of a walk.

She stuffed the letters in their oversized and well-rusted mailbox, inherited from the previous tenants. The name *HADLEY* was nearly worn off the front of the box, and she stood there momentarily, trying to decide it was part of their address that had worn off, or if it was the name of the previous owners. She made a mental note to ask her dad if he knew.

Turning to head back up the road, she noticed the boy from last night was coming around the corner, heading towards her. He slowed when he saw her, but continued walking. She noticed he also had something in his hand to be put in the mailbox. He nodded hello.

"You scared me pretty good last night," she said, with a small smile. "My name is Ari. We just moved in next door. I don't think we got properly introduced." She held out her hand.

"I'm Dane," he said simply, and shook her hand. She hadn't noticed much about him the night before, but in the sunlight she could see he had brilliant hazel eyes: jade green on the outside, with deep brown splashes on the inside. He had dark brown hair, not exactly black, as she had though last night. "Sorry I scared you. I didn't mean to. I was taking a walk and didn't know anyone had moved into the Hadley house." He had an air of aloofness about him.

"Ah. That answers one of my questions," Ari pointed to the mailbox. "The previous family was the Hadleys," she concluded.

"Well, that was a long time ago," Dane said nonchalantly, putting a letter his box. "House has been empty a long time. No one's been in it since I've lived here."

She was going to ask how long that was, but he simply turned around and headed up the road again. "Hey," Ari called. "It was nice to meet you." He half-turned his head and nodded.

Ari shrugged her shoulders and headed back to the house. "I met one of the neighbors," she told her dad as she arrived, picking up her gardening gloves.

"Oh yeah? I was going to go down the road today and introduce myself, but it sounds like you beat me to it. Do tell."

"Um, well, they have a boy about my age, maybe within a year or two, I don't know. He didn't say much. He didn't say anything about his parents." Ari headed out the back screen door, grabbing a silly straw sun hat that they'd picked up at the hardware store. It seemed much hotter here than what she was used to, and she'd noticed in the mirror that morning that a new bloom of freckles had banded across her face.

"What are we doing today, Dad? Finishing the bark dust and then what?" They surveyed what they had accomplished in the garden so far: the rose beds had been totally cleared of weeds and some of the bark dust laid, and they had mowed the knee-high wheat field that had sprouted in place of a lawn. It was a start, but there was still so much to do. "Are we going to be able to finish this before September?" Ari had her doubts.

"Oh sure, hon. No problem. We just have to keep at it, that's all. Even after we get it looking great, we'll have to maintain it. Don't worry," he said with a chuckle, "you won't be running out of things to do here for a long time. Let's edge the path and all the stone borders today," he pointed at the cobblestone path, which was obscured by weedy grass. "I'll put down that fertilizer we bought, and maybe we can get the lawn in good shape."

Ari took the odd-looking tool, aptly called a "weed-whacker" by the guy at the hardware store, and started buzzing the grass along the edge of the path. It was loud and made her arms vibrate with an unpleasant sensation. However, she quickly saw the path had better definition and looked quite lovely when completely uncovered. She stopped the tool and turned towards her dad.

"Hey, what do you know about the people who owned the house before us?" she asked him. He looked up from the fertilizer spreader.

"Oh, hmm, well, I don't know too much of the history, really, just what the real estate agent told me over the phone. She said that it had actually been built by one of the founders of Rivers and, in its day, was a spectacular home. I guess they were quite wealthy. Hadley was the family, which is what the road and hill are named for. You know, you should check the Rivers library for more information. I know it's a historical house; they'd probably have a lot of stuff on the family and the town. Just from the looks of the garden, I'm sure there was a whole crew of servants and gardeners who tended to the place. Wish we had that kind of money," he chuckled as the fertilizer spreader *tk-tk-tked* its way across the lawn.

Ari went back to buzzing the path. She followed it all the way to the edge of the pasture, where the massive stone columns were. She ran her fingers along the bronze bas-relief bees. Why were there columns here? And what was the brass circle that she'd found yesterday? She couldn't see it from the edge of the pasture; it was well hidden behind the oak with the bird's nest. Ari wanted so badly to drop the weed whacker and examine the oak grove more, but she didn't want to give away her secret yet.

chapter five

The garden looked much improved at the end of the day. Ari and her dad were both surprised how a days' worth of work made their backyard so much lovelier than it had been before. It seemed to come to life with care. Ari smiled to herself as she swayed on the rocking chairs on the back porch. The low evening sun was drenching the sky in a pinkish-purple light. They had eaten dinner on the back deck, and Ari was incrementally beginning to like this place. She still ached for her friends, and her mom and Lily, but she also couldn't remember the last time they had eaten outside. She wished so much that her mom and little Lily could be here sooner.

"Dad, can I call mom?"

Her dad was organizing his home office inside, with the jazz softly playing, and all the windows were open. "Sure, come get my cell," he called. She went through the back door, through the large kitchen, and took a right down the hallway. Pipe smoke was escaping the room in small tendrils. Miles Davis was playing on the radio. He tossed her his cell phone and she punched in the numbers, and returned to the back porch.

"Hello?" her mom's sweet voice answered.

"Mom! Oh my gosh, I've missed you so much. How are you and Lily doing? How is your job going?" She took a breath and heard all about how her mom was wrapping up her job, getting ready to transfer, and how Lily was doing in her summer camp. She then started telling her mom about the huge farm house, her magnificent room, and how she and her dad were making it as nice as possible before the rest of the family moved in. Ari left out details about the garden; however, it was *so* hard for her to keep secrets. Ari wanted to tell her mom every detail about the work she was doing in their backyard, and it took every bit of willpower she had to refrain from doing so, although she did hint that there were big projects going on.

Suddenly, Ari heard a clanking sound somewhere nearby. She

moved the phone away from her ear, straining to hear for more sounds.

She thought she heard hard footfalls. Ari quickly rose from her chair and ran through the garden, following the path. "Mom, can I call you back tomorrow? I, uh, have to do my chores." Her mom bid good-bye and Ari hung up. By now Ari was at the entrance to the grove.

She always seemed to pause here. She wasn't exactly afraid, but she didn't know what was in those woods. Finally she took a deep breath and charged ahead. She almost expected to find Dane on the path again, but as she got deeper and deeper into the woods, Ari found herself to be completely alone. She then turned to where the brass circle had been. Where was it? She knew it had been here, for there stood the oak with the bird's nest. She brushed the ground with her foot. Sure enough, there it was—under a pile of leaves. Someone had deliberately covered it up again.

What was going on here? Obviously she wasn't the only one who knew about this place. She took note of the designs on the circle; they were beautifully ornate. If the circle did indeed open, it must weigh a lot. If she ever found the key, would she even be able to open it? Suddenly, her dad's cell phone rang. Ari startled so badly she dropped it onto the circle. It made a terribly loud noise as it vibrated across the metal. "Shhhh!!" Ari hissed at the phone. Grabbing it, she ran out of the grove and answered; it was someone for her dad. Her heart was still jackhammering in her chest as she ran the phone to him.

Later that night, she was getting ready for bed and she gazed around her room. So far, she'd unpacked most of what they'd brought with them, and she was pleased with how cozy her space was. She loved how she could look down at the garden they were working so hard on. She propped her knee on the window seat cushion and heaved the old wood-framed window open. It was still wonderfully warm outside. The sky was still a bit dusky but the stars were starting to pierce through. How bright they were out here! No light pollution from distant cities, she figured.

She listened to the crickets, frogs, and buzzing bugs. Suddenly, she heard those noises again. She *hadn't* been dreaming the night before. The warm summer breeze was bringing sounds of voices, staccato shouts and a slamming door. It had to be the neighbors. *Dane's family?* she wondered. What was going on over there?

She listened for a few more moments. *Nothing.* Ari shook her head and turned in for the night, more mystified than ever.

*   *   *

The next morning, Ari's dad left for the first day of his new job. Ari stayed home and continued working on the garden. It was the first time she'd ever been alone for any real period of time. Usually she'd had a busy schedule that kept her away from home, or she was stuck watching Lily. Now, it was just her. She realized that she'd give just about anything to be able to have Lily around now.

Ari felt a little uneasy at first, but after a few hours in the garden, she had established a rhythm. She was startled when she looked up and saw Dane standing at the side yard, next to their driveway. "Uh, hey. Some of your mail was put in our box by mistake. I thought I'd drop it by." He waved an envelope in the air.

"Oh, thanks. That was nice of you." Ari walked up and took the envelope. Her curiosity overrode her normally shy disposition. She desperately wanted to know more about this tall, broad-shouldered boy from next door.

"Hey, wanna stick around for a while? I'm trying to get our yard nice for when my mom moves in, and you're welcome to hang out here...I mean, if you don't have anything else to do...like, no worries if you're busy or something..." Ari bit her lip and rolled her eyes at herself.

"No, I'm not busy, I can hang for a bit," Dane said casually. "Where are you from?"

"We're from San Francisco. I've, um, never lived anywhere but the city. This is a bit different." Dane nodded in agreement.

"Um, so, do you live with your parents up the driveway?" Ari asked.

"No," he said, shaking his head. "I live there with my aunt, Rhoda. That's it." He turned his head to the side and Ari noted his profile. He had a strong curved nose, a soft jaw, and his hair, as before, was mussed. She wanted to ask where his parents were, but thought against it. She didn't want to pry. Not yet.

She started pulling weeds out of the flower bed by the deck. "So, how long have you lived here?" she asked.

"Um, about four years," he said, with disdain in his voice, perhaps. She couldn't tell; she didn't know him well enough. He saw her weeding and knelt down beside her, picking out the weeds.

"You don't have to do that," Ari said with a laugh. "This is my project." She smiled.

"Got nothin' better to do," he said quietly and continued picking.

"Where do you go to school?" she asked.

"Rivers Union High School. I'll be a junior this year. It's not too bad. You'll make friends," he said, pulling out a long-rooted weed. She noticed a ball-chain necklace tucked under his white shirt.

"Hey, what's on your necklace?" she asked, pointing at the chain.

"Ah, nothin'. It's just a chain." He pulled at it and then went back to the weeds.

They kept working side by side for quite some time, accented by quiet conversation, but for the most part, they just worked. Ari was brimming with curiosity but she didn't want to drive away her only acquaintance with an endless barrage of questions. She didn't glean much information from Dane, only that he had a sibling somewhere, and that he didn't care much for his aunt. The whole day, he probably said about twenty words total, but Ari felt a certain sense of kinship towards him.

They heard a car drive down the road. "That's my aunt, I'd better go," Dane stood up and brushed the dirt from his jeans. "Nice weeding with you," he said as he jogged down the driveway.

Ari smiled. "Thanks for the help," she called. "Hey, wait! Dane!" He spun around, mid-jog. "Can you show me where the library is tomorrow?" she called.

"Sure," he said, then turned back to the road. Ari made a mental note to check the air in her bike tires before the next day.

The doorbell rang shortly after 10 a.m.. Ari opened it to see Dane standing there, his BMX bike laying in the front yard. "You ready?"

"Yeah," she replied, "let me get my backpack." Ari grabbed her messenger bag and locked the door. She ran to the side of the house where her old beach cruiser was parked. She thought she heard a snicker from Dane, but she turned to see him looking at her, straight-faced. "Nice bike. No, really, it's cool. But you'll need to go slow if you want me to keep up." He motioned at his smaller bike.

"No problem. It's downhill mostly anyway, right?" That much was true. They lived above the valley, and getting to the library wouldn't be the problem. Getting back would be. They set off and rolled down the gravel road all the way to the pavement. Ten minutes later, they were at the Rivers Public Library.

"What are you looking for?" Dane finally asked.

"Well, I just was wondering if there would be information on our house. I know it's old, and possibly it's on the historical record or something. Dad thought there might be some information on the Hadleys." She ran her finger along a row of books. They found the historical reference section and she began looking up the history of Rivers. She would pull out a book, check the index section under "H," and if she found the name, she'd put the book on the table. After fifteen minutes, she had only a handful of books, most of them with single-page references only. Dane had been picking at the books as well, but he was going about it a different way. "What if the Hadleys were just ordinary people, with no real importance?" he mused.

"That's ok too," she said, chuckling. "I'm not looking for anything in particular, just basic information, you know. I've never lived in a house with history. It helps me get my mind off of everything I miss." She lowered her voice. "I guess I'm just trying to like this place, because I think we'll be here for good. We might never go back to the city." She let her mind wander for a second, thinking of her friends, and the colorful beauty of the city.

"Hey," Dane looked up at her from his seat. "It's ok. I'm glad you're here." He smiled only with his eyes; she knew he was being sincere.

She pulled out another book and checked the H's. "Ooh, here's a good book; I think I've found something." She plunked down in the chair next to him and opened it up to the first reference. "Ok, this is about Reginald Hadley. It says he was a wealthy business owner and world traveler. 'Mr. Hadley moved to the city of Rivers in 1900.'" Ari flipped through the pages. "Oh! Oh! Whoooa! It's a picture of our house, I think..." Dane pulled the book over to his side and took a look.

"Yeah, I think you're right. Look at the gardens; everything is in the same place. Wow, they were really beautiful. You could probably make a copy of this page and maybe use it as a guide as you're restoring the garden," he said, actually sounding a little excited about their discovery.

"Dane, that's an awesome idea. Anything else in there?"

He flipped through the book. "Uh, there's some more history on Reginald, I think. It kinda sounds like he went to Russia and came back with a wife in 1905."

Ari snorted. "A Russian mail-order bride?"

Dane smirked and continued reading. "It says he built the house on 'the hill above town,' which I assume is our hill, 'immediately after his extensive trip to Russia, in which he returned with a well-known ballerina, Nadia Varishnikov. She was known for her gardening skills and was responsible for creating the gardens behind the main house,'" he finished.

"Hmmm..." Ari stared out the sunny window and was lost in thought for a few minutes. If Nadia and Reginald were the owners of the house, and they had settled there around 1905, how much longer had they lived in the house? Did they have children? Who else had lived in the house?

"Is Ari short for anything?" Dane questioned, breaking her momentary reverie.

"Huh?"

"Your name. Is it short for something, or is your name just Ari?" His eyes met hers.

"Oh, sorry. It's short for Aribelle. Aribelle Leigh Cartwright. What's yours?" She gave a quick smile, thinking this was a way off-topic conversation, but she found it odd that she'd forgotten to ask his full name yet.

"I'm Dane Hadley. Why do you ask?"

Ari gasped in surprise, but tried to keep her composure for the sake of the other library patrons. "*What?!*" Ari hissed at him. "You mean...are you? Seriously? Same family?"

"Yup."

"Arrgh! Why didn't you tell me this, say, before we came to the library?" She tried to keep her voice at a low whisper, despite her excitement.

"You never asked. Besides, I actually don't know much about my family at all. You know how I live with my aunt Rhoda, right? Well, that's my uncle's wife. Unfortunately, my uncle passed away right after I moved here. My dad is a Hadley, a grandson of Reginald and Nadia, and I haven't talked with my mom in a long time. Rhoda knows nothing about the family history. I don't think she even cares. So, I'm as interested in it as you are."

Ari was still reeling. "Why don't you live in our house? It belonged to them, and you're their descendant. Doesn't that mean you would've inherited it, or something?"

Dane shook his head. "Rhoda did inherit the whole property, including our house, which used to be the servant's quarters. But, eventually she had to divide the property and sell your half so she could support her bad habits." His tone seeped with distain.

She lowered her head. "I'm sorry," was all she could think to say. She almost wished she hadn't asked, but it was too late now.

He just waved it off. "Whatever. It's not a big deal to me. I'm just interested in the family history, I guess. Especially now that you're living in the house, making it nice again. It's really cool to see."

She gave a big smile, but then a thought occurred to her. If the property used to belong to his family, wouldn't he know about the brass circle? She weighed the possibility of asking him, but didn't want to chance it. If he really had never come across it, could she trust him by revealing it? She decided to wait.

They collected all the relevant books and headed back. The burning June sun was high in the sky, with fluffs of cottonwood drifting like summer snowflakes. Ari lugged all the books in her messenger bag. When the driveway became too steep to ride, they pushed their bikes up the gravel driveway to their houses. "Ugh, this is torture," Ari commented as she shifted the bag to her other shoulder.

"Here, let me take it. My bike isn't as heavy to push uphill."

"Ok, thanks. Wow, it's really hot today. You would think with all the land up here, they would've put a pool in somewhere," Ari wiped the sweat off her forehead.

"Ah, but they didn't have to," Dane said, sounding pleased.

"Whaddya mean?" Ari's curiosity was piqued.

They were rounding the corner where their driveways parted. "Follow me. Oh, you might want to get a swimsuit on," Dane mentioned. Ari dropped her books inside and grabbed a swimsuit and a towel. She met Dane in the backyard and they continued through the gardens, and then followed the cobblestone path. Ari started to get nervous and excited at the same time. Where was he taking her?

chapter seven

They entered the oak grove. It was so much cooler under dark canopy of the leafy trees. Dane proceeded along the path, but didn't pause near the brass circle. Instead, he kept walking deeper into the grove. Ari thought they might be almost halfway between her house and his, but couldn't be sure. The trees were so dense that she no longer could see anything outside the grove. Then, she saw a circle of light breaking through the fluttering canopy. Had they come to the other side of the grove?

No, it was simply an opening in the trees, perhaps about fifty feet across. The closer they got, Ari noticed the opening in the leaves. Then she saw it: a perfectly round pool of water, bordered with smooth rocks, and encircled by a four-foot rim of flat slate. Sunlight glistened on the glassy surface, revealing emerald-green water, sparkling with minerals. Dragonflies and the most elegant purple damselflies kissed the surface of the pool, sending off mini-ripples.

"Wow," she breathed. All she could do was take in her surroundings.

"Something wrong?" Dane was about to jump in, but he saw Ari hadn't even put her towel down.

"No, not at all...this is just so unbelievably beautiful," she slowly lowered down to the ground and set her towel on the slate stones. Dane threw his shirt to the side and jumped right in. Ari scooted to the edge and dangled a leg in. "Whhhooooaa! Holy cow, that's cold water!" She swung her legs out as quickly as they'd gone in. "Dane, how are you even swimming in there? It's freezing!"

Dane's head shot out of the water and he tried to conceal a small gasp. "It's not cold," he lied. As he surfaced, Ari noticed his necklace glinting in the sunlight. In the middle of his chest, a small, old-fashioned key dangled from the ball chain. Her eyes widened. *Was that the key to the brass circle?*

She gulped a huge breath of air and jumped in. She plunged into the icy water, and rocketed to the surface, gasping again.

"Hey, you made it," Dane had floated to the edge of the pool.

"I want to know about your necklace," Ari said between sputters. She swam over to him, despite the cold, and pulled the key towards her. "I want to know what this key is for."

Dane thought about it a moment. "It's something very special," he said slowly, in a low voice. "If I tell you, you have to promise me you won't tell anyone. Not your mom, not your dad, nobody. Got it?" He met her eyes, and she saw he was being absolutely serious.

Hugging her arms to her body, and with her teeth chattering, she nodded. "O-k-k-kay, I promise."

He pursed his lips and paused again. "When I first moved in with my aunt, I was putting my things in my room and I found it there. I didn't know what it went to, so I just kept it in a safe place. I didn't think anything about it until I was walking in the oak grove about two years ago. I stumbled across the brass thing that you found the other night, when I accidentally scared you. You *did* find it the other night, right?

"Yeah, I did. But I couldn't figure out what it was."

"Well, the key goes to the brass thing." Dane looked at her, then dipped under the water.

Ari rolled her eyes. She lifted herself out of the pool and grabbed her towel, wrapping herself tightly. Dane surfaced. She was about to ask if he intended to tell her about the brass circle, but suddenly a close voice broke the silence. An angry-sounding woman was yelling for Dane. His eyes widened. "Oh gosh, that's Rhoda. I need to go," he said, and in one motion hopped out of the pool and grabbed his t-shirt, throwing it over his head.

"Wait, Dane, where are you going?" Ari hopped up, still hugging her towel.

"I'm sorry, Ari, I have to go or I'll be in trouble. Remember," he said, as he headed towards his house, "don't tell anyone."

Ari nodded and Dane disappeared into the grove. She threw on her t-shirt and shorts over her swimsuit. Again, curiosity got the best of her. She waited a moment and then headed into the oak grove, in the direction of Dane's house.

Ari quickly threw on her shorts and t-shirt as she followed the path Dane had taken through the oaks. She could hear his aunt's voice angrily yelling something at him. Carefully, Ari picked her way behind the trees so she wouldn't be seen. Finally, she had a clear view of the house, Dane, and his aunt-by-marriage, Rhoda.

She was a larger woman, wearing a dirty oversized t-shirt and baggy jeans. It seemed that she was yelling at him for not doing a chore, and all Ari heard him say was "I was at the library. I'll just do it now, ok?"

What happened next made Ari cringe. Rhoda drew her hand back and threw it hard against Dane's face. He dropped back for a moment, but then returned to standing. She hadn't fully hit him, but it hadn't been a slap either. *All that for missing a chore?* Ari didn't understand. She watched as Dane reluctantly followed his aunt into the house.

Ari looked at the house. It too had once been beautiful, she could tell that much. However, it no longer resembled the tidy servant's quarters it once had been. Two windows were broken, the paint was peeling, and the front steps were falling apart. Nobody had cared for the property in ages. She turned to head back through the woods when yelling began in the house again. This time, she could hear Dane's voice yelling as well. Ari paused. Crashing sounds came from inside. What was going on in there?

Without warning, Dane came bursting from the front door. His aunt followed, but he outran her without any difficulty. "Forget it!" Dane yelled behind him. Ari suddenly realized he was headed straight for the path she was on. She froze. Could she hide? Would he see her? Not only was Dane heading her way; Rhoda was as well. Ari sensed danger in the situation. Before Dane reached her, she decided to run for it.

Turning, she headed back the exact same way they came:

weaving through the woods, past the pool, and then towards her own house. She doubled over near the brass circle; a side ache was killing her. She gasped for breath as she knelt for the ground. Heavy footsteps were close behind. Before she could react, Dane had nearly stumbled upon her. "Hey!" he caught himself, grabbing for a tree branch. "What are you doing here still?"

Before she could answer, they heard footsteps coming their way. Ari wanted desperately to avoid a confrontation with his aunt. Dane grabbed her arm, and they headed towards Ari's house. They rounded the corner and followed the path all the way into Ari's pasture. She could see her dad leaning over into the bearded irises. He turned at the sounds of fast footfalls.

"There you are," her dad said, standing straight. "Ah, this must be the neighbor. I'm Alan," he extended his hand to Dane.

"I'm Dane," he nodded once and tried to catch his breath. He furtively looked over his shoulder.

"I've been meaning to introduce myself to your family, but Ari and I have been so busy with the house I haven't gotten a chance. So, what have you guys been up to?"

"Well, Dad, let's go to the house and I'll show you what we found today," she took hold of her dad's arm and practically dragged him toward the house. She half expected Rhoda to come bursting out of the oak grove, but so far, she hadn't. "Dane showed me where the library was, and we collected some information about the Hadleys. Wanna see it?"

"I'd love to," he said, heading towards their porch.

"Um, I'd better head home now," Dane said, before Ari could protest. "Got chores to do," he muttered, glancing once again toward the oak grove. Ari shot him a worried look, but he didn't acknowledge it. "Nice to meet you, sir," he nodded at her dad, and headed up the driveway back to his house.

"I'm glad you've made a friend, Ari. Let's go check out what you found," her dad said with a smile.

For the rest of the evening, they poured over the books. Ari didn't mention that Dane was a Hadley, but with everything she read she tried to fit him into the picture. She read for so long that after a while, she drifted off amidst her books, with pipe smoke and faint strands of jazz floating through the background of her dreams.

*   *   *

Ari didn't see Dane for a few days. When her dad left each morning, she would work on the garden until it got too hot in the afternoon. Then she'd turn on the porch fan, sit on the old rocking chair, and get out her history books. She had a pad of sticky notes that she'd insert on each page that she found with relevant information about the Hadleys. She had so many questions for Dane, but she really didn't know if he'd be able to answer any of them. Each time she heard a noise outside, she'd look up, expecting to see him coming out of the oak grove. Each time, though, it was just leaves rustling in the hot afternoon breeze.

On a cool Friday morning Ari was standing at the edge of the cobblestone path, comparing the garden as it was now with a picture in one of the library books. It looked like she would have to replace some rhododendron bushes and encourage the wild roses to grow up the arched trellises. Also, there was some missing statuary. The old sepia-toned photo showed a St. Francis statue in the rose garden, and an small angel gracefully protecting the zinnias with her wings. Other than that, she thought they had a good chance of making it look almost like it once had.

A snapping twig caused her to whirl around. "Hey," Dane said, once again realizing that he had startled her. "Sorry, I didn't mean to scare you—again," he walked out of the grove and next to Ari.

"Hey, how are you doing?" She tried to sound casual, as if she hadn't seen what had happened between Rhoda and Dane a few days prior.

"Doin' ok, you know, just hanging around," he looked at the garden. "Wow, Ari, this is looking great. You've done so much work here. Can I see the picture?" She handed him the book. Tilting it, he looked at the photo, then the garden. "Do you see something missing?" he gave her a questioning look.

"Well, yeah, those statues aren't here anymore. And some plants, of course, are gone. Why? What do you see?

Dane pointed to one wall of the house. "Look here," he pointed to the photograph. "What's on the wall?"

Ari took the book back and squinted at the photo. Sure enough, hanging on the back wall of the house, there was a circular object. Ari examined it so closely that the image got lost in the halftone dots of the photo. She had missed it the first few times because it blended in as some kind of garden decoration, but now it looked quite familiar.

"Oh my gosh. It's the brass circle," she said, barely audible.

chapter nine

How did the same brass circle *get from the wall of the house to the oak grove*, Ari wondered. "Dane, c'mon. Please, I wanna see what's in there. You have the key. You can trust me. I promise."

Dane sighed and looked at Ari, as if he was trying to gauge her trustworthiness. "Ok, come on."

Ari nearly jumped from excitement. Dane headed down the path, his long legs taking giant strides, and she trotted behind. They came to the brass circle, which Ari noticed had been hidden once again. "Are you the one covering it with leaves?" she asked.

"Yeah. I can't take any chances on anybody finding it, you know?" Ari solemnly nodded.

Dane pulled the necklace from beneath his t-shirt and brought it over his head. He showed the key to Ari. It was about two inches long and had two prongs on the end, just like any old-fashioned key. The top was circular and quite ornate, with a single tiny honeybee in the center. "Ok, so the key goes into the keyhole like a regular key. But instead of just turning it one side, you have to turn it all the way around, like this." He inserted the key into the center of the brass circle, and turned it one complete rotation. There was a sound inside the lock, like something was rolling into place. "Ok, now feel around the front here," he took her hand and placed it under the front of the circle's rim. With her fingers, she could feel a button. "Push," he said, and she pressed in. The lid popped open, as if it had been tightly sealed.

"Whoa," she whispered. Though weighty, the lid wasn't difficult to lift. Immediately she looked down. Complete darkness was all she could see. "Um, how do we get down?" No ladder was evident, and she couldn't see the bottom. "Did you bring a flashlight?"

"No, we don't need one," he said. "If you turn around and lower yourself down, you can feel recessed steps in the side of the wall. Be careful that you don't slip off and hit your shin, though. It hurts pretty bad."

She turned her body and carefully stepped into the blackness. Sure enough, she could feel a solid step with her foot. Each step came slowly, but after counting seven steps, her foot hit solid ground. She looked up. Daylight illuminated only a small portion of the hole. Suddenly, she felt a wave of panic wash over her. Not being able to see what was down there with her made her extremely uneasy. She couldn't see Dane anymore. "Hey! Where are you?"

Dane's head appeared in the opening. "I'm coming. Why, you scared?" he said, perhaps with a tinge of amusement.

"No..." Ari felt her cheeks get warm. "It's just kinda dark down here; I can't see a thing." Dane hopped to the floor of the cavern. He handed her a match.

"There are candles along the wall; light them," he quietly ordered. She felt her way around. Striking the wooden match against the stone wall, she was finally able to see. Old-fashioned candles were housed in small insets built into the wall, one about every five feet. She lit each one and took in her surroundings.

They were in a small tile and brick-lined room, about ten feet by ten feet. Gold and glass tiles were inlaid in a border around the perimeter. The candlelight glinted off of each one, creating a breathtaking glow. The room was almost empty, except for a blanket and a pile of comic books on the floor, and a door on the far side of the wall. "Um?" Ari looked at the comic books, and then at the door.

"Oh, I don't have a key for that. I've tried this one and it doesn't work. I've looked all over our house and I never found another key. I don't know what it goes to." he sounded apologetic. "So this is it. It's really beautiful the way they did the tiles and stuff," he motioned at the walls, running his hands along the glass tiles. Ari gave him a questioning look and glanced at the blanket and comic books. "Oh, yeah, sometimes I come down here to get away from...stuff. You know," he shrugged.

Ari lightly brushed the tiles with her hand. "This is really weird. Why would somebody make an ornate room like this, underground?"

"Dunno. Must've been important, though."

"So you know what we have to do now, right?" Ari said, with a glint in her eye. "We've gotta find the key to this," she said, going over to the mysterious door. She examined the lock carefully. It consisted of a bas-relief honeybee surrounding the keyhole. "What's up with all the bee symbols?" she mused. "They're all over the place; in the garden, on the columns to the oak grove...and here, on this tiny keyhole...".

Dane shook his head. "I've wondered that myself. There are a ton of honeybees at our house too, like on our front door. You'll have to see it sometime."

"Hmm. So mysterious. Whatever is behind *this* door must be important. What could it possibly be?"

Dane gave the slightest smile, which was the closest thing to a real smile Ari had seen yet. "I know what's in there," he said, playing along. "It's a huge network of tunnels that go deep into this hill," he motioned with his hands.

"Where does it go?"

"Uh, nowhere. It's the sewer system," he winked. Ari laughed. "But seriously, though, what do you think is in there?"

"Um, you're the one that's been down here before," she said, pointing at the comic books. Suddenly she felt brave, and intensely curious. "Dane, what's up with your aunt? I hear things, you know...is everything okay with her?" she proceeded carefully, knowing this could be a touchy topic.

Dane shifted uncomfortably. "She's got problems. I try to stay out of them. That's it," he said simply. Ari saw she wouldn't get anything more than that, so she changed the subject.

"Hey, how about a swim?" she asked with a smile. "Race ya!"

Ari had always been good at keeping secrets, but the mystery of the subterranean room occupied her mind for a good portion of her waking hours. After their swim, Ari had returned home to find her dad back from work. She told him about the beautiful pool in the oak grove, after all, Dane never told her to keep that a secret.

"That's amazing, Ari! I'll have to take a look at it sometime. I wonder what other forgotten relics are on our land?"

Ari wondered as well. Over the weekend, she spent more time inside the house, looking at each unexplored nook, examining each room for a possible hiding spot for the missing key. Deep down, she feared it was a futile search, either long lost or possessed by someone who had once picked it up, unknowingly, and kept it, never linking it to what it really opened. Ari sighed. On Sunday afternoon, as she was carefully going over Lily's unadorned room, the doorbell rang.

"Hey," Dane greeted her as she opened the door. "I was bored and thought I'd stop by. My aunt went to town, an' I got nothing to do. What are you up to?"

Ari motioned for him to come in. "I'm just looking around for stuff that might've been left in the house by the previous owners," she said.

"Ah, sounds like fun," he nodded his head with understanding. "Need help?"

"Absolutely." She grinned.

Ari's dad came in from the kitchen, car keys in hand. "Oh, hey, Dane, nice to see you again," he nodded. "Ari, I'm going to head to the supermarket to get a few things. Can you guys hold down the fort for a bit?"

"Sure," she said, and she and Dane headed up the stairs. They heard the door close and her dad's car go down the driveway. "Okay,

36

here's what we gotta do," she said, with all the enthusiasm of an investigator. "Let's go from the top to the bottom. We have an attic, which...I, uh...well, it's kinda creepy. There, I said it. I'm weirded out by the attic, so I haven't searched it yet. Where did you say you found your key?"

"Ah, I found it in my room," he said, remembering. "It was just lying in a corner on the floor. It was as if it had been dropped or something."

"Hmm," she mused. "Well, let's get started. We have a lot of house to search," she said, motioning with her arms.

They reached the second story and Ari pointed to a hatch in the ceiling. "That's our stop."

After pulling on the draw cord, a wood ladder revealed itself from the inside of the hatch. Dane extended it, and, one by one, they lifted themselves up. Dust particles made flurries in the filtered sunlight, which streamed from two small half-windows on either side.

There wasn't much in the attic besides cobwebs and dust. Ari suffered from a sneezing fit.

"Good grief," Dane said, as Ari tried to recover from her stream of sneezes. "Allergies?"

"Yep," she said, barely. "Uh, Dane, I don't see a thing up here. Not so much as a single box." They took a cursory look at the interior, just to be thorough.

Ari's room was next in order, and she frantically tried to remember if her room was presentable as she turned the doorknob. Opening it slightly, she peeked in. It looked safe enough. Unfortunately, Dane didn't see her pause. "Ooof," he grunted as he stumbled right into her.

"Hey, watch it," she giggled, finally opening the door all the way. The sunlight was streaming in through all the windows. She had photos of all her friends and family hung from floor to ceiling. Dane slowly walked over to one wall of photos.

"This your mom and sis?" he asked, quietly, pointing to a photo of Ari, Lily, and their mom.

"Yeah, that's them. I really miss them," she said, gazing at the photo. It had been taken during their last trip to Disneyland.

"You're really close with your parents, huh?" he said, seeming to momentarily forget about their key hunt. "That's cool. Your dad seems really nice, and trustworthy."

He couldn't see Ari's confused expression, but she quickly responded. "Yeah, they're cool. I love them." Ari paused, thinking about her mom. "It's been really hard not having my mom here. I miss her more than you could imagine."

Dane turned and looked at Ari, his shocking hazel eyes caught in the sunlight. It looked like he was going to ask her something, but decided against it. His serious demeanor disappeared. He started looking at the wood panels on the walls. "Gotta look for secret passages, you know, just in case." He knocked on the wall and pretended to listen for hollowness. Ari started to laugh.

"Ok, Sherlock, let me know when you're done scaring the mice in the walls. I'll be downstairs drinking lemonade," she said, laughing.

Dane turned and really, truly smiled at her. She couldn't believe it. She had never seen him smile before, and it was incredible, like a flash of sunlight on a dark day. She stopped and couldn't help but smile back.

"You gotta do that more often," she said, quietly.

"Do what?"

"Smile," she said. Before she could say anything else, they heard someone pounding at the door. Ari moved towards the stairs, but Dane blocked her.

"Wait! It could be Rhoda," he said, his voice filled with tension. "I'm going to head into the oak grove, just so she doesn't flip out 'cuz I'm over here, ok?" Before Ari could ask why, he bolted out the back door and was gone. She shrugged her shoulders and decided to get the door. It was more likely to be the postman or a someone selling something, she thought to herself.

She opened the door. Standing on the front step *was* Rhoda—same baggy shirt and jeans. She lunged towards Ari.

"Where's Dane?!" she yelled, her face a mottled shade of red. "You'd better tell me where he is, you little freak! I know he's been hangin' 'round here instead of doin' his chores! An' I need him back! Her voice shrilled at the last word. Ari was caught so off-guard that she had no idea what to do. His aunt kept screaming. "You'd better tell me, girl, or you're gonna be sorry you ever moved here, you little wretch!" She lunged at Ari, but Ari quickly slammed the door, held it with all her weight, and bolted it. Ari started to tremble. What had just happened? His aunt was pounding on the door again, yelling like a madwoman.

Terrified, Ari ran through the backyard, down the cobblestone path, and into the oak grove. She gasped as adrenaline robbed air from her lungs. She ran hard through the woods, but before she reached the brass circle, she caught up with Dane, who was lingering just past the stone columns at the entrance of the oak grove.

"Ari, what happened?" Dane reached out for her, without waiting for a response. Taking her arm, he started to run. "Come on! Quickly, we gotta hide!"

Dane and Ari reached the brass circle, and Dane opened it with surprising swiftness. Ari jumped into the darkness, and Dane landed quickly after her. He closed the cover and latched it from inside with a little lever. Ari was still trembling; her heart stung. Before long, Dane had a candle lit. Hugging her knees and sitting on the floor, Ari buried her head in her arms and took slow, deep breaths.

Dane knelt down beside her. "Ari, look at me." Reluctantly, she obeyed. He gazed at her for a moment, and placed a hand on her trembling arm. "Ari, I'm sorry about what happened," he said quietly, his voice determined. "Please don't be afraid to hang out with me because of this," he pleaded. She looked in his eyes for a long time, trying to find the real Dane, the Dane that hid himself away to keep himself from getting hurt. "Don't let her scare you, okay?"

She nodded and took a breath to steady herself. "Ari," he continued, "this is why this place is so important to me," he said, motioning towards the brass lid. "In here, I'm safe from her. I can come here and be alone until she's done being crazy," he explained. "That's why I needed you to keep it a secret."

"I understand. I'm so sorry you have to live with her, being like that..." Ari's voice trailed off. Ari's parents had never screamed at her like that; in fact, nobody ever had. How could he live with someone like that, day after day?

"Ari, I have to go back. Don't worry about me. She never gets too crazy," he said, slowly opening the lid. "You need to get back to your house, too," he said. "Your dad is probably going to get home soon—"

"Don't worry," she cut him off. "I won't tell him about what happened today. Promise." Ari vowed. He looked at her appreciatively, and headed into the woods.

*   *   *

The next few days, Ari worked on the garden only when her dad was home, partly because there were things she needed his help with, and partly because she was afraid of Dane's aunt appearing again. She didn't think she could face Rhoda all on her own. In light of what she knew about Dane's home life, the reality of her own life seemed to change perspective. She had never known abuse or unfair treatment. Her parents had spanked her when she was little, but she had never been hurt nor feared them because of it.

"Ari, you seem lost in thought," her dad saw her staring at an empty flower bed. "Everything okay?"

"Oh, yeah," she said hesitantly. She wanted to discuss it with her dad, but she didn't know how to say it without breaking her confidence with Dane. She picked the soil with her trowel.

"So, I was at the library yesterday," her dad said with a hint of mystery in his voice, "and I found out some more information on the Hadleys. Want to hear it?" he said, smiling.

"Yeah. What did you find?"

"Well, it turns out that Nadia had been a famous Russian ballerina with the Royal Ballet. The story is that a governor of Russia had been courting her. However, somehow, she arrived in the U.S. with Reginald Hadley before the governor even knew she was gone."

"Poor governor," Ari shook her head. That's really kind of a sad story," she said. "I wonder what he did after she left?"

"Who knows. Maybe you can find that out," he said, with a glint in his eyes.

Later that day, Dane stopped by the garden, by way of the grove path. Ari's dad brought out a giant pitcher of lemonade, and they sat in the shade of the back deck, sipping from plastic cups. They discussed the recent findings about Nadia and Reginald. Dane casually brought up the fact that he was a Hadley, and Ari's dad was genuinely intrigued. Dane revealed the fact that his family had, until recently, owned the entire property. He only briefly mentioned that his aunt wasn't sentimental about his family history, because she was only related by marriage. Ari's dad nodded, and they began discussing the town of Rivers. Ari stared out at the garden, her mind running over things again and again. Where could that second key be? She listened to their voices and closed her eyes as she thought.

She awoke with a start. She was still sitting in the rocking chair; but the sun was near setting and the cool breeze of evening had hushed the chirping crickets. Dane was still sitting in the other rocking chair; when he noticed Ari was awake and leaned forward and gave the slightest smile. Ari sleepily returned a smile, then the thought of Rhoda's anger suddenly rushed into Ari's mind.

"Oh my gosh! Dane! What about Rhoda? Aren't you supposed to be home?" Momentary panic caused Ari to nearly jump out of her chair.

"Whoa, it's ok," Dane reached over to keep her seated. "It's alright. She's gone for a few days. Not sure where she went, but it's fine. We don't have to worry for now," he kept his voice low.

"How long have I been asleep?" And where's Dad?" Ari noticed Dane's hand was still gently resting on her arm.

"I think he's putting together a late dinner. You've been out for about half an hour. I think you've been working a little too hard in the garden lately, or perhaps you've been looking for a lost key late at night?"

"I haven't found it yet. I actually haven't looked for it since the other day."

"Well, to tell you the truth, Ari, I haven't been in my attic for years. I was thinking about it the other day when we were in your attic. Let's have dinner and then go over to my house, check the attic, and see if we can find anything."

They had a homemade meal prepared by her dad, then Ari let him in on their plans. "We're going to look for more information about Nadia and Reginald, see if he has anything in his attic," she mentioned. Her dad insisted they let him know if they were successful. The pair grabbed flashlights and ran out the front door.

chapter twelve

Instead of taking the pathway through the oak grove, Ari
and Dane walked up the driveway. Ari never thought she'd get a
chance to actually go inside his house. When they arrived, she noticed
it didn't have the same home-like feel that her own house had.
Perhaps she was just reading into what she already knew about Dane's
family life, but she had a definite feeling of dread as she entered the
house. It must've showed on her face, because once they entered and
Dane turned the lights on, he paused beside her and gave her a
questioning look.

"Hey, are you ok?" he asked as he closed the front door.

"Yeah, I'm fine. I...I just feel like I'm trespassing or something.
I'm worried your aunt will come home and get mad, I guess." She
took a look around. There was nobody there but themselves.

"Ari, don't worry. I won't let her freak out on you again, I
promise. Besides, her note said she'd be gone for at least a few days.
Who knows where she went. But it's great to have a quiet house for a
change," he chuckled solemnly. "C'mon, let's get to the attic."

They went to the top floor and opened the hatch in the ceiling,
just as in Ari's house. There were no lights in the attic, so they had to
keep both of the flashlights on. Ari swung up and helped Dane off the
ladder. This attic was much smaller than the one at her house, and
was packed full of old boxes, crates, and old furniture. "Wow, we
might actually have a shot at finding something here," she said,
pulling over the first crate.

They sorted through box after box. Dust swirled in the beam of
the flashlight. After about an hour, Dane excused himself, and Ari
continued working through the boxes. So far, they'd come across old
papers that belonged to his aunt, articles of clothing that had
belonged to his late uncle, and some old toys. She got up and went to
the far corner of the attic. There was an intriguing trunk in the
corner. She lifted its lid and positioned her flashlight so she could see

44

the contents.

Ari pulled out a manila folder and unwound the string that held it closed. Dozens of black and white photographs were inside. She sorted through them with excitement. Could these be photos of the Hadleys? The first one she pulled out was of a beautiful lady and older gentleman. Could it be Nadia and Reginald? She flipped the photo over. Nothing was written on the other side. *Hmm,* Ari thought. She piled through more photos, many of them likely a century old. This was just what they were looking for! Would Dane know who these people were?

Ari scooted to the edge of the hatch. "Dane! Hey, where'd you go? I think I found something! You down there?" Silence. She sighed. Dropping out of the attic, she wandered around the house. She saw a door that must've been to Dane's room. It was open a little, so she peeked inside. "Dane? Are you in here?" Nobody. She looked around for a moment. There weren't many photos in the room. A bed, a poster here and there, some clothes on the floor: a typical boy's room. She saw one photo stuck by his night stand. She gently picked it up. It was an old photo of Dane, she guessed, and his father? Maybe. They looked quite alike.

A noise startled her. She turned quickly to see Dane standing behind her. She was immediately embarrassed. "Oh, um, I'm sorry, I thought you might be in here. I didn't mean to snoop or anything—" Dane cut her off with a wave of his hand.

"It's ok. No worries. I don't mind if you're checking out my room. I mean, I've pounded on the walls of your own room looking for secret passages. You're allowed to check out my photo," he said, motioning at the picture.

"Is this you and your dad?"

"Yeah. That was a while ago." He sounded solemn. "It was taken right before he left me here with Rhoda."

45

"Do you know where he went?"

"All he told me was that he was going to look for a job and he'd be back for me when he found one." Dane swallowed hard, then gruffly cleared his throat. "That was over four years ago. He's called a few times, but hasn't ever come back. I try not to think about it anymore. If I don't expect anything from him, I can't get disappointed, right?"

She just shook her head. "That sucks. I wish you had a family, Dane. Do you ever get lonely?"

"Not lately," he said, and flashed another great smile, which washed over Ari like a warm wave. She basked in it momentarily but then realized she'd come out of the attic for a reason.

"Hey! Come see what I found up there!" They ran to the ladder and scrambled back up. Ari handed him the manila folder full of photos. "Dane, do you know who any of these people are?"

He sifted through the photos. "Hm. I just don't know, Ari. I think we might have to take all this stuff with us and compare them with photos in the history books that you checked out. Let's get this whole trunk out of the attic and take it to your house. Rhoda won't have a clue that it's gone."

"You sure about that?" She was doubtful. Dane nodded.

They carefully lifted the fairly heavy steamer trunk out of Dane's house. Each took a side and they waddled down Hadley Lane to Ari's house. Once they got inside, Ari's dad poked his head out of his office. "You guys have any luck?" he asked, intrigued.

"Maybe," she said, and they set the trunk into the living room. Dane then thanked her dad for dinner and excused himself for the night. Ari walked him back to the front door.

"Thanks for coming over today," Ari said with a little smile.

"Hey, get some sleep tonight," he chuckled. "We've got some

46

research to do tomorrow," Dane paused a moment and looked at her, then stepped off the porch. Ari watched him walk down the lane until he was out of sight.

The next afternoon, Ari was making lunch when the doorbell rang. She opened it to see Dane panting. "You gotta come over and see what I found!" He grabbed her hand and they ran to his house, pounded up the stairs, and up into the attic. Sunlight was streaming through the single window, illuminating a corner of the small space. Ari could make out a cloud of color amidst the otherwise-dark attic.

Another old steamer trunk was opened and the contents were overflowing, like an explosion of tulle and sparkling rhinestones. Ari went over to examine the glowing pile. Laying in a heap were a half-dozen ballet tutus, their enormous pancake-shaped skirts puffing out in the sunlight. There were pink ones, white ones, and tutus with petal-shaped details over the skirts. She ran her finger down the edge of a bodice, noting the hand-stitched crystal beads and pearls. "Wow, these are amazing," she said, carefully looking underneath them. Satin ballet slippers were carefully packed in the bottom of the trunk. They looked fairly similar to pointe shoes that she'd seen before, only a bit different, and definitely old. Each shoe was carefully tucked into its mate, heel to toe, with matching ribbons delicately curled inside. It looked like they all had been well-worn, the toes missing their satin.

"Dane, these are Nadia's, they have to be." She stood up and held up a white tutu to herself. She twirled once, and when the tutu's sequins touched the corner of sunlight, a thousand glittering dots of light circled the attic. Ari caught her breath and looked at Dane, who was smiling at her enjoyment.

"Is there anything else in there? Once I opened it I went straight to get you," he explained.

"Let's see," Ari knelt, putting down the tutu. Dots of reflected sunlight came to rest on the walls. She looked carefully through the trunk. I see some more shoes, and here's something else." She pulled out a stack of letters held together with some twine.

"Ooh, this might be important," she said as she untied the twine and divided the stack in half. Dane took one half and examined the envelopes, turning each one over several times. About half of the letters were scripted in Russian; the other half were in English. Dane picked out some and started reading.

"There's no return address on these, Ari. The handwriting is incredible," he said, pointing to the ornate cursive. They were all addressed to Nadia Varishnikov, at 3311 Hadley Lane. "Hey, that's my house," he mused. He turned it over, noting the red-wax seal with a fleur-de-leis imprint on it. It had been opened at the top of the envelope, slit by a knife or letter opener.

"I bet these letters would have information that we're looking for," Dane said quietly.

Ari nodded. "You're right. Hey, let's get out of here and read them outside." She traced a line in the dust with her finger.

"Good idea," Dane gathered the letters and they packed the delicate tutus and shoes back into the trunk and descended from the attic. On a whim, Ari paused at the top of the stairs.

"Dane, how many rooms does your house have?"

He paused, quizzically. "Um, three bedrooms and one large room upstairs, and the living room and kitchen downstairs. Why?"

"What's the large room for?"

Dane thought a moment. "Well, nothing is in there now. It's along the south side of the house and has a bunch of windows and about nothing else."

"Can I see it?" Ari asked with anticipation.

"Uh, yeah." He turned and opened a heavy mahogany door at the end of the hallway. Sunlight streamed out, reflecting off the still-polished wooden floor, despite a heavy layer of dust. The room hadn't been set foot in for ages, Ari could see. Along the windowed wall, at waist height, was a plain wooden rail that was delicately bolted to the wall.

"Dane, you know what this is, right?" Ari said excitedly.

"An empty room?

"Well, yes, but no, silly. That's a ballet barre on the wall, there." She scanned the room. The room looked just like the studio where she had taken beginning ballet lessons when she was a fifth-grader. There were no mirrors; however, the walls had small holes at regular intervals. "There were mirrors on the wall once, I bet. Somebody had this room made especially for ballet, I think," she ran her hands along the wall, feeling the tiny indentations that had long been filled in.

"I hate to point this out, Ari, but this just doesn't make sense. Why would the servants need a ballet studio?" Dane just shook his head and headed back into the hallway.

She followed at a trot down the stairs. "I dunno, but it's got to do with Nadia. All her stuff was in your attic, not mine. Plus, all the letters were addressed to your house. Maybe they just ran out of room in my house. I hope the letters will answer some questions. Let's go."

They took the path through the oak grove and came into Ari's back pasture. "Let's sit under the arbor," she pointed at the white bench gracefully arched by a lattice trellis. The wild roses were blooming and provided a good amount of shade. As Dane pulled out a letter and began reading it to himself, she silently noted how the perfectly filtered sunlight caused Dane's eyes to be exactly half green and half brown. Realizing she was staring, Ari took her half of the letters and placed all but one in the lush grass.

Carefully drawing the first letter out, she noticed the soft texture of the paper. Like cotton, almost. The sunlight revealed a finely-lined watermark beneath the ornate cursive. She read aloud:

"March 18, 1905.

My Dearest Nadia,

I wish this letter could have been delivered in person. Each day that passes without your kindness is another day stolen from my life, my Nadia. It is my intention to send for you as soon as everything settles.

Accompanying this letter will be a package. Just a token of my love, darling. Place it somewhere where you can see it every day, and think of me often.

Love Always, Grekov."

Ari paused, deep in thought for a moment. "So what was in the package, do you think? Who's Grekov? Reginald was her husband, right? Or was he?" Ari looked at Dane. "Read yours and see what it says."

Dane picked a letter out from his pile. He scanned over it. "This one is also from Grekov. He says he should be sending for her soon, and he can't wait to see her. Dated September 1910. Wow, five years since your letter. Why would he want to see her? Didn't she move to the States with Reginald? This is really confusing."

Ari closed her eyes and sat back for a moment, her back to the concrete bench. Instead of revealing answers, the letters seemed to produce more questions. She reached for another and read it aloud:

"Dearest Nadia,

I received your letter and it heartened me to hear of your lovely gardens. I trust Reginald is keeping you safe in my absence. I know it is your desire to return but it simply cannot be accomplished at this moment in time. Perhaps affairs will settle soon and we shall be reunited. In time, my love. In the time between, keep up your gardens that remind you of home. Hold my treasures dear and keep them safe until it is time to return.

Love always, G."

Treasures? Their eyes met, questioning. A holler startled them both.

"Ari! Hey, where are you? I need your help for a bit!" Ari's dad was calling from somewhere inside the house. She realized her dad had returned home from work. She carefully put her letter down and motioned to Dane.

"I'll be back; don't go, 'k? He nodded and opened another letter as she ran inside. Her dad had brought home several statues for the garden, and a flat of petunias. "Wow, dad, these are beautiful!" She smiled as she admired the first small statue: an angel with her wings and hands opened, looking downward. The second was a garden fairy, sitting on a rock.

"I thought you might like those," he said with a smile. "What are you doing in the backyard?" He peered around her, looking out the kitchen window.

"Ah, we found some cool stuff in Dane's attic that might give us more insight on the Hadleys," she said, avoiding detail—at least for now. "Do you want me to take these outside?" She quickly lifted the angel and headed out before her dad could reply.

She stood on the back deck, surveying the garden. Dane was now sitting on the bench under the arch, obviously concentrating on one particular letter. He looked deep in thought. She glanced at the resin angel in her hands—where should it go? The lawn was looking much greener now; completely mowed and trimmed. The rose garden was looking better; there were even some yellow roses blooming. The winding cobblestone path that visited every nook of the garden was neatly groomed. She spied a bare spot next to some purple and white morning glories that were entwined on a bamboo lattice. She carefully placed the angel amongst the blossoms.

Ari and her dad continued to work on the garden for the rest of the afternoon. Dane excused himself and took half of the letters with him, leaving the other half for Ari to peruse. That evening, as the cool summer air was drifting through her bedroom, she pulled out her half of the letters and settled in her window seat. She tried reading more, but the sound of the crickets lulled her to sleep.

chapter fourteen

July had come and gone; and the garden was nearly done. Ari and her dad had taken great care to try and restore it to its previous glory, as in the days of the Hadleys. Every historical book they could get their hands on had been referenced, and while they had found several old photos of the houses and garden, little information could be found on Nadia, Reginald or Grekov. Ari decided they needed a little outside help.

"Mom? How are you doing?" She switched the cell phone to her other ear. "Hey, I need you to find some information for me, when you get a chance. We have a bit of a history mystery with house," Ari said, smiling.

"Ooh, a mystery with the new house?" Her mom was a sucker for mysteries of all kinds, and was thrilled that their "new" house had many old mysteries. Of course, Ari left out all the really interesting details, like the brass circle.

Ari carefully spelled out the names of Nadia and Reginald for her, and hoped that the San Francisco public library would have more information about Nadia Varishnikov than the library in Rivers. After a few more questions from her mom, Ari hung up and worked on chores around the house.

Hours later, the cell rang, vibrating across the kitchen table. Ari snatched it on the first ring. It was her mom. "Ari, this is really interesting," she said with excitement in her voice. "I did some poking around, and it sounds like Nadia was one of the most famous Russian ballerinas of her time. She began dancing at the Russian Royal Ballet in 1889, and was soon courted by some notable gentlemen, among them a governor. She was actually engaged to him by 1904, but it sounds like because of political unrest, they never actually married. It says she moved to the United States in 1905 and lived out her life as Nadia Hadley. Sounds like a sad story, huh? Didn't you mention that Reginald was her husband, and that your friend Dane is a great-great grandson?"

"Well, yeah...at least that's what we think. I don't know. I mean, yes, he's a Hadley, but we've found some interesting letters that are really confusing. Anyways, thanks for doing the research." Ari chatted for minutes longer with her mom, asking how Lily was and hearing about her mom's moving preparations. Eventually they said their good-byes and Ari headed out the back door.

She wanted to tell Dane the new information, but she hesitated. Fear crept into her stomach. Ari was sure his aunt was home; her car had crunched by on the gravel driveway not long before Ari received the call from her mom. Suddenly, Ari gathered her courage and ran up the driveway. She could hear a TV blaring inside, but no other noises. Barely slowing as she reached his house, she pounded up the front steps and knocked on the door. Subconsciously, she backed away a few steps, but stayed on the front porch. Footsteps approached. Ari braced.

The door opened and Dane's familiar face took on an expression she'd never seen before; half between surprise and amusement. He ducked back but then stepped out and closed the door quietly. "What are you doing here?" he said, a small smile crossing his mouth. "What about her?" he jerked his hand, motioning toward the house.

"Where is she?" Ari whispered, hoping an enraged aunt wouldn't be charging out of the door at any minute.

"She got home from her factory job, and she's sleeping. You're safe for now."

She nodded and motioned toward the oak grove. "I gotta tell you something," Ari said with urgency. "C'mon, let's go to the circle."

They raced to the brass circle and Dane procured the key from underneath his shirt and opened the lid. Once secured inside, with candles blazing, she propped herself against the wall and began reciting what her mom had found out. Once she finished, Dane just looked at her quizzically. "Um, Ari, I hate to tell you this, but we pretty much knew all that already," he almost sounded sad.

She cocked her head. "No, we didn't, Dane. They were engaged," she emphasized.

"So?" He sounded completely, utterly lost.

Ari threw her head back, exasperated, and sighed pointedly. "At first it sounded like she eloped with Reginald, possibly to get away from the governor. But now we know that she and the governor were engaged, and even after she moved to this very spot in 1905, he still continued to send her letters, for five years after her move. Get it?" she stared him down.

"Um?"

"They were still in love," she sighed.

"Oh." He fiddled with his shoelace. "What about Reginald, then? Was he totally oblivious to the stream of love letters and packages and stuff that were arriving at his house?"

"I think you need to see this," she shoved an envelope in his hands. He opened one of the old letters they'd found in the attic, and scanned it over. "November 1910...My Nadia, I am so sorry to hear about our dearest Reginald. He lived a long and full life. Give my regards to his brother Wilhelm.

"I believe Reginald's passing will give us a new opportunity. Nadia, I will no longer be sending you provisions for your journey back. Instead, I will be joining you within the year at our home. I cannot wait to finally be reunited after our long separation.'"

Dane looked up at Ari. "Sooo....huh?"

Ari shrugged her shoulders. "I can't figure it out either. But I don't believe Reginald and Nadia were married. Look at this photo I found in the folder," she handed him a sepia-toned photo of a young lady and a grandfatherly-looking man. "This," she pointed to the lady "is Nadia. I found a photo of her on the Internet, from a page on the history of Russian ballet. The older man with her is definitely Reginald," she said.

"How do you know?" he examined the photo, scrutinizing the faces.

"'Cuz I found another history book at the library. They had a photo of the Reginald R. Hadley standing next to the city hall with a horse and buggy. This is him and Nadia. She's about 24 years old here. *He* is 88."

"Oooohhhh, hum. Yeah, that's quite the age spread there. And it sounds like he died in 1910."

Dane and Ari remained silent for a moment. "What do you think the 'provisions' were that he was talking about?" She tilted her head against the brick wall.

"I'd guess he was sending her money or something so she could get a boat ticket back to Russia; that's what it sounds like," Dane glanced at the door that remained as locked and inaccessible as before.

Ari got up, brushed her jeans off, and climbed up the ladder. "Where ya goin?" Dane looked at her from below, in the darkness of the room.

"We haven't even looked at the first trunk we found, the one that's still in my living room," Ari pointed toward the house. "That's where all the photos came from. I got through a few but not many. 'C'mon, let's go."

chapter fifteen

They headed for Ari's house and were greeted by the cool silence of the living room. The old house lacked air-conditioning, but it stayed cool despite the heat of the early August day. The first steamer trunk remained closed in the corner of the living room, where they had first put it.

Ari lifted the lid. She handed an envelope to Dane and kept one for herself. The first photo she pulled out was of an attractive girl who looked to be a teenager. Maybe fifteen, Ari thought. She was wearing a long, straight dress with a small-brimmed hat. Ari flipped the photo. "Katia Hadley, 1925. Dane, this is one of your relatives," she handed him the photo. She sorted through more, quickly flipping them to acquire more names. "Here's one with more names: Eva, Katia, and Sergei, 1924.' I think this is the same Katia as her," she poked at the picture Dane had.

Dane handed her another photo, this one much different from the others. It was almost contemporary. A once-colored photo was now rosy with age, but it clearly showed a lovely brunette lady in sixties wedding attire, posing with a tuxedo-clad fellow. "Nikolas and Abigail, wedding day," he read. "Ari, these are our family photos. Like, all of them, I think. Look how many are in here," he motioned to the trunk. "Look for more recent albums," he piled through the contents.

She pulled out a scrapbook with black pages and white photo corners on every page. As she opened it, the photos began to bend and curl off the pages; some of them were falling out of the book. One photo was in color; like the other one, it was faded with rosy tones. This one showed a family: the same couple from the wedding photo, but many years later, and with four children, one a small baby held by the oldest boy. "'William Marcus, Dina, Maria, baby Viktor. 1979.'"

"Wait, let me see that," Dane held out his hand for the photo. "Ari, this is my dad," he pointed to the one holding the baby. "He was the oldest one of the four kids; these must be my aunts Dina and Maria—I've never met them before—and the baby is Viktor, my uncle who died, Rhoda's husband. Wow...I've never seen this photo before. I've actually never seen any photos of my dad as a kid," he stared at the photo. "Can I see that scrapbook?" She nodded and handed it to him. He carefully turned the pages, as not to disturb the photos any more.

"Shouldn't we start writing down the names of all these people, so we can figure out who's who in your family?" Ari tilted her head to the side, thinking. "Kinda like a family tree, you know?" She grabbed a notebook from the kitchen and a pen. "So you, Dane—" she jotted down his name, "—and how many siblings do you have?"

He looked up at her. "Um, well, I have one other sibling; that's Molly, she was born before my parents divorced. Other than that, I have no idea about half siblings or anything like that."

"Oh..." Ari looked down for a moment. "Ok, what are your mom and dad's names, then?"

"Dad's name is Mark Hadley, and my mother's maiden name was Olivia Harrison. Dad's full name is William Marcus, but he never went by that."

"Dane, can you tell me about your mom?" she asked quietly, pausing her pen.

"She was a good mom," he simply stated. It seemed like he might be done, but then he continued. "She was a nurse and worked really long hours when I was a kid. My parents got divorced a year after Molly was born. Mom took Molly and moved to another state to take care of my grandma. She sends me cards for my birthday, but I haven't actually talked with her in the longest time."

He looked down at the photos, then the trunk. "C'mon, let's take a break," he shook off the thoughts of the family he'd long forgotten about. "Swim?"

Ari nodded, then went to grab her stuff.

*   *   *

The next few mornings were uncharacteristically foggy. Each day would begin cool and gray, just like the days Ari loved so much in San Francisco. Slowly but surely, the warmth of the day would push the fog away and a warming heat would develop in the late afternoon. Strangely, she had felt more homesick lately than when she'd first moved. Maybe it was the fog, maybe it was because her mom would be moving in with them soon and she'd have no more ties to the city; she didn't know. But she couldn't stop thinking about the bustling hills, the noise of traffic, and her favorite spots in San Francisco.

She'd loved the wharf. She'd take a trolley up and down the hills, through little Italy, and then go to Ghirardelli Square and sit by the mermaid fountain. The square was small and cozy, and she would take a book and read there for hours, a scarf wrapped around her neck. Occasionally she'd look up from her book and take in a deep breath of chocolate-laden air that was drifting from the gift shop across the square.

Early one of those foggy August mornings in Rivers, she got on her bike and rode into town to mail a letter to her mom and sister. She could've just put it in the mailbox, but she wanted to take a ride and get some exercise. She had promised her Lily that she would take pictures of their new house before she arrived.

She pedaled her bike down the crunchy gravel hill, onto the country road, and into town. The streets of Rivers were normally sparse, but mornings left it absolutely deserted. Her dad worked in a three-story office building; she passed his car on the way to the post office. She had only explored the town a few times; of course, grocery shopping and supply runs took them into town often, but nothing beyond that. A little exploring would be good to clear the mind, Ari surmised as she aimlessly pedaled away from the post office.

Just as in the Bay Area, the sunlight began clearing the sky. Ari took her bike and pedaled to the only park in Rivers. It was located where the two major streams met and made one large waterway, the

Elgin River. On warm days, it seemed the whole town showed up to play in the pristine waters. Now, however, it was a chilly summer morning and the ducks and Canadian geese were the only other visitors to the park. She dropped her bike in the grass and picked her way down the rocks along the shore. Sitting on one particularly large boulder, she breathed in the silence around her.

Ducks effortlessly glided past on the still-misty waters. She picked up a rock and skipped it across the river. A feeling of isolation swept over her. She wanted so badly to call her friends from home; her best friend in the whole world, Misha, had been faithful in calling her at least once a week, but it just wasn't the same as talking to her in person. Dane was as good a friend as any, and his presence had a certain calm that she loved, but as much as they talked, sometimes they didn't really talk at all. In all of her life, Ari had never met a person who could say so many words without revealing what was really going on inside his mind. Besides, they mostly talked about the mysteries surrounding their houses. She sighed and skipped another rock.

A sudden noise behind her caused her to turn. To her surprise, it was Dane. He dropped his bike next to hers on the grass and walked over without saying anything. Sitting on the rock next to her, he picked up a rock and also skipped it across.

"Hey," she said.

"Hey. Whatcha doin' down here?" he turned to face her, and she noticed a faint scent of soap and shampoo drift past. Must've just gotten out of the shower, she thought to herself.

"Nothing really. I miss home," she blurted out, quietly but bluntly. "I mean, I've been kinda homesick lately, and I really wish I could go back," she looked at him and quickly added, "Just to visit, you know. I do like it here."

He waved her off. "I know what you mean. No worries."

"Dane," she started, and his hazel eyes were on her again. "...if

60

you could have one thing in the whole entire world, what would it be? Like, what do you wish for above all else?"

He blinked in surprise and returned the question. "What would you wish for?"

"No way," she said, shaking her head. "I asked you first, so you gotta answer first." She resolutely crossed her arms and stared at him. He sighed.

"I...I, um, guess I would have to wish that I wouldn't have to live with Rhoda anymore, and that I'd be with my family," he said, looking at her for approval. "Okay, your turn."

"Gosh," she said, running through all the things she could wish for. "Right now, I just want to feel like I belong somewhere, you know? I don't feel like Rivers is my home yet, and San Francisco is no longer my home, an' I just have to accept that, I guess." She looked straight at Dane and memorized every inch of his face. She allowed herself to get totally lost in his eyes, if only for a moment.

"You know that it's only about an hour to the beach from here, right?" he added. "I mean, I know it's nothing like the city, but at least you could be near the ocean for a bit. Might help things," he said.

"I didn't know that. Dad and I haven't gone anywhere really since we moved here. I should convince him to go to the coast this weekend. Good idea," she said with a small smile.

It wasn't news to Ari's dad that his daughter was homesick. He could see she was keeping herself extra busy to help ease the unfamiliarity. He not only agreed that a trip to the coast would be a great excursion, but he suggested that Ari ask if Dane could come as well. Ari ran to Dane's house, and, not seeing Rhoda's car in the driveway, proceeded to the door to inquire.

After ringing the bell twice, a disheveled Dane appeared in the doorway: shirtless, wearing sweat pants, and with the messiest hair Ari had ever seen. She stifled a giggle.

"Hey, we're taking that trip to the coast, and I want you to come with us. Can you?"

"Umm, sure, I'd like to. Rhoda's gone again for a few days; let me leave her a note. And, um, I gotta brush my hair. I'll be there in five, ok?"

He appeared nearly five minutes later with a sweatshirt in hand. They piled in the car and, per Dane's directions, made their way across the low valley and into the coastal hills. Ari, Dane, and her dad all discussed the mystery of Nadia, Grekov, and Reginald, but Ari and Dane were careful to skirt around the secret of the brass circle.

"I think it sounds like a love triangle," her dad offered, chuckling.

"Ew, dad," Ari made a face. "We forgot to tell you that poor 'ol Reginald really *was* old—almost sixty years older than Nadia. So there goes your theory," she said.

"But seriously, what's up with all her stuff being in my house, not yours?" Dane said, shaking his head. "I think that's the weirdest part of this whole thing. It's like they lived in two separate houses, or something." Ari looked at him, her expression curious.

"You know, Dane, that almost seems possible," she said, but

before she could explain, they had finally come to their destination, and the topic quickly turned to where they would eat lunch.

Their first stop was a tiny fishing village called Port Callaway. They visited a small cafe for lunch. Ari hadn't had clam chowder since they had left San Francisco, so she ordered their largest bowl. Her dad ordered a Reuben sandwich, and Dane had chowder as well. With her spoon, Ari dunked the oyster crackers that floated in her soup. She wished that her mom and sister could be there with them now.

On the way to the beach, they came to a large brass fountain. It was a memorial for the fisherman who had been lost at sea in the history of Port Callaway. In the middle of the fountain, a fisherman stood with his rain slicker blowing in the wind. His hand rested above his eyes, shielding them from the storm. A water spout in the back sent water in the air. The pool of water below rippled as drops of water disturbed the surface. The plaque below the statue read:

"To all the men and women who have lost their lives to the sea,

the people of Port Callaway dedicate this memorial.

May your souls be at rest."

Ari pulled a quarter from her pocket. Rubbing it with her thumb, she closed her eyes. A wish immediately came to mind. She never had really believed in wishes coming true, but this one was important. It was more than a wish to her. She opened her eyes and tossed the coin in. Ari watched it as it see-sawed to the bottom, glinting in the sun on its way down.

"What'd you wish for?" Dane followed the coin on its way down.

"Can't tell you," Ari smiled and shook her head.

"Okay, then." Dane pulled out a coin as well, paused, and tossed it in.

"Well?" Ari looked at him expectantly.

"Nope," he looked at her with a glint in his eye. "Won't come true if I tell you." She could hear him smiling.

Their next stop was the beach at Port Callaway. The day was sunny, but the wind was brisk. A dozen or so families were on the beach; flying kites, making sandcastles, and watching the fishing vessels leave the channel and head toward open ocean. The three headed north down the beach, braving the wind. Ari shivered and she ducked her head down into her chest. Her brown hair whipped around wildly. Dane wordlessly handed her his sweatshirt. She smiled gratefully at him and pulled it over her head. It sagged on her, two times too big, but she warmed up quickly.

"How often do you go to the beach?" Ari asked Dane, at a semi-yell, trying to raise her voice over the wind.

"I don't," Dane shook his head. "Rhoda's not a big fan of the ocean," he continued. "I bet you went really often before you moved, since you lived on the coast."

"Yeah, I did. But living in San Francisco was like being at the beach all the time," she grinned, thinking back to her favorite place. "The air was salty, and the wind blows like this every day. You'd like it, I think," she said wistfully.

They made their way up and down the beach. The afternoon was giving way to early evening, and the sun was beginning to reflect off the horizon of the ocean. Ari lost herself staring at the expanse, feeling the warm sand flow between her feet. The water lapped at her feet, causing them to sink deeper in the sand. She loved that feeling. She gazed out at the water. Suddenly, a wave hit her knees, like a rush of ice on her legs.

"Wheeeeeeeooooww!" Ari half-screamed and laughed at the same time. So cold! Her pants were half-soaked and the wind was blowing straight through them. Her dad and Dane found it amusing, but she decided it was time to head for the car. They all raced to the parking lot and Ari was relieved to be in the warmth of the vehicle.

The drive back lulled Ari to sleep. When she awoke, she realized they were close to Rivers. She looked over at Dane. He too had drifted off, and his head was tilted back, eyes closed. She had been dreaming about the ocean. There were scenes of the city, and of the garden, and then places she'd never seen before. Then a string of jumbled images that didn't make any sense at all flashed through her mind. She felt relieved to be awake. However, as they approached their hill, her relief waned. 'She thought she saw lights on at Dane's house. Reaching over, she gently nudged him. "Dane, wake up. I think your aunt is home," she whispered.

Dane blinked awake quickly. They were now parked in Ari's driveway. "Dane, do you want me to drop you off at your house?" Ari's Dad asked.

"No, it's fine. I can walk," he said, getting out. "Thanks for asking me to come," he told them both. He started to jog down the lane, but Ari jogged after him.

"Dane! What are you going to do? Do you want me to come with you, or have dad walk with you?" she said, sidling up to him, whispering so her dad wouldn't overhear.

"No, I'll be fine, really. Don't worry about me," he said gruffly, and kept heading toward his house. Ari stopped short and shook her head. She didn't know what to do, so she simply turned around and went back to her own house. She climbed the stairs with a heavy heart. She hoped Dane wouldn't get in trouble for going with them, but somehow she knew that no matter what he did, he would probably would anyway.

Ari went into her dark bedroom and sat in her window seat. Cool evening winds came through her window and blew the curtains against her face. She listened intently for sounds coming from the direction of his house, but all she could see was a lit second-story window. Eventually the light went out and all was quiet. Ari grabbed a blanket and a pillow, and curled up on the window seat and fell into a fitful sleep.

Ari descended to the living room the next morning and looked at the steamer trunk. She really wanted to dig in and look for more clues about the Hadleys and the missing second key, but without Dane, it was slow work. She needed him to help her identify the people in all the pictures. Ari went into the kitchen, picked up her gardening gloves, and went to the backyard. She needed to weed some of the newly-planted flower beds, which had sprouted a healthy crop of dandelions, as well as plant a new orange tree they had purchased.

She hauled the small tree across the yard. She was just about to shake the tree loose from its planter when she thought she heard the doorbell ring. She knew her dad would get the door; besides, she couldn't let go of the tree at that moment. Ari was setting the roots into the ground when she heard a terrible sound.

Ari rushed to the kitchen and looked around the corner. Rhoda was at the front door, looking angrier than ever before. Her dad was trying to calm her down, and Ari could barely understand what she was saying. She was yelling something about Dane not being at home. Ari's dad said something and she could hear him walking towards her. He stopped short when he found Ari pressed up against the wall in the kitchen.

"Hey, Ari. Dane's aunt is here..." He skipped the unnecessary explanation and cut to the point. "She says Dane didn't come home last night and I think she wants to know where he is," he shook his head. "Ari, you need to tell me what you know," he said with a serious tone.

She was taken aback. "What I *know*?" she repeated. What did he mean? What she knew about his aunt, or where he currently was? She guessed the latter. "I don't know where he is, dad, honestly. The last time I saw him was when we said good-bye last night. Promise," she looked at him intently.

"Okay, I believe you. I think his aunt might not...not be thinking clearly," he said, shaking his head, not knowing how else to put it. He turned and headed back to the seething woman.

Ari ran out the kitchen door before she could hear anything more. She pounded down the cobblestone path and into the oak grove. She came to the brass circle, which was uncovered, a ring of dried leaves sloughed to the side. She pounded on it as carefully as she could, causing a hollow thump each time. "Dane!" she half-yelled. "Dane, please open up! It's Ari!" There was a long pause, but then she heard a rolling clink inside. The circle popped up. Ari jumped into complete darkness. The circle closed again. "Dane?" she whispered. "What's going on?"

She reached her hands out. She was frightened. Her own heartbeat racked her body, like an earthquake in her core. "Dane, what are you doing in here? Your aunt came to our house—" she felt her way around the wall "—and she wants to know why you didn't go home last night. I don't know what to do, but I didn't tell anyone about here," she was running out of breath. She took a step forward and her hands found the back of Dane's shirt. "What's going on?" she whispered.

A match was struck, and Dane lit a candle. He turned around and Ari gasped. His chin was bloody and a bruise colored his forehead. She covered her mouth with her hands. "What happened?" She didn't want to ask, but already she felt responsible. Her stomach dropped and twisted.

"Ari," he had her sit on the stone floor with him. "You need to listen to me. She has problems. I did go home last night, and this is what happened. She was already mad about something before I even got home. You're not at fault for this. I'm just waiting in here until she calms down. I can totally handle this." His well-rehearsed answer was unconvincing.

She just shook her head and looked down. Her head was spinning. The gold tiles flickered in the candlelight, making her even more disoriented. The fast dash to the underground room and the shock of seeing Dane was too much. She laid back on the cold stone. She had never been so fearful in her entire life.

"Ari...are you okay?" Dane didn't want to see her upset. Ari didn't respond for several minutes; she only held her head and lay there. Finally, she spoke.

"I want to help you, Dane. We need to call the police. She's *hurting* you."

"No, Aribelle, we can't do that." Dane's voice was gruff. "My dad has legal custody of me and I have no idea where he is. If the police get involved, I go straight into foster care if they can't find him. It's too big of a risk. It's not like I can just go and live on my own, either." Ari sniffed; she was trying hard not to let tears form. His voice softened. "Listen, Ari, I figure I've got only two more years and then I'm outta her hair. Sound like a plan?"

Ari sat up and just shook her head. *Not good enough*, she thought. "Let me at least clean you up. Will you do that?" she asked, with a forceful but quiet tone.

"Yeah, I guess," he touched his hand to his crusted chin. She had him take off his undershirt and she went to the forested pool, soaking the shirt in the icy water. Back at the brass circle, in the safety of its vaulted hatch, she examined the gash on his chin.

"How did she do this?" Ari asked under her breath. No reply came from Dane. He just sat stone-like, head tilted up, as she gingerly tried to clean the blood without causing the wound to re-open.

She knelt beside him. Carefully, with her left hand, she supported his chin while she brushed at the dried blood. The look on Dane's face was pained, and his eyes were closed. She saw the bruise on his forehead was getting darker, and the proximity to his eye was concerning. She doubled up the cold shirt and carefully placed it on his forehead, holding it with her hand.

His eyes opened in surprise to the sudden chill on his forehead, but he relaxed almost immediately. "Am I hurting you worse?" she asked tentatively.

"No, it's numbing the pain, I think," he said, and with that, he put his hand over Ari's hand, and closed his eyes again. Ari froze momentarily.

"I need to get a band-aid or something for your chin," she managed.

"It'll be fine," he finally opened his eyes and looked straight at Ari. "Really. It's not that bad."

Ari searched for the right words to convince Dane. She finally took the cold shirt from his forehead and focused on the bruise. "No, Dane. Your forehead looks terrible. And your chin isn't going to heal up on its own, I don't think. It needs a butterfly band-aid, at least, if not stitches. Can I at least go to my house and see if we have something that will work?"

He looked at her with a certain intensity she'd never seen before. "Please don't say anything to anyone about this," he urged.

"Dane, I won't. But what about Rhoda? What should I say if dad asks me where you are? He's concerned now too, you know."

He sighed and glanced at the floor, shaking his head. "I don't know."

Ari climbed up the steps and carefully lifted the brass circle, making sure nobody was near. When she got to her house, she found the first aid kit, and as silently as possible, found some band-aids and disinfectant. She could hear her father clicking away at his computer in his office. Before she returned to Dane, she poked her head into the room where her dad was, and handed him a small piece of paper with writing on it.

"I need you to find these," she said. He gave her a questioning look.

"Why? Is everything okay?" He was genuinely concerned.

"It will be better if we can find these," she said, then quickly left before more questions could be asked.

She returned to the brass circle with a glimmer of hope in her heart.

chapter eighteen

The next few days were excruciating for Ari. She
desperately wanted to talk to Dane but was too scared to go to his
house, so she waited. Her father had been respectful of her privacy
and hadn't asked too many questions about what had transpired over
the weekend. During the week, she tended to the nearly-finished
garden and hoped that everything was okay. The search for the key
had gone unfinished; she had a much more important search to
conduct at the moment.

Each night she'd sit in her window seat before she went to bed,
and she'd listen. She'd strain to hear voices, or noises, or see a light
come on in his house. Everything had been eerily still and quiet,
which made Ari uneasy.

On Thursday morning, Ari took a big mixing bowl and hiked a
small way up their road, about halfway between her driveway and
Dane's. The blackberries were plentiful, and she wanted to get just
enough to make a pie before her dad came home from work. She
picked her way through the brambles until she came to her first
cluster. After being stuck with thorns at least a half-dozen times, she
managed to get three berries in her bowl. "Hmph," she mused,
reassessing her strategy.

"It's going to take you longer if you don't have one of these," a
familiar voice said from up the road.

Ari whirled around to see Dane holding out a small branch that
forked at the end. More relieved than curious, she whooped and ran
to him, stopping short of giving out a hug. "You're okay," she said.

"Yeah, I'm okay," he repeated. "I think my chin is getting better.
But your blackberry picking sucks," he said with a small grin.

"Well, you'd better show me how, then. And you have to tell me
why you haven't been around the past few days," she demanded.

"First thing's first," he said as he held out the branch, "you need this to pull the vines toward you. You'll never get the good berries if you don't get the ones in the middle of the patch. And," he said, looking into her bowl, "you gotta get the ones that look like they're so full of juice that they look like they're going to explode," he explained. "The red ones you have—well, you won't want to eat those. If they almost fall off in your hand, that means they're ready."

She nodded and began looking for bigger berries. "So, what happened with Rhoda? Is she still mad at you?" Ari asked, carefully avoiding thorns.

"Well, she's still insane, if that's what you want to know. She was mad because the government caught her avoiding paying taxes. I think she's going to lose the house," he said, nearly at a whisper.

"But Dane, that belongs to *you*. It's your family's house. That's not fair!" Ari exclaimed, shaking her head. "You can't move..." Her voice trailed off as she set down the bowl. Ari reached for her pocket and pulled out a folded piece of paper. Holding it in her hand, she rubbed it with her thumb. "There's something you need to have," she said, placing it in his palm.

"What's this?" he asked, not unfolding it.

"I found your mom, and your real aunts, Dina and Maria. Their addresses and phone numbers are there too."

Dane stared at the piece of paper for a moment, his eyes cast downward. It was so silent Ari could hear each breath he took as he examined the unfolded note. "Wow...I can't believe you did this..." he said slowly.

"Aren't you going to look at it?" she asked.

"Um, yeah, I will...were you able to find my dad?" he asked, without much hope in his voice.

"Nooo, I'm sorry, Dane. We couldn't find him anywhere," Ari explained, sorry she'd found everybody but the one person who'd meant the most to him.

"It's okay," Dane said, and suddenly he wrapped one of his arms around her. "Nobody's ever done something like this for me. Thank you," he said. For a brief second. she heard his heartbeat next to her ear, then he was gone. "Gotta go make some calls," he yelled, as he ran towards his house.

*   *   *

Later that evening, Ari and her dad were rocking in the chairs on the deck, watching the first stars of the night make their appearances. "So, Ari, less than a month 'till your mom and Lily arrive. Are you excited?" her dad asked with a smile.

"Of course," she said, turning her brown-freckled face toward him, returning a smile. "And I can't wait until she sees the garden. I hope she likes it." Ari surveyed their backyard. It was truly beautiful now; every inch was manicured and cared for. "Thanks for helping me with it," she said.

"No problem." He leaned back in his chair, sighing. "Well, Ari, I think I'm going to turn in for the night. You staying up?"

"Yeah, for a little while. I'm not tired yet. Geez, dad, it's only 10 o'clock. Getting old?" she teased him, giving him a little punch on the arm.

"Well, yes, I am, thank you," he said, laughing as he rose from the rocking chair. "Don't stay up too late."

"Why not?" she said jokingly.

"Hmmm...I don't know," he chuckled back. "'Night."

"Good night," she called as he left.

Ari sat in silence, the only sound being the creaking floorboards of the deck. The crickets were echoing their chirps around the garden. She could hear a freight train at the base of their hill, clicking over the tracks. Suddenly, she heard a familiar clink in the distance. The brass circle had just been closed, and Ari knew of only one person who

73

could be there.

Rising from her chair, she jogged into the oak grove, which proved to be ten times eerier in the black of night than during early evening.

She felt her way through the trees to the brass circle. Finding it, she knelt down and rapped gently on the metal. "Hey, open up," she hissed.

A moment passed before the circle slowly popped open. "Dane, what are you doing down here?" she asked, leaning her head into the opening. Only one candle was lit in the room, barely illuminating the space.

"I just needed some space," he replied gruffly.

She heard the warning in his voice but proceeded anyway. "Can we talk?" she said. No reply came, so she tried again. "Come on and sit on the porch with me. It's scary out here when it's dark."

Ari swore she heard a snort, but her plea worked. "Fine," he said, climbing out. She looked at him, puzzled, but held out her hand anyway. He grabbed it and hoisted himself out of the circle. He tried to pull his hand away to close the hatch, but Ari tightened her grip.

"Wait," she demanded. "Are you mad at me or something?"

For a moment, Dane tensed, but then eased. "No," he said quietly, shaking his head. "C'mon, I'll tell you when we get to your house."

chapter nineteen

They quietly sat on the rocking chairs as a harvest moon began to rise in the southeast. "Well?" Ari looked at Dane intently, waiting to hear what, exactly, had caused him to retreat to the brass circle in the middle of the night.

"I called my mom today, right after you gave me the phone numbers. She sounded surprised—I mean, *really* surprised—to hear from me. I asked her how she and Molly were doing, and if I could come and live with them. I told them everything about Rhoda and how we're gonna probably lose our home pretty soon," he said, staring at nothing.

"And?" Ari leaned forward.

"Basically she said she was sorry, and reminded me that my father has custody of me, even though he left me with Rhoda. She said she barely makes enough to support Molly. There's no way she could take care of two kids, even if I got a job after school. So that's it, in a nutshell. Plus, Rhoda heard me talking to her, and she completely freaked out, telling me how ungrateful I am and all that crap. You know, the usual. Hence the trip to the ol' underground room." He spoke in hushed tones.

Ari felt a funny ache in her stomach. It started at the bottom and moved its way up to her heart, and then she felt like every inch of air had been sucked out of her lungs. How could she have such good intentions, with such bad results? She cleared her throat and tried to speak.

"I'm so, so sorry, Dane. That's not what I had hoped would happen. What about your aunts?"

"Rhoda grabbed the piece of paper from me and tore it up before I could do anything. But I'm pretty sure they wouldn't care about some kid they hadn't seen in years. Ari, you did all you could do. Don't be sad about it," he said, glancing at her with a kind look.

She nodded, wanting to believe that he was okay with how things turned out, but deep in her heart she couldn't shake the feeling of extreme disappointment. "But, hey, I'd probably better go home now," he said, rising from his chair. "I'll see you tomorrow, okay?"

Ari nodded and got up as well. "I'm really sorry," she said once more. He disappeared into the night; as soon as he entered the oak grove she lost sight of him. She was hardly surprised when she faintly heard the brass circle clink shut for the second time that night.

*　　*　　*

The morning came too soon for Ari. Sunlight streamed through her windows and announced that yet another beautiful late summer day had already begun. She turned and buried her head in the pillow, hanging on to every last moment of hazy sleep. Eventually, even her half-awake mind began thinking of how to remedy Dane's family problems. At first, the excitement of Nadia's mysteries had overshadowed the reality that she knew he lived with every day. But now, knowing that he could lose even his house, she wanted to give every possible solution a chance.

Why do I care so much? Ari suddenly thought to herself. She raised her head from the pillow and brushed fuzzy strands of brown hair from her face. Instantly, she realized why she wanted to succeed in helping Dane: she didn't want to fail him. His father, Rhoda, even his mom—it seemed they had all, in some way, failed him miserably. Ari just couldn't let him down.

Immediately after she got up, Ari searched the Internet for the phone numbers of Dina Ray Hadley and Maria Ellsworth, Dane's real aunts. Their addresses were listed on the Internet white pages as both being residents of San Luis Obispo, California. Ari smiled as she recalled several family vacations spent in that part of southern California. She jotted down the phone numbers and picked up the phone. *Who to call?* Dina was listed first, so she took a deep breath and punched in the numbers. The phone rang twice, and then a pleasant-sounding lady answered.

"Um, hello. My name is Ari, and you don't know me-" Ari prayed Dina wouldn't think she was a telemarketer and hang up— "but I'm good friends with your nephew Dane," she paused, hoping for some recognition from his aunt.

"Oh, of course, Dane. Is everything alright?" she sounded genuinely concerned. Ari took this as a good sign and continued on.

"Well, actually, not really. That's why I'm calling you," she said, and began explaining exactly what was happening.

chapter twenty

Twenty minutes later, Ari was beyond excited to tell Dane what she'd discussed with his aunt Dina. But before she could go find him, she had to call her father.

"Dad, I'm really sorry to bother you at work, but I have to ask you a really big favor. I don't have much time to explain, but this is what's going on," she spilled everything to him as quickly as she could. After a brief moment of silence, her dad recovered.

"Okay, Ari. I'll allow it. I think it's really good of you to be helping Dane. I just hope everything works out okay. So, what are you going to do about his aunt Rhoda?"

She sighed, and admitted she hadn't thought that far. She had two days to think about it, she reminded him. She thanked him and hung up. Running out the back door, she flew down the trail in the oak grove till she came to the brass circle. She tapped on it and it popped open. "Hey," she said breathlessly. "I'm so glad you're still here," she said, smiling. When he gave her a funny look, she waved her hands to explain. "I have some fantastic news, Dane." She jumped down the steps and pulled the circle closed.

"So this morning, I took the liberty of calling your aunt Dina," she said, not waiting for him to interject. "I let her know about some of the things going on—mostly that you might have to move soon— and in two days she's flying up here to visit," she said. "Dad was totally okay with her staying at our house, so we don't bother Rhoda. Anyway, Dina really wants to help you out. She lives alone in San Luis Obispo and has room for you to stay if you want," she finally paused to see his reaction.

It took some time for him to digest Ari's rapid-fire stream of words, but he finally nodded and smiled a bit. "Thanks, Ari. I really appreciate it. I don't know if I want to go live with her though. I mean, I don't even know her," he said. "But thank you. Really. It will be great to actually meet another family member who cares," he said.

"But, um, what are we going to do about Rhoda? Likely she won't be any kinder to a relative of mine than she is to me."

"Maybe Rhoda won't notice she's around, since she'll be staying at our house," Ari offered.

Dane just shrugged. "Well, if I only have a few more days here, maybe we should start really looking for the key to that second room."

*   *   *

Two days went by, with Ari and Dane searching high and low for the missing piece of their mystery: the second key to the door in the underground room. Every time Rhoda would leave the house, Dane and Ari would manage to sneak up to the attic and dig through every box they could get through. Finally, on a Monday night, a rented sedan pulled up to Ari's house. Ari and her dad met Dina Ray Hadley at the door. She looked to be in her late thirties, with mousy brown hair streaked with a bit of gray. She had friendly brown eyes, and Ari liked her immediately.

"So you're the young lady who cares so much for Dane," she said, shaking Ari's hand. Ari blushed, unnoticed, but nodded. "I'm so glad you made me aware of the situation with Rhoda. And what a coincidence that you moved into Nadia and Grekov's original house. You know, I've always wanted to visit this house," she said, looking around. "It's absolutely beautiful. And I've seen pictures of the original gardens. They were spectacular once."

"Well, if you'd join us on the back porch, I think we've got a surprise for you," Ari's dad said, beaming. "Ari's summer project has been to restore the garden. Take a look," they went through the kitchen and exited onto the porch. Dina gasped.

"*You* did this?" she said, turning to Ari. Ari just nodded meekly. "Why, Ari, what a beautiful job you've done!" Even though it was evening, they could see most of the garden in the last light of day. Their doorbell rang, and Ari excused herself.

"Must be Dane," she said, running to the door. She opened it to a pensive-looking Dane.

"She here?" he asked.

"Yeah, come on back," Ari pulled him by the hand through the house. "She's really nice," she whispered to him.

On the porch, aunt and nephew met each other. It had been years since Dina had seen Dane, and he had been only two at the time; far too young an age for him to remember her. They shook hands, and after a few minutes of light conversation, Ari and her dad excused themselves so that the two could talk in private.

When they were inside, Ari's dad hugged her. "You did a good thing, Ari," he said. "You saw your friend was in need and you did more than was required of you. Your mom will be so proud when she hears what you did."

"Yeah, but dad, I really wish that he didn't have to move. I wish mom and Lily could meet him, you know? If he leaves with Dina, they won't get to."

"I know," he said, with a sigh. "That must've been a really hard decision to make for you. You might never see him again if he moves to California with his aunt," he concluded.

Ugh, Ari thought silently. The thought had not completely occurred to her. Even though they had only been friends for a few months, she felt like she'd known him for much longer. It would be so lonely when he left.

Her thoughts were interrupted when Dane popped his head in the back door. "Ari, Aunt Dina knows all about Nadia! She can tell us the whole story!" He sounded more excited than Ari had ever heard him, and she bolted to the back porch.

Dina chuckled and began the story. "Dane tells me that you have bits and pieces of information on Nadia and Grekov. I can set the record straight," she said, with a glimmer in her eye. "My mother told

80

me the story of our family from the time I was a small child. My bedtime stories consisted of almost nothing else than the glamorous story of Nadia Varishnikov, the famous ballerina, and her royal husband. Well, here's the real story:

"Nadia was a talented ballerina from a young age. At nine, she had the opportunity to join the Russian Royal Ballet, where she studied for ten years. She came from a fairly well-to-do family who could afford her schooling.

"Now, the principal dancer at the ballet wasn't fond of having his students enjoy any other activities other than ballet. In fact, it was the strictest school of ballet in Russia at the time. The students had to eat, breathe, and sleep ballet. That meant no boyfriends or husbands," Dina said slyly. "In fact, if a dancer was found to have a boyfriend, they were suspended from the ballet. So, when Nadia began dancing leading roles, many men took notice of her, but only one was bold enough to court her."

"Grekov?" Ari asked.

"Yes. The governor Grekov. He was smitten with her, and she was very fond of him. So fond, in fact, that they were married in secret in Russia. She couldn't tell anyone, because her ballet career would be over as soon as it had started. She swore Grekov to silence, and all was well until things began to heat up politically. Then Grekov did a daring thing: he sent for his good friend from America, Reginald Hadley. They had met while Reginald was in Russia studying at a university, and had remained good friends. Reginald was, of course, many years older than Grekov, but when Grekov contacted Reginald with a very unusual request, Reginald consented without hesitation.

"Grekov had asked Reginald to take the lovely Nadia back to the United States with him, to keep her safe, and to allow her to practice ballet without personal scrutiny. He intended for her to come back to Russia when things settled down, but it soon became apparent that her stay in the U.S. would be much longer than he, or she, had intended. The first house, the smaller one, was built first."

"Wait, Nadia's house was the smaller one?" Dane asked.

At that, Ari nearly jumped from her chair. "I knew it!" she exclaimed. "That's why there's a whole ballet studio in your house, Dane! And why her tutus are there!"

Dina looked at her, surprised. "Really? You guys have all of her things? And there's a ballet studio?" she asked, incredulous.

"Yeah, you've gotta see it," Ari said, but quickly realized that might be impossible with Rhoda around.

Dina continued on. "Wow, that's amazing. It wasn't until Grekov moved to the United States that the larger house was built. After that bigger home was finished, the smaller house became the servant's quarters. But in the almost five years she was here with Reginald—until he died, in fact—she awaited the time she could be reunited with her husband. She later became famous for her gardening skills.

There were rumors that Grekov sent her vast amounts of money, both for her personal use, and for a trip back to Russia. But, when Reginald died, Grekov figured he had an unplanned opportunity. He was given permission by Reginald's family to assume the Hadley name upon entering the United States. That's why it's been reported that Reginald was Nadia's husband. The history books just got the wrong Hadley," Dina said.

"Wow," Dane and Ari said, nearly unanimously. They mulled it over silently for moments before speaking.

"What happened after Grekov and Nadia were reunited?" Ari asked.

"Well, they had three beautiful children; two daughters and a son. And Reginald and Nadia passed on, having lived very full lives." She smiled and had a far-off look in her eyes for a moment, then recovered and looked at her watch. "My, it's late. Ari, Dane, I think I'm going to turn in now. See you two in the morning?" She smiled and excused herself.

When she was inside, Dane and Ari looked at each other. "She didn't say why there are bee images all over the property," Ari whispered.

"She didn't say anything about the brass circle either," Dane added.

"I know. I honestly don't think she knows anything about it," he replied. After a moment, he got up as well. "I'm gonna head home too," he said, turning for the oak grove. "Oh, Ari?" he asked, looking straight at her.

"Yeah?"

"Thanks," he smiled broadly, and Ari felt a twinge of sadness. She'd grown to love that smile.

Over the next two days, Ari saw little of Dina, and even less of Dane. Of course, meals were shared with them, but Ari assumed that the two were getting to know each other, and Dane was likely in the process of weighing his options, as well as figuring out how to deal with Rhoda. Ari and her father were busy too; the end of next week would bring her mother and sister to their new home. As happy as Ari was to have her family reunited, she dreaded the possibility of Dane leaving.

At the end of the second night, Ari and her dad set out an elaborate meal on the back deck. Dane and Dina joined them, and her dad had even requested Rhoda be invited; whether or not she was, they never knew, but she never appeared. Candles were lit amongst the garden landscape, glass hurricane lanterns hung from the porch ceiling, and a strand of white Christmas lights circled the porch railing. Jazz wafted from the open windows of the office. They had cheese fondue, roast beef, and a scalloped potato dish that Ari had spent much time perfecting.

A cool breeze signaled the possibility of autumn; Ari wore a light sweater for the first time in months. In between cooking dinner and putting dessert in the oven, she had taken a few moments to put on some eye shadow and lip gloss. She wasn't exactly a girly-girl, but she liked looking nice. She'd brushed her straight, brown hair, which had gotten quite long over the summer. A small pair of sparkly earrings were her last addition. She looked in the mirror. *Not bad*, she thought, before rushing off to check dessert.

Once everything was ready, they sat down to eat. The evening couldn't have been more beautiful; it was getting dark earlier now, but at seven-thirty, sunlight still filtered through the trees before it set behind the hills.

Ari's dad clinked his glass and held it high. "I'd like to toast Ms. Dina Hadley for putting aside her calendar to come up and visit us," he said, carefully avoiding anything that would embarrass Dane. They all raised their glasses in agreement. Dishes were passed and light conversation was made, mostly about the history of the Hadleys. Dina had viewed the trunk containing her family's photos, and she desperately wanted to see Nadia's ballet accouterments, but Ari guessed that she hadn't even been introduced to Rhoda yet, much less been inside her house. Ari wanted to grill Dane about all they'd talked about, but waited for a more private opportunity.

Dessert was a broiled pear with drizzled syrup, with the option of Ari's homemade blackberry pie. After more conversation, Ari's dad and Dina retreated to his office for a discussion of jazz and blues, while Dane and Ari sat on the porch railing.

"So, has Dina met Rhoda?" she inquired.

"Yeah. Two days ago, Dina came to the door and introduced herself to Rhoda. Dina simply told her that she was here to visit me, and mentioned that she was willing to take me back to California with her if it was okay with Rhoda. Rhoda grunted and said whatever I wanted to do was fine and dandy with her."

A ripple of disbelief moved through Ari. "She was actually alright with letting you go? All she has tried to do is control you and now...that's it? You're free to go?" Ari shook her head in shock.

Dane shrugged. "I was just as surprised as you are."

Ari wanted to ask the next question, but it was stuck in her throat. She opened her mouth, but it refused to ask whether or not he'd chosen to go back with Dina. The twinge of an inner ache kept her silent.

"I...I've decided to go with her," he quietly said, without any question from Ari. Although her head was turned, she could feel him looking at her. "Part of me doesn't want to, but Rhoda is already packing her stuff, ready to move to who-knows-where." He paused, not really knowing what to say next. Ari still wasn't looking at him. In fact, her hair was covering most of the side of her face, so he couldn't really see a reaction at all. "Ari?"

85

She nodded. She was blinking fast to clear the tears that had formed. *This is ridiculous*, she thought. *I did this for him; I wanted him to go somewhere better.* But her emotions ruled out rational thought. She put her hand up to wipe away a strand of salty tears when Dane caught it and pulled her hand away from her face.

"Aw, Ari...come on," he said apologetically, taking her hand in both of his. She froze and silently caught her breath.

"I know, I know," she eventually said, and managed to smile. "I'm happy for you, really I am. And I do want you to live somewhere better. It's just gonna be really lonely without you, you know?" She finally turned to him and caught his gaze, dead-on. Words she had formed in her mind disappeared and a minute could've been an hour. He waited for her to say more, but all she could manage was, "When are you going?"

He put her hand down. "Two days from now." Ari nodded. He hopped from the porch railing to the ground. "I'd probably better go home now. I have to figure out what I'm taking with me," he said, brushing off his jeans. Ari jumped off as well, landing right next to him. Impulsively, she reached out and hugged him. He had no choice but to hug her right back.

*   *   *

Two more days came and went. Ari's dad had helped Dane pull out all of his family's possessions from Rhoda's attic, and they loaded them into a rented moving truck. They were going to start the long journey back to San Luis Obispo in less than a day. Ari helped a bit, but it made her sad to think that they're fantastic summer mystery had ended, as well as her friendship with Dane. She didn't hold onto much hope of hearing from him after he moved; she knew all too well how distances had an uncanny way of unraveling even the tightest friendships. Ari was moping, and she knew it.

The morning of Dane's move, she opened her bedroom door to find one of Nadia's trunks blocking it. On top was a plain white envelope that said, "Ari." She carefully opened it to reveal the key to the brass circle, on Dane's ball-chain necklace. Next to it was a note:

"Ari, This necklace is yours now. Because of you, and your unselfishness, I won't be needing it anymore.

Love, Dane"

"P.S. I wasn't able to find the second key- that's your job now."

A smiley face was drawn at the bottom. She smiled and slipped the key over her neck.

Reaching down, she lifted the lid to the trunk. Yards of tulle sprang out. Ari gasped. He was leaving Nadia's tutus for her? She couldn't believe it, nor accept them. As lovely as they were, they were part of Dane's history, not hers.

She jogged up the lane and saw Dina was loading the last of their family belongings onto the truck. Once outside, she asked Dina where Dane was. "Ah, he's inside, getting the last boxes. Can I be of help?" she said, noticing Ari was flustered.

"Ah, um, well, maybe. He left Nadia's trunk of tutus for me, but I think you guys should have them. They're amazing, but they're part of your family history," she said quietly.

Dina just smiled kindly and waved her hand. "Dear, I told him to give them to you. You're part of our family history now, too," she motioned at the house. "You restored her gardens, and you tend to her house. And you're a dear friend of her great-great grandson," she winked. "It's all yours, honey."

Ari blushed and smiled, but suddenly, her eyes caught hold of Dina's necklace. A flash of sunlight revealed a tiny, ornate key that was identical to the one Ari had around her neck, only smaller. Ari gasped.

"Oh my goodness," she said under her breath.

"Is everything alright?" Dina asked, concerned.

"Umm, Dina, where did you get your necklace?" Ari pointed at the dangling key.

"Oh, this?" she said, looking down her chin. "This has been in the family for as long as I can remember. My mother gave it to me, and it was given to her by her mother. I believe it's belonged to one lady in each generation of our family. Why?"

In an instant Ari bounded up the steps and yelled for Dane through the open door into the nearly empty house. "Dane! You have to come here! *Hurry!*"

Looking alarmed, Dane bounded down from the second story at the sound of Ari's cries. "What's going on?!"

"She has it!" she gasped, totally out of breath. "She—Dina—has the key. It's on her necklace. She's had it the whole time! We gotta see if it works!"

Dane took a minute to process Ari's mile-a-minute delivery, then sprung down the driveway, Ari in tow. They reached a befuddled Dina. "What's so important about my necklace?" she said, chuckling in half amusement, half curiosity.

Ari pulled out her key from the ball-chain necklace. "See, they match," she said, mainly to Dane. "Dina, there's this circle thing— ah, nevermind. Can we borrow your necklace for just a few minutes?"

Dina blinked, then reached back and unhooked the necklace. "Here you go..." she said, looking confused but handing it to Dane anyway.

"We'll be right back," Ari and Dane disappeared into the oak grove. Ari paused at the brass circle, waiting for Dane to procure his key.

"You have it now," he said, motioning at the necklace that once had been his.

"Oh!" Shoot, sorry," she quickly inserted the key and made a full turn. The hatch popped open and they barely even used the steps to descend. They quickly lit the closest candle and Dane carefully pulled out the small, delicate key. Holding their breath, Dane slipped the key into the keyhole. It fit.

Exhaling, Ari managed a "*whooaaa*," but Dane just paused. "What are you waiting for?" she asked impatiently.

"I don't want to get my hopes up," he said. "I don't want to be disappointed if it's empty."

She nodded, understanding, but was so anxious about opening the mysterious door that she started jumping up and down with mini-hops. Dane cracked a smile and chuckled. "Geesh," he said, shaking his head. "What do you think is in there?"

"Um, I dunno. Something wonderful, I think. I really think whatever is in there, it's important, you know?"

He shrugged his shoulders. "Here goes..." A single rotation of the key caused the heavy door to slide open. Darkness prevented them from seeing anything at first. "More candles," he ordered, and Ari found the lighter and illuminated each candle. They both held one inside the doorway. In unison, they gasped.

Reflecting the light of the two candles were glints of gold, silver, and gemstones, all arranged on small shelves around the perimeter of the safe-like room. One shelf housed cut diamonds, each stone nestled carefully in a silver tray lined with black velvet. Below that, stones of ruby, sapphire, citrine, emerald, jade, and opal were arranged in a similar fashion. Jewelry—necklaces, earrings, tiaras, and headdresses—were carefully lain in display. Ornate boxes were stored on one half of the closet. Dane gingerly lifted the lid on one. Russian money was stacked and banded inside. A stately vermeil box sat in the corner of one shelf. Delicate Russian antiques were stashed here and there. In the middle of the top shelf, a singular gold honeybee pendant hung from a thread of silver. Ari couldn't believe what she was seeing.

"Dane, this is incredible. I've never seen anything like this in my entire life," she breathed. "You know what this means, don't you?"

"Yeah. I don't have to move anymore," he said, smiling at Ari.

chapter twenty-three

Over the next few days, Dane and Dina had the challenging task of discreetly assessing the value of the pieces found in the underground vault. Dina wanted to make sure that the press didn't get involved; a fantastical story of an underground treasure would surely draw unwanted attention to Hadley Hill.

Nadia's treasures were carefully catalogued and appraised by an antique dealer from the closest city, while the jewelry and gems were reviewed by a jeweler from Rivers. The jeweler looked at each stone, each article of jewelry, and shook his head each time he looked up from his loupe. "These are fantastic examples of hand-cut stones. I've never seen anything quite like these. You say these are yours, young man?" he gazed curiously at Dane.

"They're my family's collection," he murmured.

"Exquisite," the jeweler commented, and went back to his loupe.

*   *   *

Two days later, Ari was brimming with excitement as she listened all morning for the telltale crunch of a car on the gravel driveway. At noon, Ari was in the kitchen when she heard car doors slam somewhere in the front of the property. She bolted out the front door and nearly tackled her mom and Lily in a giant hug. Before they even had a chance to take a single item into the house, Ari begged her mom to close her eyes while she led her through the house and out the back door.

"Mom, Dad and I have a surprise for you. We've worked on it the whole summer, and we hope you like it." Ari paused and made sure she'd placed her mom in the perfect spot to see the entire garden. "Open your eyes now," Ari said, beaming.

Ari's mom did as she was told, and when she opened her eyes, she gasped and smiled. The black-eyed Susans were in full bloom, an unbroken field of yellow and black. Petunias trailed from hanging baskets that bordered the garden path. Birds swooped and dove above their heads, using the birdbaths and houses she and her dad had posted all over. The statues peeked from behind clusters of cosmos and lupine. Every hedge was trimmed, the grass was lush and green, and everything was in full bloom.

Her mom walked along the cobblestone path and admired the garden that Ari and her dad had worked on all season. "Ari, this is amazing. You guys did this for me?" Ari nodded and hugged her mom. "Unbelievable. I finally have the beautiful garden I've always wanted."

Ari walked with her and Lily, describing every detail of the project: how she'd worked with the neighbor to uncover historic documents that Ari and her dad had used to accurately recreate the garden. As Ari and her mom admired the latticed arbor with its rambling roses, Ari recited the history of Nadia and Regniald and Grekov. The story itself was as stunning as the gardens that surrounded them.

Ari led her mom to the glass-paned greenhouse. "I have always wanted a real greenhouse," her mom gushed, opening the door and peeking inside. Ari's dad had placed a few tropical plants within, and Ari had chosen a small crystal chandelier candle holder and hung it inside from the highest point of the roof.

"It took a bit of work to get the glass cleaned up and the metal frame polished," Ari admitted.

Lily had since become disinterested in the garden tour and was darting around the garden paths, chasing butterflies. As Ari and her mom were chatting among the tall gladiolas on the edge of the formal garden, Lily had made her way down the pasture and was pointing up at the brass bee plaques on the stone pillars.

"Those are beautiful bees," Ari's mom commented.

Ari nodded. "Bee symbols are literally all over the property. Dane and I haven't figured out why, though," she mused.

"Sounds like another mystery to be solved," her mom said, with glint of excitement in her eyes.

*   *   *

Later that night, after Dane had been introduced to Ari's mom and sister, Dane and Ari sat on the front porch of his home for the very first time.

"So Rhoda has already moved out?" Ari asked, incredulous.

"Yep. Dina was able to sell enough antiques and jewels to not only cover the back taxes on the house, but she's in the process of purchasing the home from Rhoda," Dane explained. "We also decided to give Rhoda a little extra cash to cover moving costs."

"I bet she was thrilled to have some money in her pocket," Ari mused.

"Absolutely," Dane grinned. "She even smiled at me as she took the check," he nodded. "I think she was happy to not have to worry about her taxes anymore, and not having me to deal with. It was a win-win for both of us."

Ari nodded. "And your Mom and Molly?" she asked.

"They get here in two weeks. Permanently. She won't have to worry about supporting me now. Dina set up a Hadley family trust fund for Molly and myself, too. It's unbelievable how many 'tokens of love' Grekov shipped to Nadia over those five years, and how they have changed the course of my entire life in the span of a single week. It feels like a lifetime since I've seen my mom," Dane continued.

"I can't wait to meet her and your sister," Ari smiled, relieved that she and Dane no longer had to avoid living in his own house. "Hey, I'd better head home and help mom and Lily unpack," she said, stepping down the front stairs.

"Wait. I...I want you to have this," Dane pulled something from his pocket, and reached for Ari's hand. A small velvet bag was placed in her palm. She opened it and pulled out a delicate silver chain, from which dangled a small round pendant. The pendant was a silver disk with a honeycomb pattern. A tiny golden bee sat right in the middle of the disk.

"Whoa," Ari said, examining the necklace. "Dane, I can't take this. It's too precious. And it belongs to your family," she said, quietly.

"Ari, you're the whole reason things turned out like they did. Without your persistence, I'd be out on the streets with Rhoda, or worse. Now I have a home. I have my family. And we—" he motioned to Ari, "—are able to stay friends. So if you think that necklace is precious, well, that's how I feel about what you did for me."

Slowly, she tried to put it on. Dane stepped closer and sweeping her long hair to the side, latched the clasp on the necklace. Ari looked down at it, and a broad smile spread across her face. Things couldn't have turned out better.

PART TWO

chapter one

The crisp late summer morning was beautiful, but Ari decided that sleeping in would've been a better alternative to riding her bike to her first day of high school. She had just glided down the long driveway that connected her house with the main country road when she heard a second set of tires crunching down the gravel. Dane skidded to a stop next to her.

"Hey," she said to him, nodding. "So, school, huh?" Apprehension filled her voice.

"It's not so bad. You'll make friends fast," he said, acknowledging the fact that she'd didn't really know anyone, besides him, from Rivers. "C'mon, we're gonna be late," he said, and they started out onto the highway, towards the tiny country town. Dane would be starting eleventh grade, Ari was starting tenth, and although she was glad to have someone she already knew, she had no idea what her first day would hold.

They arrived at school and Ari got out her schedule. The building that housed Rivers High School was impressively huge. Numbers in bas-relief above the front doors indicated the building had been built in 1924. Geometrically-styled walls hinted toward Art Deco architecture, like many of the buildings that made up the town. She glanced at the piece of paper in her hand and read the first class. "Hey, point me in the right direction. Where's Room 312?"

"Floor three, room twelve," Dane said, with a glint in his eye. Ari rolled her eyes. "Hey," he said, snagging her backpack loop as she turned away. She looked back. "Good luck," he said, with a small smile. Ari loved his smile, and her nervousness melted away. Even though she'd seen Dane smile more than usual since the arrival of his mother and sister, his grin hadn't lost its effect.

"Aaaand that's your homework tonight," the teacher finished writing the long list of assignment pages on the chalkboard and Ari rushed to scribble them down. As she was writing, she noticed the bee pendant Dane had given her. She always wore it and smiled at the thought of the memories of her first summer in Rivers. Suddenly, the bell rang and woke her from her reverie. Her first day of school had ended without incident.

She was unlocking her beach cruiser from the bike racks when she heard Dane talking behind her. Two boys and a girl were laughing and talking to him as he approached. "You guys should meet my neighbor," he said. "This is Ari Cartwright. She moved here this summer from San Francisco."

She nodded at the group. "Ari," he said, "This is Ray, Alex, and Jenelle," Dane smiled at Jenelle. She was slender with wavy blonde hair, which she tossed to the side as she smirked a silent hello at Ari. Immediately Ari felt a twinge in the pit of her stomach, but she didn't know why. They walked on as Dane unlocked his bike.

"How'd it go?" he said as they wheeled down the road.

"Fine, I guess," she said, still feeling uneasy. *Neighbor,* she thought. He'd introduced me as his *neighbor,* not friend. Why would he call me that? Was it because of the blonde girl, Jenelle? She wanted to ask but knew it was a detail that probably didn't matter.

"You sure it was ok?" He glanced at her as they got off their bikes to walk up their steep driveway. They both noticed a white van slowly coming down the driveway; Ari knew she'd never seen it before. She took a mental note of the New Mexico license plates, but her concentration was broken by Dane's questions.

"You're awfully quiet. Were people nice to you today?" he sounded genuinely concerned.

"Oh, yeah, everyone was fine," she said. "Hey, does your family know anyone from New Mexico? she asked, motioning towards the van that had just passed.

"Nope." He said, looking behind him. "They probably just made a wrong turn."

Ari nodded and mustered a half-hearted smile as they came to the forked driveway. "I, uh, I have a lot of homework that I have to get done" she said. "I'll see you later."

"Oh. Ok, yeah, I have some too. Well, bye until tomorrow, unless I see you at the circle," he said, and they parted ways; Dane going straight up the road, and Ari turning right. Since they had discovered the Hadley's immense family treasure in an underground room, the items had been removed and safely stored elsewhere. Since the weather was still dry, the brass circle was usually left unlocked, although Ari always wore its key around her neck.

Often, Ari would go to the underground room to think, and sometimes Dane would go there for some peace and quiet. Sometimes, they'd happen there at the same time.

When Ari opened her heavy oak front door, silence greeted her. Her mom and dad were still at work. Lily was still at daycare. Ari went to the kitchen and made herself a small afternoon snack of apple slices, peanut butter, and popcorn. She sat down at the table and opened her history book, figuring she'd use the few quiet hours before everyone came home to get her work finished. However, somewhere between reading about the turn of the century and the Great Depression, her mind wandered.

She turned and glanced at her reflection in entryway mirror. Her hair remained untouched since summer. It was long and straight and just brown. She considered her face. It was still sporting a myriad of freckles from summer's strong sun. Ari sighed. *Time for a change,* she thought. Grabbing a pencil, she scribbled a note and jogged for the front door.

When Ari returned home two hours later, her mom and Lily were already there. "Ari?" her mom called from the kitchen. "Is that you? How was your first day of school?"

Ari quietly walked into the kitchen and Lily squealed. "Whoa, sissy!" she said, her little girl voice raising excitedly. "You're hair's different!" With that, Ari's mom turned and a look of shock, then an approving smile, came over her face.

"Very nice!" her mom nodded as she stirred dinner. "When your note said a haircut I didn't expect anything like that, but it's really flattering. You got it colored, too!" Ari nodded, a little embarrassed, but she was glad she had done it. Her long hair had been cut short, the back cleanly layered to a bob, with the front a bit longer. It was parted on the side, and a few blonde highlights accented her newly coppery-brown hair.

"Yeah, I just wanted a change, you know?" she said.

"Yup. Every girl needs to change things up once in a while," her mom agreed. "Makes life fun, you know?" she smiled as she put the lid back on the stew pot. Ari was glad her mom agreed. Even Lily seemed to like it, as she reached up to touch Ari's hair.

"Dinner won't be ready for half an hour," her mom said. "How about your homework?"

"Um, yup, gotta get that done," Ari said, grabbing her backpack and a blanket. "Call me when dinner's ready," she held up her cell phone and her mom nodded.

"I knew that thing would come in handy," she heard her mom chuckle. "Thank goodness for the family plan."

Ari bounded out the back door and into the oak grove. The trees were absolutely brilliant this time of year. She had never experienced such beautiful color, as trees along the California coast were generally evergreens. The trees themselves were like sunshine, glowing yellow in the low evening sun. It made the oak grove one of her favorite places to be. She could smell wood smoke coming from both houses, her own and Dane's, and she wrapped her knit scarf around her bare neck once more. The air was chilly, but once she dropped down underneath the brass circle, it was cozy.

She lit the candles, one for each small nook in the wall. Besides providing light and causing the wall tiles to sparkle, she liked how they quickly warmed the small space. *Now* she could start her homework.

She breezed through history and math, but when it came to biology, Ari wrinkled her nose. It wasn't an easy subject for her, and she sat there, staring at the diagrams of cells and DNA. She startled when a cold stream of air hit her. The brass circle had been opened.

chapter three

"Oh, hey," **Dane looked down** into the room. "Whoa!" He did a double-take, then hopped down into the hatch, staring her down. "Your hair wasn't like that earlier today, was it?" he gave her a quizzical look, but was smiling one of his fantastic smiles.

"Um, definitely not," she couldn't hold back a laugh. "I just wanted a change," she said simply, then held out her homework. "How good are you at cellular processes?"

Dane just shook his head. "Uhh, what?" He sat down next to her and was still staring at her head. "Whoa, it's a different color, too..." With that, he ran his hand through her hair, examining the highlights. She froze at his touch, but eventually turned her head so she was facing him.

"Well, does it look ok?" she asked, not exactly looking for his approval, but deep down she knew she cared what he thought.

"Of course it does. It looks really nice. You just look a lot different now, you know? It's cool though."

"Thanks," she said quietly, but then pushed her worksheet back at him. "Cellular processes," she reminded him. He shook his head but looked at it anyway. "I think I remember this stuff," he said, and they worked away at the problems on the sheet until Ari's ringing cell phone caused them both to jump.

"Dinnertime," Ari said, collecting her things. "Thanks for your help," she added, and he helped pull her up from the ground. He didn't let go of her yet, but instead glanced at her bee pendant.

"You're still wearing Nadia's bee," he said, smiling.

"Of course. I never take it off, you know that. It reminds me of the best summer I've ever had," she said, gently smiling, but unsure of what to say next.

He was still holding her hands. A serious look came over his face, and the candles barely illuminated his deep hazel eyes. "I need your help with something," he said quietly. "Please don't let anyone know about this," he said, "but I think I know where my dad is."

"Huh?" Ari paused a moment and then tilted her head. "Why didn't you say something earlier? I gotta go to dinner now, but where do you think he is?"

They started up the steps and exited the circle into the evening. "That's what I need your help with," he said, walking her to the backyard. "You're obviously a lot better at finding people than I am. I have a hunch, but that's all right now. Mom doesn't know I'm looking, and she probably wouldn't want to know where he is. But...I *do*. I guess he's the missing piece, an' I just gotta know why he disappeared four years ago..." He looked down and Ari recognized his introverted gaze.

"Ok, I'll help you," Ari said quietly, nodding. "We'll talk more tomorrow," she said, running up her deck stairs.

"Later," she heard him say as he disappeared into the dusk.

She opened the back door to a flood of warmth and the delicious scent of dinner. Her parents were already at the table, and her dad did an identical double take at Ari's new haircut. "Good grief! Where'd your hair go?" he said with a big grin. "Looks great, Ari. Goodness, our little girl is growing up, Jess," Ari's dad smiled at her mom.

"Hardly," Ari smirked. "Just wanted a change, that's all." She poked her spoon into the stew and took a hefty bite. Quiet conversation filled the warm house and soon Ari's mind drifted to Dane's request. Why on earth would he want to find the father who had abandoned him? What would Dane's mom think if she knew he was looking? They had just settled in and finally had begun living life as a real family. Ari just shook her head and continued eating.

*   *   *

The next day was a whirlwind. Another set of classes awaited Ari, as her schedule alternated days. Math, history, and biology were three days a week, and English, art, and gym were two days a week. She had meant to ask Dane more about his request for help finding his father, but didn't have a chance until art class. The art and music classes were generally mixed between grades, and she'd smiled at her good luck when Dane walked through the door of the studio classroom. Her smile faded when she saw the tall blonde girl from yesterday walking beside him. Jenelle slinked to a seat at the end of Ari's table. Dane hesitated, and then pulled out the chair next to Jenelle's and sat down. Ari suddenly felt her face flush.

She barely heard anything the teacher said through the entire class. Now she knew she hadn't been imagining things yesterday. She tried to focus on the class syllabus that was laying in front of her, or the teacher—anything to avoid catching Dane's eye. Not that he was looking at her. He seemed more intent on Jenelle. Ari shook her head. *This is silly*, she thought. *Why am I upset he has a friend? He's allowed to.* She tuned back in as the class ended. She simply got up from her table, nodded at Dane, and headed to gym class. As she entered the crowded and noisy hall, she thought she heard Dane calling after her. She resisted the urge to turn back, and continued down the hallway, weaving through the mass of people.

At the final bell, a sweaty Ari quickly unlocked her bike and hopped on, but not before Dane jumped out in front of her with his bike. "Where you goin'? I have a little bit of information I found on the internet, but I need your help with a couple of things. You still wanna help me, right?"

"You could've asked me, oh, earlier, like in *art class*," Ari just couldn't help herself. She winced as soon as she'd said it.

"Wha...? Ooooohhhhh...*Jenelle*. Right. Um, about that... I'm sorry. We've been friends since last year, you know?" he explained, and Ari was sure he was sincere. But she still felt the sting of being ignored.

"And I'm just your neighbor, I guess." Ari swerved around Dane's bike and pedaled off. She partly felt bad about what she said, and she kept telling herself that Dane was allowed to have whatever friends he wanted, but she just couldn't shake the pit in her stomach.

At home, Ari sat at her desk with her English book, notebook, and an assortment of pens, but yet again, concentration failed her. Her gaze fell on the old steamer trunk that had once belonged to Nadia, Dane's great-great grandmother. He had given it to Ari at the end of the summer, and time and time again she'd gone through the contents: beautiful old tutus, notes, and letters. After Ari had painstakingly read each of the letters, she'd discovered more family photos, some of them labeled, and some of them hopelessly devoid of any markings. Four generations of photos sketched out a jigsaw puzzle of Dane's lineage.

She was fascinated with history in general, but living in one of the houses where this family called home for so many generations truly invested her interest. Ari went to the trunk and sifted through the family photos. One of them showed two beautiful girls standing in front of a building that looked vaguely familiar. It wasn't Ari or Dane's house, but a much larger structure. She flipped the photo. "Katia, Eva, at school. 1926."

Ari furrowed her brow. The only schools in Rivers had been built at the establishment of the town, right around the time Grekov had begun building the house Ari currently lived in. Did that mean these girls had attended the same school she went to? And could she possibly put the pieces together the pieces to help find Dane's dad?

She went to her computer and brought up a search engine, typed in a name. Thousands of entries came up. *I need more information* she thought to herself. *A middle name, a birthday, something.* She shook her head out of frustration. A knock on her door brought her out of deep thought, but before she could call out to come in, the door swung open. "Hey," Dane said.

chapter five

"Geesh! Dane!" Ari jabbed the power button on her computer screen and all went black.

"Whatcha looking at?" Dane said with a curious grin. "Is it... homework?" He slid over to her desk and poked at the power button, despite a fast swat from Ari. The screen flicked on. *"Ahhhhhh,"* he said, nodding. "So I see you do want to help me, but when I try to talk to you, you run away. I see how it is," he said, obviously not upset.

"I do want to help you, but it's like you don't want to be seen around me at school. I don't get it," Ari said quietly. "So I'm not as gorgeous as Jenelle. I get that. But you can at least *pretend* I exist, right?" Frustration strained her voice.

Dane opened his mouth as if to say something, but closed it after a moment. "It's just that things have been really weird lately. I mean, my mom and sister, both who I barely know, just moved into my house and became a part of my life. I'm trying to adjust to that, and it's tons better than living with Rhoda, but it's like starting over with two almost-complete strangers. It's weird." He stared at her computer screen. "School is the one thing that hasn't turned upside down on me. And Jenelle is just a friend; don't worry."

Ari narrowed her eyes, staring Dane down with the most intense glare. "Fine," she cautioned, "but beware. I think she's one of *those* girls, though." Ari glanced at him knowingly.

"What kind is that?" Dane looked at her innocently.

"The kind of girl that likes you, or pretends to like you, and then backstabs you or does something horrible. And they get away with it every time. Mark my words." She brought her pencil eraser down hard on her desk for emphasis. Dane flinched.

"Don't worry about me," he said, taking the pencil from her hands. "Let's talk about what's on your computer screen before you kill your desk with that pencil. There are an awful lot of Mark

Hadleys out there, aren't there?" Dane said, pointing at the screen.

"Yeah. I need more information. What do you have?" Ari said, preparing to start a new search.

"His full name is William Marcus Hadley. He went by Mark for short. I don't ever remember him using his first name for anything, except we'd get the occasional piece of junk mail with his full name on it. I'm pretty sure he's in Texas or Arizona."

"How do you know that?" Ari said, already typing the name into the search engine.

"Because I looked on a people-finding site on the internet, and there were four William Marcus Hadleys, two in Texas, and two in Arizona. Of those four, only two of them were the right approximate age of my dad. One was in Texas, the other Arizona." He pointed at the two entries that matched, though they had no phone number or address listed. "So that's where I'm at. I need you to help me figure out which one is him."

Ari tilted her head to the side. "That's weird. It doesn't seem like his full name would be so common." Furrowing her brow, she suddenly declared it was time for a hot chocolate break and got up from her computer.

They went downstairs and Ari prepared two mugs of steaming hot chocolate with marshmallows bobbing on the top. She grabbed her coat and headed out to the back porch.

"So why don't you just call both of them?" Ari asked, once they were seated on the rocking chairs. The creaking floorboards and rustling leaves were the only sounds heard in the cold, dry air.

"I don't want to do that. What would I say? 'Hey, you might be my dad and I want to know where you've been for the past four years?' Is that what I should do?" he spoke slowly and evenly, though a hint of frustration tinged his voice.

"That's what I did with your aunt, and she was a complete

stranger," Ari said.

"Naw, I'm not gonna do that." He took a sip of the hot chocolate. Wispy strands of steam rose from the cup. "I think I want to know something about his situation, you know? I want to know the reason he's been gone so long, *without* him knowing that I know. Ari, what if he has a wife and a new family? I don't wanna be a part of his life if it's like that."

Ari nodded, understanding. "Yeah, I get it," she said quietly. "I think we need to work backwards on this. We need to start with your dad's family, like your Aunt Dina. Somebody has to have heard from him, Dane. People don't just disappear."

At that, the back door opened and her mom poked her head out. "Hey, guys. Ari, dinner's ready. Dane, you're welcome to stay if you'd like," she smiled.

"Thanks, Mrs. Cartwright, but I've got to go home and do homework. Later, Ari." He hopped off the back steps and disappeared into the oak grove.

The next couple of days went by quickly. The routine at school became more familiar, and although Ari enjoyed most of her classes. biology was still troublesome. Most of the lectures seemed monotonous and unintelligible despite copious note-taking on Ari's part. It didn't help that she had chosen a seat right next to one of the second-story windows. She looked down one of the streets bordering the high school, sometimes counting how many cars stopped at the stop sign below.

During one particular lecture, Ari's pen deviated from the lines of her loopy cursive notes and she began making a secondary list in the margin. "Exact birthday, employer, address, phone number, email address, last known phone number, family(?)" She put the pen to her head and concentrated. What else would she need to know to find which William Marcus Hadley was Dane's dad?

"Ari," the teacher looked down his glasses and glared at her.

"Can you tell me what mitochondria does for the cell?"

Ari paused. "It, it, uh..." she faltered. "No, I can't," she said quietly.

"Miss Cartwright, I'm aware that you're new to this school. I don't know where you're from, but around here, we make a point of actually trying to learn the material. Understood?"

Ari felt her cheeks burn hot. She nodded and kept her eyes down to her paper, though she could feel a stare from the girl sitting next to her. She looked slightly to the side and caught eyes with the girl. The girl gave an apologetic smile, and Ari felt a twinge of relief. After an eternity, the bell rang and she made a point to escape the class as quickly as possible, but not before the girl quietly sidled up to her. "He can be a real jerk sometimes. I'm Riley. You're Ari, right?"

Ari nodded. "Yeah. I'm new...you probably figured that out."

Riley smiled. "If you ever need help with class, let me know. This is my second time through biology," she gave a rueful laugh. "But I think I'm actually getting it this time. We can work things out together if you'd like." She handed Ari a strip of paper with a phone number on it.

"Thanks. I need that. I suck at this stuff," Ari just shook her head. "See you later."

When she got to her beach cruiser, she noticed that Dane's bike, usually placed somewhere near hers, was missing. A note was stuffed between the springs of her seat, however, and she unfolded it. In Dane's neat all-caps handwriting the note read, "Meet me at Cinema Coffee right after school. Urgent!"

chapter six

The Cinema Coffee shop was housed in an elegant turn-of-the-century theater building. The lobby area was the main coffee shop, but on Friday and Saturday nights, the theater section opened up and vintage films were shown for fifty cents per show. Ari arrived at the coffee shop and spied the back of Dane's head in a far corner of the room. Taking off her scarf and hat, she plunked down in the seat across from him. "Well? What's so urgent?" she asked, rubbing her hands together for warmth.

"Aren't you going to get something to drink?" He motioned at his cup of coffee which was steaming up the window next to the table. Ari took in a deep breath. The scent of the warm coffee was delicious.

"Mmm...a mocha would be perfect on a day like today, huh?" she mused, and before she could rise, Dane got up.

"Then a mocha it will be. Don't go anywhere," he said, heading towards the counter. Ari smiled inwardly. She gazed out the tiny coffee shop windows. The little town of Rivers bustled at this time of day. People dressed in warm coats hustled from one place to the next, pulling scarves and coats tight. It hadn't rained or even frozen over yet, but a crisp autumn bite had settled on the valley floor with a permanency unlike what Ari was used to.

A heavy stoneware mug was set on the table, jarring her back to reality. She smiled at Dane in thanks and took a sip of the fragrant mocha. "So, what's urgent? I'm dying to know," Ari said inquisitively.

"So this morning as I got ready to ride to school, I noticed that white van you saw awhile ago," he said, looking intently at Ari.

"What van?" she shook her head, trying to recall.

"The one with New Mexico plates. The first day of school, you asked me if I knew anyone from-"

"Oh!" Ari exclaimed, cutting off Dane mid-sentence. "Yeah, I totally remember now. Where did you see it again?"

"Well, that's the weird thing. I didn't see it until I was riding down our driveway, and I didn't notice it until it passed me. That means," he lowered his voice and leaned in, "that it was parked somewhere where I couldn't see it when I left my house, and I don't know where that would be," Dane said, nearly at a whisper.

Ari was momentarily lost in her close proximity to Dane. Her eyes were locked on his. For a moment, she felt like her memory was taking a photograph of exactly what he looked like in this singular moment, down to every fleck of green in his eyes. Her brain registered that she *had* to say something, but she froze and rational thought was suspended. She blinked slowly, breaking the mesmerizing connection. "I...uh...that's really strange," she finally managed. "What do you think the van has to do with anything, though?" Ari finally collected herself.

"I don't know. That's where you come in, again. I need your skills," He gave her a smile. Ari automatically smiled back, but her eye suddenly caught the form of a familiar figure out the window. A big-haired blonde girl and several of her friends had just entered the coffee shop. Inwardly, Ari groaned.

Dane saw the shift in her smile and quickly turned around. "Oh, it's Jenelle," he said, giving a small nod. Immediately, Jenelle beelined for the table and gave one of her big, lipstick-outlined grins.

"Hiya, Dane! Oh, this is your friend, Arnie...Arby...um-"

"Aribelle," Ari said, quietly.

"Well, don't be a stranger, Dane. Let's hang out like old times, you know?" She winked as she turned back to her pack of friends. Ari just stared downward at her coffee mug, watching tiny orbs of oil collect around the rim of coffee. That funny twinge twisted in her stomach again, but she tried to ignore it. Finally, she recalled what they had been discussing.

"You need a license plate number," she said, still looking down. A strand of her short hair fell across her eyes and she brushed it away. "If you see it again, be sure to remember it. And look to see if you can tell who's driving. For your dad," she continued, "I need to know his birthday, and any addresses he previously had. If he ever sent you any letters, I need them." Dane didn't respond so she looked up, and her hair flopped back across her eyes. Before she could react, he leaned over and brushed the stray hair from her forehead, but his hand lingered right at the side of her face, brushing her cheek. A small smile crossed his face, and his eyes reflected the waning light from the window. This time she knew it was permissible to be looking at him without trying to pretend she wasn't. But as quickly as it had happened, Dane drew a deep breath and quickly got up.

"Alright, I'll try and get any information I can," he promised, grabbing his coat. "See you later...and thanks for your help." He almost sounded apologetic, Ari thought, but her mind was still stuck at the moment where his hand touched her cheek. She sat there a minute, but then her glance darted to Jenelle's table. Jenelle's friends were snickering in her direction, but Jenelle was glaring at Ari. Quickly, Ari gulped her coffee and exited the shop. She needed some space to think.

Riley was laying on her stomach on the plush rug in Ari's room, and Ari was laying on her bed. Biology books were spread open, with notes covering the floor. In desperation, Ari had called Riley for some much needed help. Without hesitation, Riley had agreed.

"Hey, I really appreciate you spending part of your Saturday helping me with this," Ari smiled at Riley, silently thankful that she had a new friend to talk to. She hadn't seen Dane since the coffee shop.

"No prob. Besides, we gotta get it done anyways. May as well do it together. Probably increases our chances of doing better, right?" Riley smiled, her blue eyes framed by glasses. Ari thought Riley was pretty, but Ari guessed Riley was more concerned with academics than appearances. Ari found this reassuring, somehow. Ari was currently lacking in self-confidence. Removed from anything familiar, she was in the process of rebuilding who she was. It didn't help that Dane was being more confusing than ever.

"Hey, Riley, how about a non-biology question?" Ari reluctantly ventured.

"Shoot," Riley answered, still looking at her notes.

"Do you like anyone...I mean, *like* like anyone at school?" One could almost hear Ari wincing as she asked, but she was curious if a self-confident, pretty, and most importantly, smart girl could stoop to liking an immature high school boy.

Riley's expression indicated she wasn't irritated by the question, but instead a sly smile spread across her face. "Maybe," she said, but offered nothing else.

"Well? Enlighten me," Ari joked. "He must be pretty special. You're too smart to fall for the creeps at school."

Riley let out a snort and kept smiling. "He's just some guy in my calculus class. I'm a nerd, so I'm in with the juniors. His name is Jace. He's pretty smart and pretty cute, but I think he has a girlfriend. It doesn't hurt to dream though."

"Have you talked to him?"

"Nothing besides, like, class stuff. I'm cautious when it comes to conversation." Riley giggled.

"You mean you're chicken," Ari concluded. "I bet we could figure out something for you two to talk about—"

Riley cut her off with a raised hand. "Nope. I seriously get too nervous. I'd totally say something dumb and it's just not worth it. Besides, if *he's* the one who starts a conversation, then there's a possibility that he might like me too. Until then, I'm just admiring from afar," she said wispily, half joking.

"Dang. You *are* smart," Ari nodded, grinning.

"What about you? I've seen Dane Hadley hanging around you a lot. Does he like you, or do you like him? He must be a real interesting guy," she said, dryly.

"What do you mean?" Ari was curious.

"Well, he seems really quiet. Like, there's a wall between him and reality. Although this year he seems a lot more convivial, and I see him smile a lot more. What's the deal with him?"

Ari paused. How much could she tell Riley? She figured Riley was trustworthy, but there were a lot of things Ari knew Dane wouldn't want other people to know. Heck, Ari didn't even know how she felt about him...or maybe she did, but she didn't want to confess anything yet.

"Uh, he lives up the road. That's how I know him. He's nice, but there's a lot of family stuff that he has to deal with. He was the first person I met when I moved here," Ari concluded.

Riley narrowed her eyes and peered at Ari. "You didn't say whether you liked him or not."

Ari shrugged. "He's nice, but I think he likes Jenelle Thomas," she said honestly.

Turning the page in her biology book, Riley nodded silently. "Too bad for him," she remarked.

After another hour they finished their homework, and school books were traded for magazines. Although Ari didn't consider herself a girly-girl, she wasn't above reading an occasional beauty magazine. She flipped through the pages and sighed at the photos of flawless models. Before she knew it, Riley had pulled a compact, mascara, and some other items from her purse and was working on Ari's face. Ari chuckled; she'd never really paid too much attention to makeup, but once she looked in the mirror, she was astonished at how a little color here and there had made a huge difference.

"You looked great before, Ari, don't get me wrong," Riley smiled kindly as she capped her mascara. "But your eyes are just too big and brown to go unnoticed. I think the shadow really works, too.

Ari just smiled at the transformation. "I didn't know you were a makeup artist," she chuckled, and Riley took the compliment. Ari silently noted that this was the first time since they'd moved that she'd had actual girl-time with someone other than her mom or sister, and she liked it. Even though it partly made her miss her old friends, she was glad she was finally comfortable meeting new people.

They continued chatting until Riley noticed it was time for her to be back at her house. Ari walked Riley to the door, and, after Riley got on her bike, Ari was about to shut the door when she saw the same white van drive down the road. She ran out into the drive just in time to see the plate number. "YRD 934," she said, repeating the set in her head until she found a pen and scrawled it on her hand.

chapter eight

Ari slowly turned the combination lock on her paint-chipped locker. Twenty-three, fifteen, then nine. She dropped her books from the previous class into her locker, and they hit with a thud. She quickly glanced at the magnetic mirror on her locker door. She'd spent a few minutes on her makeup this morning: her brown eyes were framed by long, brown lashes, and she'd dusted just a bit of sparkly gold eyeshadow on her lids. She smiled at the effect it made; with her new haircut, she actually looked like a tenth-grader instead of a misplaced middle-schooler.

She gathered her books needed for the next classes and was about to stuff them in her bag when a hand came down hard on them, sending them crashing to the floor.

"Hey! What the heck?!" Ari swung around, only to see the back of Jenelle and her friends walking away, giggling. Ari felt her cheeks burn hot as she bent down to get the strewn books. *What's her problem?* she scowled to herself.

She glanced to her right and left, hoping nobody had seen, but suddenly she saw a familiar face. At first he wasn't looking, but, as if he had sensed her gaze, his eyes caught hers. She tried to look away, but wasn't fast enough. Dane walked over and bent down to pick up her last book.

"What happened?" He hadn't seen. "You ok?"

"Um, yeah, I just dropped my books." A long awkward pause begged filling. "Hey, we have to chat sometime." She tried to get a lock on his eyes, but he looked down. *I don't like it when he hides like that,* she thought to herself.

"How about you meet me by the pool or something? Four o'clock?" he asked. During the summer, they had often visited the stone-circled well that was located between her house. He finally looked at her straight, and she thought she saw a questioning glint in his eye.

"Ok. See you then."

*   *   *

Her wool scarf couldn't be wrapped any tighter around her neck, and her gloves just didn't help keep her hands from aching from the cold wind that was blowing through the oak grove. Ari hadn't much reason to visit the beautiful circular pool that had been built by Nadia and Reginald since the weather had gotten colder, but she realized that even in the cold of late fall, it was as beautiful as ever. Yellow-red oak leaves danced along the dark surface of the water. She stood there, listening to the papery rustle of the remaining leaves on the nearly-denuded trees.

Shivering, Ari chided herself for not wearing a heavier sweater. A glance at her watch showed it to be fifteen minutes past the agreed meeting time. *Ugh, he's forgotten. I knew it.* She turned to leave and ran smack into him.

"Ooof!" she stumbled backwards as if bouncing off a wall. He reached out to keep her from falling into the icy pool. "Whoa, thanks," she said, as she steadied herself. "Where did you come from? I didn't even hear you. You're like a ninja or something," she smirked. "I was actually just going to leave. I thought you'd forgotten about me." Her teeth chattered with each word, and she hugged her arms to herself.

"Sorry," he said. "I didn't mean to be so late. And I didn't forget." He paused, wrinkling his nose. "Here, take my coat. You forget yours?" he asked.

"No," she said, taking it gladly. The coat surrounded her with his warm scent, and she was thankful she stopped shivering. "I just didn't know it would be so darn cold out here." It was big enough that she was able to wrap it tightly around, and the sleeves covered well past her gloves. "So, I have information for you." He gave an interested eyebrow. "I saw the van again on Saturday. I only saw the back, but I got the plate numbers. Sorry I didn't see who was in it."

116

"Naw, good work, Ari. Who do you think they are?"

"I'm really not sure. But, I gave your Aunt Dina a call. She said the last time she talked to your dad was about one year ago, in the spring. He was driving through Nevada, and he mentioned there was a job prospect in Arizona. Do you think that's a coincidence? I think it's a pretty good chance that he's in Arizona still. It's just too bad there's no number or address listed."

Dane nodded. "I know. Did she say if Aunt Maria had heard from him?"

"No. I mean, your aunts practically live next door to each other, so he probably only needed to call one of them. Sorry..." her voice trailed off. Dane nodded in understanding.

"Hey," he said suddenly, "Would you like to have dinner with Mom, Molly, and me tonight?" He gave her a little smile, and suddenly a reassuring warmth washed over her.

"Sure, I'll give mom a call and make sure it's ok," she said, pulling out her cell phone. As she received permission from her mom, she could hear Dane snickering.

"What?" she demanded, as she snapped the phone shut.

"You, like, live one hundred steps that way and you just called your house..." his voice trailed off in a chuckle.

"Psssh, whatever. Maybe I'm just really hungry." She allowed a small smile to escape.

*   *   *

Ari hadn't been in Dane's house since Rhoda had moved out. It had taken on the beautiful sheen of a home well loved, instead of a house just lived in. It was warm and smelled wonderful inside. Ms. Hadley had made a meatloaf dish with a mix of vegetables, as well as a loaf of homemade bread.

They sat at the table, Ari between Ms. Hadley and Dane, and across from Molly. A large silver candelabra held tall tapers that cast a warm glow. "Dane," Ms. Hadley said, "Why don't you say the blessing tonight?"

Automatically, the Hadleys joined hands around the table, and Ari obliged and took Ms. Hadley's hand as well as Dane's. She could scarcely concentrate on the blessing he was giving as she felt her hand in his. She'd never held hands with anyone before; if this could count as such. His hands weren't quite soft, though they were bigger and easily enveloped hers. For a split second she thought she felt his thumb brush across her hand. She snuck a peek at him. She'd never thought of him in terms of strong or weak; but seeing him with his head bowed, it came as a strange juxtaposition to the aloof attitude he personified. He immediately struck her as being decidedly strong. She snapped her eyes shut as he finished the blessing.

"Amen," he finished. Ari tried her hardest to concentrate on the food before her. She conversed with Ms. Hadley; although they hadn't talked at great lengths, Ari thought she was sweet, and Ms. Hadley seemed genuinely interested in Ari. She was a small lady, with dark hair and dark eyes, and her smile matched Dane's like a fingerprint. Molly liked Ari as well; she regaled Ari with stories of her school day and her friends and her favorite toys. Ari was glad that she didn't have to do much of the talking.

After dessert, Ari excused herself and thanked Mrs. Hadley. Dane followed her out to his front porch. "You want me to walk you home?" he asked quietly. Ari glanced at the inky darkness. Although it was only 7:30, night was coming earlier and earlier. Ari shook her head.

"I'll be fine. Thanks, though. Oh—" she started to take off his coat, which she realized she hadn't taken off at all during dinner. "Totally forgot about your coat—"

He just waved his hand. "Wear it home, it's fine. I'll get it from you tomorrow." She smiled in thanks and headed down the driveway.

"See you in the morning," Ari called as she rounded the driveway, out of sight from Dane's house. She once again hugged his coat tightly around her and breathed in his lingering soap-and-detergent scent. She thought she heard soft footfalls behind her. Inwardly, she smiled, thinking Dane had decided to walk her home anyway. But instead, she suddenly felt a gloved hand claw at her neck and an arm tightly circled her around the waist! Ari gasped in surprise and automatically screamed as hard as she could. A single thought seared her mind: *HIT HARD.*

Panic covered pain as Ari buried her elbow in her assailant. With two hard blows she'd dislodged the hand from her mouth and she hollered with all the air in her lungs. A stomp to the feet below her loosened the grip around her waist. She turned to face whomever had grabbed her, but as soon as she turned, he scrambled away into the woods on the other side of the road. Another figure running towards her caused a fresh wave of panic. She braced herself and screamed again, but the figure didn't stop. "Ari! It's me, what happened?!"

When Ari realized the running figure was Dane, relief washed over her. Her legs and hands began to shake with the adrenaline drain. She wanted to explain what had happened, but just as he got to her and his arms went around her waist, everything went silent and black.

"Ari! Ari, come on, wake up!" Slowly, Ari realized the buzz in her ears was receding, and she was beginning to hear clearly again. She opened her eyes slightly, but fuzzy vision gave few details. She felt she was no longer on the ground, but was firmly in Dane's grasp and was being carried somewhere.

"What?...whoa..." Her mind clouded. They arrived at his porch steps, and he carefully set her on the bottom one. He continued to support her head and torso, elevating her in an attempt to keep her conscious.

"What happened? Did you see his face?" Dane's voice was strained and tense. Suddenly, Ari realized the person could still be nearby. She gasped in fear, suddenly bolting upright, but Dane had a vice-like grip on her. "Whoa, it's ok, just relax. He's gone. I heard a car start up down the road and drive away after you passed out." Ari drew as much air into her lungs as she could and slowly let it out, closing her eyes.

"Ari! Come on, stay awake," Dane insisted.

She opened her eyes. "I'm ok," she said weakly. "Thanks for coming for me. I think you scared him away," she said, finally.

"I should've walked you home." Dane said, simply.

"Don't worry about it," Ari said, and she slowly lifted herself up.

"We need to call the police, Ari. Somebody just tried to kidnap you, I think." Dane led her into his house. Minutes later, a squad car and two officers pulled up. Ari's parents had been called by Dane's mom, and they all listened with concern as Ari and Dane went over the event.

"You didn't see his face?" one officer jotted down something on his notepad.

"No, it was too dark and it happened way too fast," she shook her head. Suddenly her hand went to her neck. Her key necklace was still there, as was her beloved honeybee that she always wore. She sighed with relief. The officers then questioned Dane about the car he heard driving away. Ari looked at Dane, and Dane knew at once what she was wondering.

"One more thing," Dane added. "We've seen a van up here a few times and we don't know why. There aren't any other houses up here." Ari gave the officer the piece of paper she'd taken the license plate number on.

The officers finished up their note taking and assured the parents that they would be sending patrol cars up the hill on a regular basis. "And," one of them added, "make sure you don't go out alone until we catch this guy. We don't know if this was a random event or if it was planned."

Falling asleep that night proved to be nearly impossible for Ari. Every creak, every bump, made her snap back to full attention, even if she'd been close to dreaming. Her skin crawled with goosebumps at every close sound. After two hours of near sleeplessness, she got out of bed and grabbed Dane's coat that she had worn home. Pulling it around her, she noticed it still smelled just like him. She smiled at the thought of him saying the blessing earlier that night, and within minutes of getting back into bed, she was soundly asleep.

Morning came too quickly. Ari's mom waited until Dane appeared in front of their house before she let Ari start off for school, much to Ari's dismay. Dane could see her look of scorn as she handed his coat back.

"Short night?" he gently chided, but Ari's scowl noted warning. "Are you doing ok?"

"Yeah, I just didn't sleep much and mom is worried about everything, you know?" She got on her bike and they started down the road.

"Well, you almost got kidnapped last night. Did you expect her to be OK with that?" He sounded reasonable. Ari just shrugged.

"Please don't tell anyone at school, ok? Not a *soul*," she stressed.

"No problem."

Ari was grateful the daily schedule was different that day, on account of a school assembly. The sleepless night had drained her energy and she chose a seat in the darkest part of the auditorium. As students filed in, she considered what she'd just come across in her locker. A hastily-scribed note warned *stay away from Dane!* in angry handwriting, clearly penned by a girl. It had fluttered from her locker as she'd dropped off books before the assembly. Ari suspected Jenelle had written it. *It's nice to feel so welcome in a new school,* she thought with a sigh. Ari had crumpled the lined paper and dropped it to the bottom of her locker.

Most of the students had filed in by now, and the lights soon fully dimmed. It was so warm and dark that Ari slouched in the seat and closed her eyes. *What if he comes back?* A sudden frightful thought caused her to furrow her brow in concern. The gravity of the previous night's situation was just beginning to sink in. Someone had actually tried to kidnap her last night. Even when she'd been living in the middle of San Francisco, she'd never felt threatened. Then, in the most unlikely of all places, she almost gets taken from her own driveway. *How could that be a random act?* She shook her head at the thought. A hand on her shoulder nearly caused her to yelp in surprise. Riley looked apologetic as she sat in the seat next to her.

"Are you alright?" she whispered. "Sorry I startled you. You look like you got run over by a truck."

She nodded and smiled. "I'm just really tired. Thanks for asking." Ari was relieved she wouldn't have to explain further, as the assembly began and she once again closed her eyes, hoping to catch up on some sleep. Halfway through, she felt a nudge. Riley leaned over.

"Hey, one row up. He's been glancing back at you the whole time. What's goin' on?" she asked with a wink. Ari looked out the corner of her eye and caught Dane looking back. He quickly straightened his gaze toward the stage.

To Riley, she just shrugged her shoulders. "No clue," she said, but as soon as the assembly was over, she caught up with him in the lobby of the auditorium. "Hey," she said, taking his arm. "What's up?"

"Well...what are you doing tonight?" Dane asked, and Ari swore she heard a hint of timidity in his voice for the first time ever.

Ari's mom dropped her and Dane off at the Cinema Coffee ten minutes before *North by Northwest* was slated to show. They got their fifty-cent tickets, picked up some coffee, and headed into the theater.

Ari had never actually been inside the theater portion of the building, and she gasped as they brushed past the burgundy velvet curtains. Gilded statues held small lamps that lit the aisles. Ornate carved mouldings bordered the screen. They chose seats in the middle of the theater, and, like the ones in the school auditorium, they were thin, curved wood seats, but these had threadbare velvet padding. In the silence before the film began, Ari felt a twinge of awkwardness. *Is this a date?* she wondered to herself. She took a sip of her coffee, trying not to burn her tongue.

"Do you think your relatives came here to watch movies like these?" she asked quietly.

"Probably. All of my family lived in our houses until my dad moved out, and I know everybody grew up here, and stayed here. The town was more prosperous back then," he explained. She noticed he kept glancing around the theater, as if looking for someone. She wanted to ask who, but the lights suddenly dimmed. Monochrome images and a scratchy soundtrack filled the auditorium, and inwardly Ari smiled. She loved old movies; and she'd never seen this one. She was glad Dane had asked her to come, whatever the reason.

An hour into the film Ari excused herself to the restroom. After exiting the honeycomb-tiled washroom, she glanced at the patrons sitting in the cafe lobby. One man in particular seemed vaguely familiar, and suddenly she felt the hair on her neck prick up. Momentary panic washed over her, and she thought he glanced up just as she slipped between the curtains. Rushing back to her seat, she sank down into the hard wood chair. She felt Dane looking at her.

"What's wrong?" he leaned over and whispered.

She hesitated. What had caused her heart to race? What was familiar about the man?

"I don't know," she tried to keep her voice as low as possible. "I think I saw someone..." She shook her head in frustration.

Dane paused, still looking at her. He furrowed his brow in concern, and glanced over his shoulder at the dark velvet curtains. "Who did you see?"

She just shook her head. It had probably been her imagination. "Nobody."

Trying to focus on the movie and not her unfounded fears, she took comfort in the fact that she was with somebody. Lots of people, in fact, were in the theater that particular night. She watched the screen, though now her concentration for the movie was thin. As if he were sensing her unease, Dane took her hand and held it tightly in his. She squeezed his hand back, and blushed, but looked at him with a grateful glance. She felt completely secure and safe, her hand in his, at least for now. Just as she was getting back into the film, the final credits rolled and the aisle lights came back on. She and Dane headed up the velvet aisle. Her legs were wobbly and numb from sitting for so long.

Her mother hadn't arrived to pick them up yet, so they chose a cafe table next to a window. "Do you see the person here still?" Dane asked quietly, looking around, although the majority of the movie-goers were steadily streaming from the theater to the exits. Ari didn't see him any longer, but through the movie she'd been developing a new theory.

"Dane, where did all of Nadia's underground treasures go, anyway?" she asked, her voice barely audible.

He raised an eyebrow, questioning, but answered quietly. "Her jewelry and gems were divided up between myself, Dina, Maria, and Mom. There's even a portion set aside for dad. We sold the currency to collectors but divided the coins. I don't know where they decided to

125

secure theirs, but I have mine in a safe deposit box at the bank. Why?"

Ari just shook her head but questioned, "Was there anybody else who knew about the treasure?"

Before he could answer, the lights in the lobby dimmed and remaining patrons left. Ari looked at her watch. The theater was about to close.

"Your mom knew what time to picks us up, right?" Dane asked.

Right as she pulled out her cell phone to give her mom a call, her car pulled up to the curb. It had begun to rain and they rushed out to the car, ducking out of the downpour. Once they got in the car they noticed Ari's mom wasn't the only person in the front seat. Dane's mom glanced back at her son and Ari with a nervous look.

"Hey, mom, what're you doing here?" he asked in surprise. Ari's mom just glanced at Dane's mom.

"Mom, what's wrong?" Ari saw concern pass between the mothers.

"Well...while we were gone, somebody broke into both our houses."

Ari and Dane both gasped. "Who? What did they take?"

"Well, we haven't really checked very well. We called the police immediately when we found out. Whoever it was, the police thought they were amateurs. They were either in a really big hurry or very inexperienced. The police were also wondering why it seems our hill has been targeted twice in a week now. They've ruled out Nadia's treasure because it wasn't publicized. At any rate, they've opened an investigation."

Ari's dad and sister were at home when they arrived. Items were strewn around the house in disarray. She gasped as she wandered through a house in disorder. Dane followed her as she bounded up the staircase to her room.

"Oh no...Dane...*no*..." she gasped under her breath. Nadia's trunk was open and photos and letters were scattered across the wooden floor, but the antique tutus were nowhere to be found. Ari couldn't speak; her hands covered her mouth. Dane just put his hand on her shoulder.

"Who would take tutus?" was all he could say as Ari shook her head.

"This doesn't make sense. We need to see if anything was taken from your house," she said, finally recovering.

They ran up the driveway to Dane's house. His mom was slowly arranging the house back to its original order as they went up the narrow stairs to Dane's room. Ari had only been in his room once, and that had been some time ago, during the summer. As she had remembered it, it was much the same, only it hadn't escaped the wrath of the thieves. He just shook his head at the mess.

"I didn't have anything important in here...but they sure made a mess." He sighed and looked around.

"Did you guys have *anything* valuable in the house?" she began picking up books from the floor.

"Naw." He sounded defeated, even so.

They cleaned up the room and Dane made sure Ari got back home safely. She helped her family organize before she went to bed. A lamp had been broken by the front door, and ceramic bits had worked themselves between the smooth cracks of the worn wooden floors. Something had fallen between the wall and the floor. She tried to get her fingers in between but there wasn't enough room. A bent paperclip easily dislodged the item. She unfolded a piece of paper the size of a Chinese fortune; on it was a phone number that she'd never seen before. Before she headed upstairs she carefully stuffed it in the small pocket of her jeans.

The next morning came far too soon for Ari. Heavy fog seemed to drape over the valley and even by late morning when she shuffled downstairs, it hadn't been dissolved by the rising sun. After greeting her parents good morning, she got dressed in a heavy coat and boots, tucked a blanket under her arm and slung her backpack over her shoulder. A cup of coffee steamed in her hand.

"Honey, where are you going?" Her mom peered over her own cup.

"I've got to get homework done, so I'm going to the underground room. Don't worry, I'll lock it. It's completely safe." Ari felt a twinge of annoyance. Their own house wasn't even safe anymore.

Her mom glanced at Ari's dad, obviously concerned. She started to speak, then paused. "Ari, we're not really comfortable with you going there anymore, especially with everything that's been going on. Aren't you scared that whoever is doing all of this will find you there?"

"I *said*, I'll lock it. And I have my cell phone. I'll be fine," and before they could protest, she jogged out the back door and down the cobbled path.

Fall had taken its toll on the oak trees; the grove was so nearly bare that, on a clear day, she could see the color of Dane's house through the skeletal branches. She disappeared into the fog, and by the time she'd found the brass circle under a layer of decomposing leaves, her house was obscured by the misty white bank.

The brass circle had been locked since the first rain of the season, and although there wasn't anything still in it, Ari was glad it had remained secure despite all the unsettling events that had transpired in the past week. She procured her key and descended into the subterranean room, making sure to lock it behind her. All the candles were soon lit, and the camping lanterns were blazing. She wrapped herself in the blanket and opened her history book. An hour of silent studying had passed when she remembered about the phone number she had in her jeans.

She pulled out her cell phone. What would happen if she called it? A sudden pounding on the brass circle sent her into an adrenaline attack. She tensed until she heard Dane calling. Ari flipped the interior latch and he jumped down into the room. He looked angry.

"Ari, what the heck? Are you seriously *trying* to get kidnapped or something!?" His voice was more than a bit raised, and Ari stumbled back in complete surprise. She just shook her head and mumbled something about locking the hatch behind her, but Dane cut her off.

"Ari, you *can't* just go places anymore. Don't you get it? Whoever is doing this has been watching our hill. They knew when our houses were empty last night. It's just not safe." He paused to catch his breath but Ari battled back.

"Geez, you sound just like my parents. Nowhere is safe, Dane. I'm not going to be afraid, so don't try and scare me away." She didn't mean to sound upset, but her voice was steel. "I came here to feel safe, and to get stuff done."

"I'm not trying to scare you; this is just how it is now," he strained his voice, halfway between anger and apology. He took a few steps back. "I just feel like something bad is going to happen. This is all because of me, Ari." She looked up sharply at him. "Remember last night you asked me if anyone else knew about the treasure? Well, somebody must. Whoever tried to kidnap you...both our houses getting ransacked...it's *not* a coincidence."

Ari held her head in her hands, took in a deep breath, and finally spoke. "I'm scared, Dane, but I don't want to hide. I didn't move from a big, bad city to a backwater town to be afraid of the boogeyman." Her voice was small and weak. The stress of everything that had transpired weighed heavily on her, and she buried her head in her sleeves. "I just want to go home," her voice cracked.

"I'll walk you," Dane offered, but Ari held out a hand to halt him.

"Not *here*. San Francisco. I just want to go back to where I came from. People didn't hate me there. I didn't get threatening notes in my locker and nobody tried to kidnap me," Ari felt like she was venting a month's worth of stress in a sentence.

"What note?"

"Last week Jenelle left a note in my locker that said to stay away from you."

"How do you know it was her?" he asked, sounding worried again.

"Who else would it be? Any other girls I need to watch out for?"

"Listen, Ari, I'm sorry she's being mean to you...and I didn't know you hate it here so much. Do your parents know you want to go back to California?" He once again sounded apologetic. She just shook her head.

"Doesn't matter if they do. We're here for good." She sighed and looked up at him. He was just standing there, in front of her, his hands in his pockets, unsure of what to say. The silent, aloof confidence that seemed to go with him everywhere was, for once, missing. "What's wrong?" she finally asked.

His eyes, shadowed in the dim light of the small room, met hers. "I know what it's like to hate where you're at. It sucks. For four years I tried to avoid Rhoda." He knelt down in front of her. His voice was quiet and soft. "Remember how you felt when she split my chin open? You were pretty upset about that. Now it's my turn to help you."

*   *   *

Riley leaned up against the locker next to Ari's. "I read in the paper what happened at your house on Friday," she said in a low tone. "I'm so sorry. That's so scary. Do you know who did it?"

130

Ari shook her head as she took out her art folder and drawing pad. "It's already in the paper, huh?"

"Well, yeah, under the police reports. Don't worry," she said, sensing Ari's dread. "Nobody here reads the newspaper. And I haven't talked about it to anyone. I was just really worried about you."

Ari gave her a reassuring smile. "We're fine. The police thought they were amateurs. Probably just a random break-in," she lied. Even though she trusted Riley, she didn't want to talk about it at school— not with other people around. She really wanted to entrust Riley with all the distressing details, if for no reason other than to get it off her chest. But she would have to wait for a more confidential location. A million people were streaming past her locker; besides, she had to get to art class.

"Before you go," Riley said, pushing a flier at her, "have you seen the posters? There's going to be a winter dance in December. They're just planning it right now, but it's never too early to go dress shopping," she grinned.

"You don't strike me as the dancing type," Ari said as they walked down the hallway.

"I'm not in it for the dance, per se. I actually do love dressing up though. Getting ready with your friends is the best part...don't tell me you've never been to a dance before?"

Ari just chuckled. "Nope. But, I'll totally go with you...and go dress shopping too," she said, ducking into the art studio.

Ari was one of the first people to arrive in class; she took her normal seat in the back of the room. Jenelle arrived with two of her friends and sat just one table up. Ari was a little surprised to see Dane enter the room and sit down right beside her without even giving Jenelle a nod. "Hey," she said. He nodded back and leaned close to talk.

"I found the things that were taken from your room," he said, in the quietest voice possible.

"You mean the tutus? Where?" she said, trying to keep her surprised voice down.

"I called all the pawn shops and antique stores in Rivers and in nearby towns. It sounds like they ended up in an antique store in Allendale. That's not too far from here. I let them know that it was stolen property, so they're holding onto them for us. But I don't know if it's all of them. Only you knew how many of them there were."

"Oh my gosh, Dane, that's awesome!" She was so happy she'd forgotten about the table in front of them.

"You lovebirds going to share your story with everyone, or is your girlfriend just being stupid?" Jenelle's cutting voice extinguished Ari's smile.

"How 'bout you leave her alone?" Dane said in a tone with a hint of warning.

Jenelle and her flanking friends just turned back around, scowling at them. Ari gave Dane a thankful glance.

chapter twelve

Ari's mom was standing on a stool, teetering precariously as she reached for the clock above the kitchen stove. "You sure you don't need help with that, mom?"

"I'm fine, I've got it. One hour back; one hour more of darkness. I really don't like it when it gets dark so early in the winter," her mom said, sighing. "It makes the days feel so short."

"I know. But it makes for spookier trick-or-treating," Ari remarked as she pulled the needle through the silken bodice of a tutu.

"Out here, I don't think it can get any spookier. Are you sure Dane said that people come up here to get candy? It seems much too far out of the way for trick-or-treaters." Her mom placed the clock back on the wall.

"He said there are some. I guess in a small town you have to really hit all the houses or you miss out on the candy. At any rate, I'm going to dress up whether kids come or not. I mean, look at this costume, Mom!" Ari held up one of Nadia's recovered tutus. It had a deep red bodice with thousands of gold glass beads glimmering in the light. The pancake tutu flounced; despite it being over a hundred years old, it was in near-perfect condition. And the best part was that it fit Ari exactly. "I just need to finish repairing this seam. I think whoever stole it wasn't very gentle with it."

She had been ecstatic when all of the tutus had been recovered at an antique store in Allendale. Not only had every one of the tutus been recovered, but, unbeknownst to Ari, some of the Hadley family photos had gotten caught within the dozens of layers of tulle in some of the skirts. Even those had been returned unharmed.

"You sure it's okay that you wear it? Dane didn't oppose?"

"No, he actually suggested it. I'll be really careful. But, it looks like these things were made to be tough." Ari smoothed out the tulle ruffles on her lap.

133

"Thank goodness we haven't had any more incidents. I think I'm starting to feel safe again," her mom said, glancing at Ari. It had been almost three weeks since the break-in, and there had been no van sightings or anything out of the ordinary. Even Jenelle had been avoiding Ari since Dane had defended her. Ari smiled to herself thinking about it.

Two days later, Ari was standing in front the mirror in her room. The tutu's *basque* was on over her barely-pink tights; the stacked layers of tulle stood nearly straight out from her hips. Next, she put on the bodice and secured it as much as she could on her own. Lastly, she pulled out a pair of barely-used pointe shoes that she'd found at the local thrift store. To keep her short hair away from her face, she'd used a red silk ribbon as a headband and combed her hair back into the smallest ponytail ever. She'd rimmed her eyes lightly with brown shadow and a hint of red glitter, which looked quite dramatic. Altogether, the effect was pretty amazing. She lifted herself up *en pointe*, for a second or two, and stretched her arms above her head. *I could almost pass as a real ballerina,* she thought as she giggled at her faux pose. A knock at her door brought her out of her plie, and she opened it an inch and peeked around.

"Just me," Dane said, a curious look on his face. "I wanted to see how your costume looked before we left. Mom and I are going into town to take Molly trick-or-treating."

She fully opened the door and Dane gasped audibly. "Wow. That's incredible, Ari. Some costume, huh?" He finally settled on her eyes and smiled. "The glitter is a nice touch. Very theatrical."

"Thanks. I thought so. Oh, can you get the top hook back here?" She strained to point at the one hook that remained unfastened.

He nodded and she turned around. "Pull your shoulders back a little," he directed, and she could tell the small hook was a bit of a challenge for him to overcome. Finally she felt it pull taut as he hooked it. "Got it. Too bad we didn't dress up as a pair," he snorted. "I could've worn a mean pair of tights."

Ari giggled and he exited her room. "Have fun trick-or-treating," she called as he descended the staircase.

*   *   *

At school the next day, Ari caught up to Dane at lunchtime. "Hey," she hissed, "We had *three* kids come to our door. You said a ton of kids usually come. What's up with that?"

He looked at her with a glint in his eye. "Well, maybe it was the weather or something. Or maybe I just wanted to see you as a ballerina. Either way, you still have a lot of candy all for yourself. What's the complaint?"

Ari rolled her eyes and shoved her hands into her pocket. She felt a scrap of paper folded inside. Pulling it out, she realized it was the phone number that she'd found the night of the break-in. She'd completely forgotten about it. *Thank goodness I didn't wash these jeans,* she thought to herself.

"What's that?" Dane looked over her shoulder curiously.

"Um...well, I meant to tell you about this a long time ago. I just forgot about it. On the night of the break-in, I was cleaning up by our front door and I found this. I don't think it was in our house before. Maybe it was dropped by one of the thieves."

He took it from her hands and shook his head. "Hm. This might be really important. What are you going to do with it?"

"Before we report this, you might want to know that I looked it up on the Internet the same night I found it. The area code is in Arizona." At that, Dane's eyes fell to the floor.

"You think my dad has something to do with this."

"I don't know. I hope not. I'm just saying, your Aunt Dina said he called about eight months ago. He mentioned he was living in the southwest. Maybe it has nothing to do with him."

135

"How are we going to find out?"

"How about we call the number? I could be a telemarketer or something. It won't take long to figure out who it belongs to."

"I dunno," was all Dane could say before he turned and strode out of the cafeteria. Ari called after him, but something in his voice offered fair warning. She decided not to pursue.

chapter thirteen

"Six weeks to go, Ari. I hardly think that's enough time to find a dress for you," Riley joked as she passed a long satin evening-style gown to her. They were surrounded by rows and rows of dresses of all kinds: long, short, slim, and poofy, and Ari couldn't seem to decide on a single one. Riley had already selected a half-dozen, all in shades of lilac and plum, and was leaving Ari for the fitting rooms. "You better be nearby when I need you to check these out," she called from one of the chandeliered rooms. Two minutes later, she floated out in a floor-length gown with an empire-waisted, sequined bodice.

"Nice," Ari approved, nodding.

"Well? Have *you* found anything yet?"

Ari shrugged and pulled a few dresses from her arm. She'd picked a ballroom-type dress with a huge flounced skirt, an A-line dress with a scoop neck, and a strappy black satin one. But none of them really inspired her. "I don't know, Riley. Like, what kind of dance is this? What's the theme? A little help here would be great..."

"Well, to start, it's a winter dance. So you can go as fancy as you'd like. And, to make it even better, it's being held at the Old City Hall. You've probably never been there before because the city only opens it on special occasions, and sometimes they rent it out for weddings and such. I've only been there once for one of Dad's work banquets. Oh, it's gorgeous, Ari. You'll love it. It's got a huge marble dance floor and the biggest crystal chandelier you've ever seen in your life. When Rivers was an up-and-coming town, it was the heart of the city. So I guess my best suggestion is to really go nuts, Ari. I mean, do we really need an excuse?" She twirled around and curtsied. "Now if you'll pardon me...more selections to come."

The pair spent the rest of the chilly afternoon looking at dresses and warming up at the coffee shop. Unsuccessful in their hunt for the perfect frock, they eventually ended up back at Riley's house, which was located right on the edge of downtown in a historic Victorian turn-of-the century house. Unlike Ari's house, this one was very vertical and compact, with detailed flourishes all over. Riley's room was high atop the third floor; a window seat looked out upon the streets below.

"Gosh, this is an awesome house," Ari breathed as she looked out.

"Yeah, it's pretty cool. Speaking of houses, did they ever find the people who broke into yours?"

Weighing her thoughts, Ari decided to tell Riley everything about what she and Dane had gone through. "Dane thinks it has something to do with his family, but we don't really know. You gotta swear to not tell anybody, though," Ari pleaded. Without hesitation Riley agreed, and Ari tried to include most of the story, except the secret of the underground room. She only briefly alluded to Nadia's treasure; at this point, Ari figured, the less people who knew about it, the better. Riley seemed to absorb the story with interest, and Ari was relieved when she didn't ask too many questions.

*   *   *

"Why would my dad have anything to do with it? It's his family's stuff, after all. He doesn't *have* to steal it; all he has to do is just show up and it's his." Dane threw a stone into the ebony water. Ripples radiated and made a gentle slosh against the rim of slate stones. There had been a break in the rainy weather but the pervasive fog seemed to settle on their hill.

Ari just shook her head. "Why do you think it's him?" She traced a moss-filled crack with her finger and snuck a sideways glance at Dane. She knew he was frustrated, but couldn't gauge if he was angry or not.

"Who else would it be? Some random person? No way."

"Have you asked your mom if she's heard from your dad lately?"

Dane just shook his head. "Never. I don't want her to know I'm looking, remember? I'm sure she doesn't want anything to do with him. Also, I don't want her to think I'm unhappy with our current situation..." He gave a labored sigh. "I can't explain it, Ari. It's like this big piece of my life is just...gone."

She watched a single leaf drift to the water's surface. "My offer to call the number I found still stands," she said, as a fat raindrop just missed her eye. "Uh oh." She looked up at the sky. "We'd better head to the circle." With that, they wound through the skeletal oaks and jumped down in to the darkness of the underground room. After lighting the candles in the room, Ari pulled out her cell phone and the tiny wad of paper. "You ready to find out who this is?"

Dane looked at her for a long moment. "What's your plan?" He finally asked, a dubious tone in his voice.

"I'll say I'm calling from a political survey or something. I'll try to get his name and I'll ask if there's anyone else living in his house. What else do you want to know?"

He just shook his head and looked up at the ceiling. "I dunno, Ari. I guess I wanna know why he's never come back, but I don't think you could work that into a political questionnaire."

"Yeah...well, you ready for this?

Dane took a deep breath and nodded. "Whenever you are."

Ari punched in the long-distance number. A dial tone rang once, twice, and a third time. Ari clicked the speakerphone button and looked up at Dane. He started to shake his head. Suddenly someone picked up.

"Hello?"

Ari quickly glanced at Dane. It was a female voice. "Yes, hello—" Ari mustered her most professional voice. "I'm calling from Voters of America." Dane raised an eyebrow. "If you have a moment, we're doing a survey about your household and possible voting positions in the upcoming election." Ari continued without giving the woman a chance to refuse. "First of all, can I have your name?"

The woman audibly sighed and gave an emphysemic cough. "Uh, Karen Zeller. What's this for again?" She sounded bored and unlikely to continue. Ari thought fast to keep her on the line.

"Mrs. Zeller, can you tell me how many people are living in your household? It *is* Mrs., correct?"

"Uh, yeah, it's Mrs. Um, there are, um, three people in the household..."

"And how many of these people are of voting age?"

"Uh, they all are."

This time Ari raised an eyebrow but kept her tone even. "Mrs. Zeller, it would help our survey be more accurate if we had the names of the other voters in your household as well. Can you give those to me?"

Mrs. Zeller faltered and Ari knew she'd asked too much. "Uh, listen, I...I don't want to take the survey." With that, the line clicked with disconnection.

Ari looked at Dane and snapped her phone shut. Shrugging her shoulders, she sighed. "Well, we tried."

"No, you did great. That was the most professional prank call I've ever heard. Really, Ari, you had some good questions. I guess it wasn't my dad after all."

"But why would Mrs. Karen Zeller's phone number be in my

house?"

"Who knows. I guess it doesn't have anything to do with the thieves at all."

They sat in silence for a moment. "Are you happy it wasn't your dad?" Ari finally asked.

Dane didn't answer immediately. "Yeah. I guess part of me is relieved but the other part just wants to know where he is." He smirked. "That didn't answer your question, did it?"

She shrugged again and dared changing the subject. "Hey, are you going to the winter dance?" she asked as nonchalantly as possible. Now that she'd just made a fake call to a totally unknown person, asking Dane if he was going to the dance didn't seem like such a big deal.

"Um, I don't really ever go to dances," he said simply. "Are you going?"

"Yeah. Riley and I are going, I guess. We were looking at dresses the other day." She suddenly felt a strange sense of deflation, and she didn't know why.

"That's cool. I, um, I'd better get going. I have homework." He sounded awkward, but suddenly he looked straight at her. Even though the candles shed little light, she could see a gentle expression come over his face. "But, Ari, really—thanks for making the call. I wouldn't have done it on my own."

She just smiled and nodded. "No problem," she said, as Dane climbed up the steps. He held out his hand to help her up as well, but she waved it off. "I'm going to stay here for a little while."

He gave her a funny look. "I can't let you do that, Ari. It's just not safe. Come on."

She rolled her eyes but took his hand. "How long are you going to escort me everywhere?" she smiled, and they both appeared above the brass circle. Ari carefully locked it, and they headed toward her house. The day had turned to dusk and fog still hovered close to the ground, and large plops of water dripped from branches above.

They carefully wound their way through the trees. They weren't a hundred steps from the brass circle when a loud *snap!* caused them both to whirl around. Ari saw a shadow dart through the trees and definite footfalls crashed through the underbrush.

chapter fifteen

"Go!" Dane hissed in Ari's ear, and he grabbed her by the arm and ran. Though her heart was pounding in her ears, she had no choice but to keep up as he deftly avoided trees. They shot out into the field and she tried to pause along the cobblestone path, but Dane pulled her ahead. He didn't come to a complete stop until they were safely on her back porch.

"What *was* that?" Ari caught her breath as she realized she was still gripping Dane's arm.

"No, *who* were *they?*" he corrected her. "I saw two people, Ari. They were really close. You—" he lowered his voice—"need to be really careful. Somebody is still watching us." He straightened and looked out into the woods. There was no noise now; nothing but silent trees, wispy fog, and the dim garden lamps on the perimeter of the upper lawn. Ari was still trembling as she scanned the tree line.

As they opened the porch door, the warmth of the house did little to comfort Ari. She dreaded telling her parents—who would in turn report it to the police—but she knew not telling them could have worse consequences than some limitations on her freedom. Reluctantly, Ari and Dane recounted the events of the evening to her father.

*   *   *

"So you can't even ride your bike to school anymore? Wow." Riley gave Ari an apologetic look. Biology class hadn't started yet, and the teacher wasn't in the room. They had at least a few more minutes of free time before the bell rang.

"Yeah. His mom and mine take turns driving us to and from school now. It *sucks*. I can't even ride my bike into town. Do you know how embarrassing it is to be picked up from school? Almost the whole student body lives within walking distance of the school and we have to have our *mommies* get us. Ugh."

"But aren't you scared? I mean, I would be if I knew somebody might be after me," Riley kept her voice down, and Ari was grateful for her tact. "Besides, you don't really mind Dane's company, riiiight?" She snuck a wink at Ari. Ari just rolled her eyes and smirked. Riley lowered her voice even more. "Are you going to ask him to the dance?"

"I told him that you and I were going but he said he 'doesn't do dances.' But I guess I can't really picture him at a dance, anyway. I know it really isn't something he'd do." Ari tried to sound as aloof as possible. The bell then rang, to her relief.

Before the teacher entered the room, Riley leaned over and whispered to Ari's. "Can you go dress shopping again after school? I haven't found one yet." Ari mouthed that she'd call her mom before the end of school. Riley smiled and snapped back to her desk as the biology teacher approached his podium.

Biology class seemed longer than usual that day, even though it was the same ninety minutes as always. After class, Ari dialed her mom and assured her she would be with Riley during the afternoon. She had just finished talking as she opened her locker, only to jump back upon seeing its contents. Papers inside were crumpled and shredded, her photos were cut up, and the entire inside was vandalized with black marker. *GO AWAY*, big black letters yelled at her from inside the door. Expletives were angrily scratched in the interior paint.

"Oh my gosh..." Riley had come up behind her and was absorbing the sight. Ari was still gaping at what had been done to her papers: assignments were ruined, her photos were destroyed, and a dozen hurtful words were all stabbing at her like knives. Even though she could hear Riley's voice trying to comfort her, she mostly felt her face turning red hot. Tears were welling in her eyes, her throat felt like it was closing, and panic was starting to build. She heard herself mutter something like *I'm sorry I have to go,* and with that, she jogged as fast as she could down the stairs and out the school.

*   *   *

It was four o'clock that afternoon when Dane's mom went up to his room. "Dane, when was the last time you saw Ari today?"

"I saw her in passing between classes in the morning. Why?"

"Her mom just called. She was supposed to be shopping with a friend, but an hour ago, the friend called and asked if Ari had come home during school. It sounds like Ari left suddenly and nobody's seen her since. If you could help us out, I'm sure her parents would be grateful. They're so worried, especially after everything that's happened lately—"

Before she could even finish, Dane jumped to his feet and pounded down the stairs. "I'm checking the circle first, and if she's not there, I'm heading into town," he called to his mom. Before she could even get down the stairs, the front door had slammed shut.

chapter sixteen

The circle had been dark and empty. Dane hadn't expected to find her there, but he knew he had to make sure. He dropped by the coffee shop. Most tables were occupied, but none of the patrons were a smallish, brown-haired girl. His next stop was the Elgin River waterfront; he'd found Ari sitting at the river's edge several times before. Unfortunately, he wasn't so lucky this time. The park was almost empty. Dane had no choice but to head back into town.

He knew she didn't have her bike with her; unless something terrible had happened, she had to be within walking distance of the school. *What if she* had *been successfully kidnapped this time?* He tried to subdue the rising panic and shut down such thoughts.

Canvassing the neighborhood near the high school, he spotted the last plausible place he thought Ari might be: the newer movie theater that showed first-run movies. Only three were playing, and of the three, only one was something he thought Ari would watch. He noticed nobody was manning the ticket booth, so he slipped in. Once inside, he deftly went through the curtain and immediately took a seat in the back. Moments passed before his eyes were totally adjusted to the darkness.

The show was a romantic comedy, but his attention wasn't on the movie. He was slowly scanning the heads in the giant room. Luckily, the 3:00 p.m. showing wasn't a very popular time and few people were in attendance. There was an older couple to the far right. Two teenage girls were giggling several rows ahead. It looked like a man and woman were sitting in the very middle. And far to the left side, almost against the wall of the room, there was a girl who obviously wasn't watching the movie.

Dane slowly got up and placed himself a row behind her. He tried his hardest to be quiet enough that she didn't notice anybody was nearby. The girl was quietly sniffling, her head down. He saw her hand come to her face a few times. A tissue went to her nose twice.

From this close proximity he could clearly tell it was Ari; he even recognized the scent she always wore.

Several minutes went by and Dane considered what to do next. Finally he got up from his seat and sat right next to Ari. She startled but then tried to look away. He simply put his hand on her arm and leaned over.

"You need to call your parents, Ari. They're really worried," Dane whispered, not looking directly at her, his head down. She paused, and after a moment, pulled her cell phone from her backpack and quickly exited the auditorium without a word. He stayed behind. She returned about five minutes later and sat down in her seat, still not looking at him. Again, he leaned over to whisper. "Do you want to go get some coffee?" All she could manage was a nod, and in the reflection from the screen he could see wet streaks shining on her cheeks.

She was absolutely silent as they walked the two blocks to the coffee house. It wasn't until she'd finished half her cup that she seemed ready to talk.

"Did anyone tell you what happened?" Ari's voice was raw, and barely audible.

"No. My mom said a friend had called wondering where you were. What happened?"

"Somebody destroyed everything in my locker. My assignments were cut up. Horrible things were scratched in the paint. It freaked me out, Dane. I just ran away." She looked at him plainly, successfully holding back a flood of hurt, and hoped she'd discover some sort of comfort in his eyes. However, he seemed worried, almost disturbed.

"Did you tell anyone? Like a teacher?"

"Um, no, I didn't." She had long before realized this was probably the first thing she should've done, but she knew talking about it to an adult would've sent her into fits of sobbing, in front of everyone. "Maybe Riley did..." Ari sighed, "I was supposed to do something with her this afternoon. I just left her there at my locker."

"She'll understand. Who do you think did it?" Dane questioned.

Ari looked down at the heavily-lacquered wooden cafe table and shrugged. "It has to be someone we go to school with. I mean, I don't think the kidnapping attempt and the locker have anything to do with each other. Do you?"

Dane narrowed his eyes. "No. I don't. I think it might be my fault, again...maybe. The other day after lunch, Jenelle asked me to go to that dance with her. I said no. She looked pretty pissed."

"I don't understand. Why would she take it out on *my* locker?"

"Maybe because I much prefer to hang out with you this year instead of her. She used to be more fun to be around, last year. Now it's like she's too good for everyone, so I'd rather not be her friend."

Nodding, Ari accepted that. Going out on a limb, she asked, "So, last year...did you *like* her?

She thought Dane almost blushed, but eventually he just shrugged. "Maybe I thought I did, or maybe *she* thought I did. Who knows." He looked up from his coffee and his nonchalant manner seemed to clear away, and he looked straight at Ari.

"I'm so sorry this is happening to you, Ari. I really am," Dane said in a low voice. He took both of her hands in his, and she felt her face flush again, but she dare not look away from his eyes. Her hurt was finally starting to recede. After a moment, he let go and he pulled something out of his back pocket. A scrap of paper fluttered onto the table.

"What's that?" Ari smoothed it down with a finger.

"It's my dad's phone number."

chapter seventeen

"Is it *really*? How do you know?" Ari read the numbers to herself.

"I called Aunt Dina and asked her if she could get the phone records from the month that she talked to my dad last. Sure enough, eight months ago a call was placed from Flagstaff, from a cell phone. That was him, and this was his number."

"Wow. I never would've thought to do that. So, when are you going to call him?"

Dane looked at her plainly. "I'm not."

"Why?" Ari was more than a bit surprised.

"I've given it a lot of thought. I guess it comes to this: a year ago, I had no family at all. And then you came—" he almost smiled as he talked, and set his hand back on top of hers— "and everything was turned upside down. Rhoda moved away, Mom and Molly came back, and you helped me find my family's heritage. So, I'd say what I have now is way more important than chasing someone who hasn't even made an effort to be a part of our lives."

It's probably the most he's ever said to me, Ari thought.

*   *   *

"Do you recognize this note?" The principal of Rivers High School pushed a once-crumpled paper across the table. *Stay away from Dane.*

"Yes. I found that in my locker about a month ago." Ari had never met the principal, but he seemed reasonable enough. Diplomas and degrees lined his walls. His desk was extra high, and Ari felt like a third-grader peeking over the top.

"Your friend Riley alerted us to what happened earlier this week. We took photos of the damage. She pointed out that the handwriting on that—" he poked at the paper "— looked similar to this." He pointed to a phrase on a close-up photo of her damaged locker. She could only glance at it. "Again, at Riley's suggestion, we compared it to handwriting of a particular student—" he pulled a manila folder from his desk "—and we questioned her, reminding her of the seriousness of vandalism, and she admitted to it. Now, Miss Cartwright, I'd like to know why Jenelle Thomas has such a problem with you." He looked over the top of his bifocals and waited.

"I really don't know, Mr. Jesser. I've never even had a conversation with her." Ari shrugged. "Sorry." And she was; this would've been easier if there was a real reason for Jenelle to be vengeful. As it was, Ari just figured she was a mean person, period.

"Well, she has been charged with the repairs and was given detention. In addition, she has been suspended from any school-related activities for the remainder of the term."

Internally, Ari smiled. *Jenelle Thomas is going to miss the Winter Formal this year.*

chapter eighteen

The tremendous storm outside had failed to relent, and, with her backpack in hand, Ari's mom drove her up to Dane's house. "I'll call when I need a ride back. It might be a while," she hoped. The sky was already darkening; it was only four forty-five, but grayish-black clouds seemed to absorb all light. She noticed the wind seemed stronger than she'd ever seen it. When Dane answered the door, he already was holding a flashlight.

"Our lights have been flickering. Mom's got the evening shift at work and Molly is terrified of the dark," he explained. "I heard you had to go to the principal's office today," he mentioned.

Ari nodded. "So it turns out it was Jenelle all along—the notes, the locker—the principal said she's been banned from all school-related activities, which means she can't go to the dance. "Ari tried not to sound too proud, but she couldn't hide the relief in her voice.

"I'm really sorry about her. I had no idea she'd be so cruel." Dane looked truly sorry. Before she could respond, the lights in the old house flickered one last time and extinguished. They could hear Molly squeal in the kitchen; Dane called out to reassure her as he snapped his flashlight on. Molly joined them, sticking close by, until Dane was able to find a small electric camping lantern. "It's like we're camping," he suggested, and Molly seemed satisfied with the thought. Soon she was playing by herself in the living room, unaware of the howling storm or darkness.

"I guess we'll have to go over your biology here at the table. I'll help you by holding the flashlight," he chuckled, and Ari glared at him.

"You're so much help. To think, I could've stayed home and Lily could've done the same," she jested back, and even in the dim swath of the flashlight, she could see him grinning. After twenty minutes, Ari was pleased that her assignment was almost completed. She hadn't realized how dark and silent the house was until there was a lull in the conversation. Hail and rain alternately smattered on the windows, and then something sounded like a car door slamming outside.

"Weird, Mom's not supposed to be home yet," Dane got up and peered through the vertical blinds. "Does anyone you know drive an old truck?" he asked slowly.

Alarm gripped Ari. "No. Why, who's here?" she said, barely whispering. She shot to the window and peeked through the slats. The cab was empty. "Why isn't there anyone in the truck?" Her throat felt tight.

"Take Molly upstairs *now*," Dane insisted.

Wordlessly Ari did as she was told. Molly gave protest, wanting to "camp" some more, but Ari scooped Molly into her arms, and ran up the stairs two at a time. "Bedtime!" she cheerfully lied. Molly was tucked in firmly when Ari crossed over to the window and knelt down. From Molly's room, Ari could see the driveway below, but the porch roof blocked any view of the front door. The empty truck could barely be seen in the darkness, and Ari realized if someone was around, the stormy darkness could easily hide them.

What if someone had cut the power?

What if they're going to break into the house?

What if they try to take me again?

A million scenarios at once flooded her mind. She was shaking, her breath coming in jagged gasps with her racking heartbeat. She held the sill for balance as she crouched down. Footsteps behind her caused her to whirl around.

"It's just me," Dane said softly, as if he read her fear. He'd turned off his flashlight and was carefully moving through the dark room. He crouched down beside her as she clutched the window. "All the doors are locked. Maybe if they think nobody is home, they'll go away."

"No...no, they'll break in if they think nobody is home!" Ari was panicking at a whisper. "That's what they did last time!"

"Whoa..." Dane braced the windowsill with his arms, behind Ari. His mouth was almost to her ear. "Ari," was all he needed to say. She closed her eyes and focused on breathing slower. She could feel his cheek almost against her face. Suddenly a noise from downstairs caused them both to start: a doorknob was being rattled. She could feel Dane tensing, but he didn't budge, despite Ari's attempt to struggle away. "Don't move," he hissed. "Just listen," as the same time Ari gasped, "what do we do?"

"Shhh....we need to call the police. Where's your cell phone?" he finally whispered.

Ari swallowed hard. She'd left it on the table downstairs, right next to her homework.

"You don't have it?" She shook her head slightly. "We'll have to go into the kitchen then. Come on."

She was unmoving, planted at the windowsill. *Focus, Ari.* She locked onto Dane's eyes, searching for some shred of strength within him. His eyes were like steel; resolute, but empathetic. She bowed her head, drawing in a breath. When he took her head in his hand, she willingly met his gaze. "We need to go. *Now.*" It was all he needed to say, and, taking her hand, they quickly but quietly felt their way down the stairs.

"Is the truck still here?" Dane looked through the vertical blinds again. "I see someone..." he hissed. Ari peered through the blinds as well. A man was backing away from the house, as if he was trying to see through the upper windows. A hood covered his head, but through the rain, Ari could see he had a defined profile.

"Wait." Dane stood straight and furrowed his brow. "*Dad?*"

Before she could protest, Dane darted out the front door. The man seemed startled at first, but he ran to Dane after a moment, ducking out of the rain. She heard them come through the entryway. "What are you doing here?" she overheard Dane's voice, a mixture of surprise and disbelief.

Ari stayed as close to the wall as possible, inching her way towards the conversation. "What are *you* doing here?" she heard the unfamiliar voice respond.

"What do you mean?"

"Rhoda told me you'd run away. I didn't think anyone even lived here anymore." His father's voice was gravelly, like an older, harsher version of Dane's.

"I never ran away; I've been here the whole time. Mom and Molly live here now, too."

Even in the dark, she could see Dane's father was taken aback. "I had no idea."

Ari edged into the entryway, and both men turned towards her.

"Dad, this is my friend Ari. She lives in the other house now." Ari was still trembling, but she managed to approach Dane's dad. They silently shook hands and Ari suddenly felt very shy, and out of place. "She was actually the reason Rhoda moved away and mom and Molly were able to come back."

His dad just shook his head. "I didn't know any of that, son. Really I didn't. In fact, everything I've heard about the past few years sounds like a complete lie. I can't even believe it..." his voice trailed off to a grunt. Suddenly the lights flickered back on, and Ari felt herself jump as the electricity popped.

She then could see Dane and his dad clearly: both had the same curved nose, the same stature. But where Dane's eyes were brooding and soft, a striking hazel, his dad's eyes were hard and tired.

They went into the kitchen and Dane made coffee. "I was in Arizona for some time, then New Mexico," his dad started. "I stayed at a job for a year or so, but I was really trying to find a better place for us to live. I got sidetracked, son. I didn't mean to leave you for so long. I lost my way. I never called because I never had any good news for you. And then Rhoda showed up, an' told me she needed money." He sighed hard. "I told her to get lost," he shook his head, "an' then she told me you'd hit the road months before. Said you'd snuck out in the middle of the night and never come back. Now that I think about it, she was just ticked that I wouldn't give her booze money. Once I heard that, I started driving up here to look for you, and this was my first stop."

Dane took this in for a bit, sipping his coffee. "So Rhoda didn't mention the treasure," Dane said.

"Treasure?" His dad had the first twitch of a smile that Ari had seen. "What treasure?"

Alternating, Dane and Ari filled in his father with all the unbelievable details of Nadia's hidden fortune. "We even have a portion set aside for you, even though I didn't know if you were ever going to return." Dane's voice dropped. "But for a few months, somebody has been after us. They tried to kidnap Ari, and our houses were robbed. We don't know who's doing it. And we thought *you* were one of them tonight."

"Unbelievable. There's an underground room, huh?"

Dane nodded, but before he could elaborate, the front door swung open with a rattle of keys, and Dane's mother appeared in the doorway. She nearly dropped her purse and a bag of groceries she'd been carrying. "Mark?"

*   *   *

Dane's mother had been shocked to see him sitting there, in her kitchen, talking to Dane. Years had passed since they'd seen each other last; even longer than when Dane had last seen him. That night, as Ari was trying to sleep despite a restless mind, she wondered what would happen next, and what would change for Dane. Her final thought seemed to ease her: *His dad finally came back. He must love Dane, after all...*

chapter twenty

Unfamiliar voices in the living room woke Ari to full
attention. Donning a robe, she made her way down the hall and
halfway down the stairs. Two officers were talking to her parents.
"She convinced her sister and brother-in-law to join in," the skinny
one said. "She reportedly promised them a percentage of the
treasure." The shorter officer saw Ari on the stairs and motioned her
over.

The skinny one nodded to her. "You must be Ari. I'm Detective
Snyder. This is Officer Rodgers." They extended their hands in
greeting. "We've been working on the case, and luckily, that phone
number you gave us was the clue we needed. Karen Zeller is your
former neighbor's sister."

"Rhoda?!" Ari shook her head. *No way.*

"That's her. When Mark Hadley refused to give her money, she
figured getting her hands on Dane's treasure would be easier than
robbing a piggy bank. She convinced her sister and brother-in-law to
join her, promising them fast cash. That was the Zeller's van you and
Dane saw, and it was Mr. Zeller who you thought he could snatch the
key to the underground room from your neck. Unfortunately, none of
them were smart enough to figure the items wouldn't be around here
at all, even after they both broke into your houses."

"Stupid Rhoda," Ari muttered under her breath.

"You'll be glad to know Rhoda has been taken into custody, as
well as the Zellers. They've got so many charges against them that I
don't think anyone will be hearing from them for a very long time."
Officer Rodgers tipped his hat as they headed for the door. "I hope
you can feel safe again in our little town. This kind of thing doesn't
happen very often around here."

*   *   *

It was four in the afternoon on Saturday when Ari was ready to be driven to Riley's house. She had her dress zipped carefully in a garment bag, and her shoes and accessories were in another bag, all ready for the winter formal. The small amount of makeup she owned was in her backpack; she was hoping Riley or another friend would help her with it.

Her mom was shuffling around in the kitchen, looking for her car keys, when the doorbell rang. To her surprise, when Ari opened the door, Dane was there.

"Hey...what's up?" Ari asked, curiously.

"Well, there was something I wanted to show you before you left to get ready for the dance..." He seemed to be hesitant.

"You caught me right in time. I was just about to go," she said, motioning towards her bags.

"But the dance doesn't start 'till eight, you know." He gave her a funny look.

She giggled and shook her head. "Girls take a lot of time to get ready. If you don't know that by now, Dane..." her voice trailed off in a good-natured smirk.

"Well, let's go then. It won't take too long," he assured her.

They headed up the driveway to his house. The day was positively gray and foreboding; wind was beginning to whip through the tree tops, but no rain had fallen yet. Ari and Dane dodged the murky puddles in the gravel road.

Once inside the house, Dane told her to wait in the entryway. She heard him rustling around in the living room for a moment. He returned with an old-looking blue velvet box, about seven inches square. He handed it to her, seeming unsure.

"I don't know what your dress looks like, but if you think this would look alright with it, you're welcome to wear it tonight." He shrugged nonchalantly and Ari opened the case carefully. She gasped.

Inside was one of Nadia's treasured necklaces. This one was delicate, despite every inch being solidly adorned with diamonds set in white gold. Each length of necklace had a repeating pattern of two leaves, one blossom (with one tiny diamond for each petal), then two more leaves. A pair of blossom earrings accompanied it.

"Dane, I can't wear this. If something were to happen to it, I don't know what I'd do! It's so beautiful—"

"Will it go with your dress?"

"Yes..."

"Then you *should* wear it. Please. Nadia would want her things being worn and enjoyed. Trust me."

Ari nodded and closed the case. "Okay. And...thank you." She smiled and paused. "Um, I'll bring it back first thing tomorrow, ok?"

He just shrugged. "Whenever. Have a great time tonight, ok?"

Ari turned and looked at him. She wanted *so* badly to convince him to come with her. He just smiled at her as she turned to leave. She opened the door and, clutching the velvet box, dodged into the blustery afternoon.

*   *   *

Four girls and four hours later, Ari, Riley, and Riley's friends Amara and Julie were ready for the dance. Riley's lavender dress practically floated in the wind as the four made their way from the car up the impressive marble staircase leading to the doors of the Old City Hall. Ari had to bustle the layers of her silk skirt as they ascended, praying she wouldn't step on it.

Nobody—not even Riley—had seen the dress she'd chosen at the last moment. It was the lightest cream color, strapless, with a fitted waist. Beyond the waist it flared into a flounced skirt that had several gathers on the front, with a slight train in the back. Her favorite part, however, was the neckline: it was straight across, with scalloping along the edge. The embroidery continued across the bodice, with tiny crystals threaded here and there. Nadia's necklace was the finishing touch.

Though her hair was short, Ari had sought help from Amara, who had expertly curled the back of Ari's hair so it slightly accentuated her A-line cut. She'd also smoothed out the front of her hair, pinning the sides with small bobby pins. Overall, Ari was ecstatic with how everything had looked together. The other girls looked fantastic, too. Riley's satin and chiffon dress was stunning; and her hair was just as glamorous, all piled into a cascade of curls and rhinestone pins.

Once they arrived inside, a collective gasp could be heard from the girls. The Old City Hall was even grander than Ari had imagined: a massive crystal chandelier was the focal point of the large, circular entryway. Two sweeping staircases descended from the second floor. Beyond that, music could be heard streaming from a double doorway at the back of the room.

Their heels clicked on the marble floors; they were speechless at the beauty of the building as they hung their coats and made their way to the ballroom. Two tuxedoed attendants opened the double doors as they entered. The loud music of a fast song caused the floor to vibrate with energy. Although the ballroom was even more impressive and detailed than the entryway, the room was dark and Ari could only see glimpses of the chandeliers as the colored spotlights flashed on them.

"Wow, this is beautiful!" Ari half-yelled to Riley, who nodded in agreement. In keeping with the winter theme, glittered snowflakes and thin silver streamers had been hung from the high ceiling, and the buffet tables gleamed with silver confetti. Only after a few moments, Ari realized she'd been smiling to herself. *This is like a fairytale*, she thought. *I wish Dane could see this.*

No sooner than she'd headed for the punch table, one of Riley's friends grabbed Ari's arm and dragged them all onto the dance floor. Although she hadn't ever really danced much, and her dress didn't make moving easier, Ari couldn't help but get swept away into the swaying crowd.

After about twenty minutes of fast dances, the chandeliers—many more than Ari had imagined—were turned on to their lowest light. The colored strobes ceased, and the only other light was from the strands of white Christmas lights on potted trees around the ballroom, and the slowly rotating mirror ball in the center of the room. Little stars of light traveled in circular orbits as dozens of couples made their way to the dance floor.

The four girls split off in separate ways; Amara and Julie found friends to dance with, Riley found something to drink, and Ari picked up her skirt and made her way to one of the luxuriously stuffed chairs in the darkened corner of the room. She sighed and took in the sight in front of her. She couldn't help but observe the dancers: some seemed to make awkward pairs, holding each other at arm's length; while others danced slowly and closely. Ari wondered how she would dance if Dane had attended, but before she could draw a conclusion, she saw Riley gliding over.

"I just thought I'd let you know that Jace is dancing with—get this—*not his girlfriend*. In fact, Julie said she hasn't seen them together in weeks..." Riley gave Ari a sly smile.

"Well? Are you going to ask him, or are you going to be a wallflower and sit in a corner like me?" Ari giggled and pushed Riley back onto the dance floor. Riley just gave a hopeful shrug and headed in the general direction of her crush.

Several more slow songs followed. She was watching Riley approach Jace, then Jace nodded and they joined the dancers on the floor. Ari smiled and butterflies tingled in her stomach. *I'll never be that brave*, she thought to herself. Edging around the floor, Ari traversed to the windows on the long side of the room, which framed the streets lining the edge of Rivers. The little town below was still and empty; it seemed Ari and the rest of the dancers were the only people awake at that hour in the tiny town. She turned around and gazed back at Riley and Jace, but her eye was drawn to the main doors as they opened. A tall, dark-haired boy paused, scanning the room. Ari was so surprised she froze, her stomach fluttering.

chapter twenty-one

Maybe he's looking for someone else. *Maybe he's not even looking for me*, she thought. But once he spotted her, Dane crossed the room, weaving through the edge of dancers. He was wearing a white shirt with the top button undone, and black pants. His normally-messy hair was not quite as tousled as it usually was.

It was hard enough getting over the sight of Dane all dressed up; she couldn't help but catch her breath at the thought of him actually at a dance. *This* dance. Standing right in front of her, now. Ari was still rooted in place.

"You showed up," she said. He bent his head low, as close as possible without touching her face, so he could hear her above the music.

An almost-mischievous smile played across his face. "I decided to come and see what I was missing out on," he said into her ear. "Now that I'm here, would you like to dance?"

"Really?" Ari beamed and finally unfroze. "Of course." He put his arm around her waist and wasn't timid about leading her to the center of the ballroom floor. Even though she previously couldn't picture him dancing, especially with her, he seemed unruffled and confident as he took her right hand in his while his other hand guided her back. The song had just begun, though the floor was already shoulder-to-shoulder. *So this is what dancing with Dane is like,* she inwardly smiled to herself. Riley saw Ari from across the room and gave her a surprised thumbs-up.

The dots of light cast from the mirror ball traveled across Dane's face, and the dim chandelier glow was barely enough to catch the light in his eyes. She strained to get a glimpse of them, always so captivating; their calm green with bold splashes of hazel in the centers. As he gazed down, though, they were half hidden by his curly eyelashes, which were dark as night.

He then met her gaze, then unexpectedly pushed her into a slow twirl under his arm and to the side. Ari's voluminous skirt flounced out as she spun. She felt like a ballerina as she wound back into his hold. Everything almost seemed to move in slow motion, and she wished she could stop time and stay here, dancing with Dane.

Wordlessly they finished the dance and returned to the windows. "You said you weren't the dancing type," she half-joked. "I disagree."

"I've never had a reason to come to one of these," he shrugged. She watched as he looked out the rain-splattered window, the orange streetlights reflecting on his face. Another slow song started. He smiled with his eyes and offered his hand.

"One more dance before I go?" he asked quietly. Her heart raced just a little as he took her hand and held it, going once again to the center of the floor. This time, he put both hands around her back. She was just at the right height where she could hold one hand to his shoulder, and he rested his chin on the side of her forehead. She realized she was holding her breath, scarcely breathing. *Trying to hold on to this forever*, she thought. Frozen in a way she'd never felt; tingling, and more aware of the person who was holding her than ever before.

All too soon the music ended and the colored strobes began with the next fast song. Dane hadn't let go, but pulled her in just a bit closer. "Thank you for dancing with me," he said, then looking at her for an eternal second, let go and disappeared through the crowd.

*   *   *

In the haziness precluding full awareness, Ari wasn't exactly sure if the night before had been an elegant dream or unbelievable reality. Her dress, neatly hanging on her closet door, reaffirmed it had been truly real. She smiled as she stretched. *He really danced with me*, she thought. Her gaze fell to the blue velvet box where Nadia's necklace safely rested.

PART THREE

chapter one

The howling wind and heavy splattering rain made a deafening drum on the brass door that sealed off the underground room from the storm above. Dane was sitting on the floor as he scanned a sheet of parchment with his flashlight. His hazel eyes were unrecognizable; only brief rims of deep green were visible in the dim light. Ari hovered close and watched him read line for line.

"And you found this *where*?" Dane didn't look up from the page, but pulled the blanket tighter around him.

"I know I've been through it a million times, Dane," Ari assured him, "but it was underneath a photograph in that leather-bound photo album that was in the trunk with the tutus. It has photographs of Nadia as a ballerina, and contains a few of her notes to Grekov." Ari's breath came in jagged gasps because of her sprint from her house to the underground room. "I hoped you'd be in here because it freaked me out a little."

"Yeah..." Dane just nodded his head. "I guess I never wondered where they'd be buried. I always assumed they'd been shipped back to Russia, or something." He returned the piece of paper to Ari. "Now the question is, where was her 'most beloved spot on the hill?'

Ari's hands were trembling as she read the note quietly to herself. "My love, we know the time is near, but I wish not to weigh you down with decisions after my passing to the next life. Please bury me at our most beloved spot on the hill, for my heart wishes to remain nowhere else but here. Eternally, Nadia."

She raised her eyes from the paper. Silently she scanned her thoughts for plausible burial locations, glancing up at Dane. "Where are we going to start looking?" she mused quietly, almost pleading. The thought of unknown grave site near her home bothered her more than she'd admit openly.

"Uh, I think you're going to have to tackle this one on your own, Ari." His voice was softer with her now. Something had changed in his demeanor since the dance a few weeks' prior. Still, she shook her head in protest.

"Why? I'm not looking for them alone!"

"I have to go to Arizona with my dad over winter break. We'll be gone the whole week. I have to help him move his stuff up here." Ari's face must've fallen, despite her honest attempts to be as excited for Dane as possible. "You'll be fine," he reassured, sealing his promise with a glint of a smile.

Ari had more than a few questions for Dane about his dad, but she knew to be selective about which ones to ask. "How do your mom and dad get along these days?" She winced even as it came out, but there wasn't a delicate way to ask. A gust of wind whistled through the brass lid above them, and Ari involuntarily shivered. Dane handed her his blanket, and she was grateful for the warmth.

"It's not like they're going to get back together," he said dryly. "But they're civil." Something in his tone lacked optimism.

"What's wrong?" Ari searched his eyes, but they were silent. She pulled the blanket up to her nose and rested her head on her knees.

"Nothin," he shook his head. It was the kind of 'nothing' that really meant everything, but Ari knew enough to not ask anything more. An awkward silence filled the tiny room, broken quickly by a sudden slamming sound on the hollow brass lid. Ari startled and Dane ducked down.

"What was that?" Ari didn't move, but Dane climbed to the lid and propped it open. A sizable rotten tree branch rolled off the top, and dead leaves and dirt swirled forcibly into the little room.

"I think we should probably go home. The storm is getting crazy out there," Dane remarked, but Ari caught a stressed inflection in his voice. She stood and climbed up right next to him on the recessed ladder and pulled the lid down. One rung higher, she was exactly at face level with him.

"Is something going on?" she asked quietly, with as much sensitivity as possible. He shifted on the step, not away from her, but no closer, and sighed.

"I have a memory of my family—especially my dad, before they divorced, when he and I got along and did things together all the time," he said, looking past Ari. "I see who he is now, and I'm not sure if I want to know him more than I do."

"You're afraid he'll disappoint you," Ari filled in.

"Yeah," he nodded, finally meeting her eyes. "It won't be the same as before. I wish it could be, but..." Dane shook his head. "I just don't see that happening. I—*we*—spent all that time looking for him, and after we couldn't find him, I'd finally accepted that things were fine as they were. Then he showed up and it's like he's changed so much I don't know who he is."

Ari dared playing the devil's advocate. "He probably feels like he doesn't know who you are, either, Dane, and he knows it's completely his fault because he left you. And with everything that happened with Rhoda, maybe he feels doubly at fault. You'll only be with him a few weeks, and if things don't work out....well, you still have your mom and sister...and me. We'll still be here for you."

Dane looked at her for a moment, processing. She'd wished to see him smile his perfect grin, but another clanking sound on the brass lid reminded them of the terrific storm above. Dane unlatched the lid and helped Ari out. "When are you leaving?" she asked, pulling her hood tight over her head.

"Tomorrow afternoon. We're flying down and driving back up with his things."

Ari nodded. "If I don't see you before then, have a good trip," she hollered over the howling wind. One of them lingered, and the other stopped as well, resulting in a half-awkward pause. Dane finally grinned, and though it had a hint of sadness, it was enough for her. It would have to be.

*   *   *

If the storm had been petulant while they had been in the subterranean room, it was unbelievably forceful by the time Ari arrived home. Dusk had settled and the wind was past sporadic gusting; it now was a constant rush, and she noticed the windows and walls of the old house flexed against the pressure. Storms weren't uncommon in San Francisco, in fact, she could remember some incredible ones. However, she had never experienced a storm in an old house—all alone, no less. She was dismayed to find the house dark and empty upon her arrival, with only a note on the table. Her parents had taken Lily with them to parent-teacher conferences.

Coincidentally, this was the first time she'd been allowed to stay home alone since the Zellers had tried to grab her outside of Dane's home. Ari was grateful for the fact her parents had noticeably loosened their watch over her; after all, there was no chance Rhoda would be back. Despite that, Ari's nerves apparently hadn't gotten the news. Every rattled window and creaking wall sent her into a small panic. She shook her head, thinking how ridiculous her fear was. She headed upstairs to her room and flopped on her bed with a book. *This should be a good distraction*, she thought.

Just as her attention was fully focused on the story, a loud *pop!* echoed through the house and the lights snapped off. Ari yelped involuntarily, and was suddenly glad nobody was around to see her panic. She picked up the phone to give Riley a call, just to have someone to talk to. Ari grimaced; the phone lines were down. She found her cell phone in her jeans pocket and dialed Dane's house, but realized they wouldn't have phone service either. Ari sighed, pulled on a jacket, scribbled a note, found a flashlight, and headed up the road to Dane's house.

chapter two

It was eerily dark at Dane's house when Ari knocked on the heavy door. She knew they had to be home; his mom's car was in the driveway, and she'd seen Dane half an hour prior, but she was still relieved when Mrs. Hadley came to the door, a candle in hand.

"Ari! Is everything alright? Come right in!" she said, her sweet, soft voice smiling.

"I'm fine, Mrs. Hadley. Our lights are out too, and, uh, my parents are at conferences." She was embarrassed to say more, but didn't need to, as Mrs. Hadley waved her off and guided her in the house.

"Well, come right in. I'm glad you came over here. Dane's in his room," she said, taking Ari's coat, and handing her a candle. She carefully picked her way upstairs and knocked on Dane's door. There was no response; she opened the door a crack. The light of a single candle was illuminating one corner, and Dane was sitting in his desk chair with his back to her and earphones in. She crossed the room and gently put her hand on his shoulder, hoping to not startle him, but from his reaction, he'd either been deep in thought or dozing. His head flew up, and his arm swung around and smacked her right on the side of the head.

"Ow!" Ari managed to keep her candle out of his arm's path, but her free hand went to her head.

"Crap, Ari—I'm so sorry. I didn't know you were there," he said, and his hand automatically went to her head as well. His touch froze her in place, as she awkwardly leaned to the side. "Do you need some ice?" He parted her hair, and she suddenly realized how warm she felt. "I don't think it's bruising," he said, looking apologetic.

"I'm fine," she said, hoping he wouldn't ask why her face was red. "I didn't mean to startle you," she said, recovering. "What are you listening to?" She grabbed the one earbud that was dangling and listened, failing to realize how close she'd have to stand to hear properly. Her face flushed once again.

A familiar rock tune was blasting full-volume. She looked up at him and smiled. "Good choice," she said.

"So," Dane looked at her curiously, ducking his head to find eye contact. "You couldn't stay away from me, huh?" he joked.

Ari stammered. "What? No—um, our electricity went out," she managed. "My parents and Lily are at conferences. There's nobody at home."

She wasn't looking at him directly but she could feel the concern in his voice. "Why are you really over here, Ari?" She was still hooked to his earbud, and suddenly felt entirely too close to him. It didn't help when he put his hand on her cheek so she'd look at him. "What's up?"

The words wouldn't form correctly, due to a mix of embarrassment over the reason why she was really there, the fact that she was inches from Dane, and he was touching her. He realized what was wrong before she could put together a sentence.

"You're scared to be alone," he stated, without accusation.

"Not scared," she insisted, stepping back. She sat on his desk. "It's just been a long time since I've been in that big, old house by myself. And, have you heard the storm outside?! It sounds like our house is going to blow over. It's freezing cold over there, too." She looked over her shoulder and out the window. Occasional thunder and lightning had been added to the repertoire; shocking blue flashes overexposed Dane's room. "And, apparently there's a grave somewhere out there. So, yes, I was a little uncomfortable." She crossed her arms.

"Well, I'm glad you're over here." He took a half-folded blanket from his bed and wrapped it around her shoulders. "I would hate to have you freeze to death in your own house," he joked. "Do you know when your parents will be home?"

She shook her head. "The note said the conference is at eight. I wonder if they didn't go out for dinner first," she mused. Sitting herself up against his bed's headboard, she wrapped the blanket tighter. "Don't let me interrupt what you were doing before I came," she said, and Dane just shrugged.

"I should probably start packing," he said, opening up a duffle bag from his closet.

The warmth of the blanket and the security of not being alone lulled her to a quick and light sleep. An unknown passage of time was broken by something lightly brushing her cheek. Her eyes fluttered open to Dane, an arm's length away. "Ari, wake up. Your parents are here," he said, nearly at a whisper.

The night's storm had barely lessened as Ari fell asleep in her own bed. She'd been woken by sudden crashes of things being blown about by the wind, or whips of rain, violently spattering across her window. Worst of all were the near crashes of thunder; some rumbles never seemed to stop. Morning revealed the full wrath and extent of the night's tumult; Ari awoke to see the effects. Roof shingles were flung across the yard, tree branches from the oak grove littered pathways, and in the front yard, a sizable branch had nearly missed her mom's car. Backyard ornaments, planters, and deck furniture had been dragged and tossed by the wind.

Ari was in the kitchen when her mom shuffled in with her robe and slippers on. "It looks like you got as much sleep as we did," she surmised, looking at Ari's tired expression. Her mom lowered her voice to a whisper. "Lily was terrified by the storm; she was in our bedroom all night last night. Did the thunder keep you up?"

"Yeah. The whole house was creaking. I thought it would blow away with the rest of the stuff out there," she shrugged towards the backyard.

"Well, after breakfast, get your boots on. We'll need some help getting it all cleaned up," her mom smiled. "Hot chocolate afterwards."

*   *   *

The yard clean-up had barely distracted Ari from her thoughts of Nadia's grave. Worse, she was afraid of accidentally stumbling across it in their own backyard, maybe even feet from the house. She thought about all the renovation on the back yard that had been done over the summer; no headstone nor grave nor any other indicating monument had been found. She mentioned her search to her mom and dad over lunch preparations, as Lily was out of earshot. "No wonder we got the house at such a good price," her dad had jested, and her mom had rolled her eyes.

"If you find it, I could live without knowing where it is," said her mom, slightly repulsed.

Even worse was the fact Dane was gone, and winter break crawled by at a pace completely loathed by Ari. Days seemed to lengthen to years, and the foul weather and cabin fever gnawed away at her. She was completely thankful for Riley's presence most days, especially when she showed her the newly-found note regarding Nadia's burial.

"What?! Oh, that is so completely gross," Riley said, examining the frail note, then she started laughing. "You've got to be kidding me, Ari. There's seriously a dead person buried on your property?"

"Sounds like it. What do you think?"

"I think I feel sorry for you. No wonder your parents got a deal," she giggled.

Ari rolled her eyes. "That's what my dad said. Anyway, Dane left before he could help me look for it—"

"You were going to look for it? Ari, I think that's one thing I'd leave alone. Speaking of Dane—" she dug around in her backpack, "—I took these at the dance. I thought you'd like a copy." She handed her an envelope with several photos enclosed. "You guys looked great."

Ari opened the envelope and looked at the first photo. It was a shot of them dancing, when Dane had twirled her. The second was of Dane holding her as they were slow dancing. She stuffed them back into the envelope and smiled. "You take great pictures, Riley. I appreciate it."

Riley smiled. "Sooo....how are things going with him?"

Ari tried her hardest to be nonchalant. "Um, he's gone with his dad in Arizona. He won't be back for a week," she said, honestly. Riley eyed her.

"That's not what I meant."

Rolling her eyes, Ari huffed. She'd never been good with expressing herself, and she felt guarded about Dane. On the other hand, she knew Riley could be trusted.

"I want to help him out and be a good friend to him, but I think there are some things he has to figure out," she explained. "I don't know if he likes me or not. Maybe he sees me as a good friend—he must—since he really went out of his comfort zone to come to the dance." She must've started smiling at that point, because Riley squealed.

"He must like you, Ari!" she exclaimed.

Ari just shrugged, but silently wanted to agree.

*   *   *

The window seat was, hands-down, the coldest place in Ari's room, due to the proximity of the window, but it was also her favorite place, no matter the season. On this particular night, she had a heavy down comforter wrapped twice around her. Only her dim mini-lamp was on so she could see the bright winter stars out her window. She tilted the shade more towards her and pulled the envelope of photos from inside the blanket. She hadn't examined them in front of Riley; but now that she looked closely, she not only noticed that Dane was looking at her in the photo, but *how* he was looking at her. It made her smile; it was almost as if she was holding conclusive evidence of something unspoken.

chapter three

The next few days were gray and dull, but fortunately the rain had stopped. A fine, wispy mist had settled on the hill, and to Ari, it seemed the skeletal trees of the oak grove had grown increasingly morose in stature. In the middle of the day near the end of winter break, she decided to venture out into the grove to search for Nadia's burial plot.

She wasn't even sure of what she was looking for. She didn't know enough about Nadia to decipher what her most beloved place would be, besides her ballet studio, perhaps. She shook her head at her own silent train of thought. It was probably somewhere outside, somewhere on the expanse of property that was Hadley Hill.

Ari had wandered past the brass circle and, where the well-worn path between her house and Dane's forked, she turned to the right, away from the path to Dane's house. This less-worn path led to the earthen pool, and during the winter, the path was littered with windfall from the trees. Dead twigs and debris snapped under her feet, until she reached the wide opening of trees that surrounded the pool. A ghostly fog hovered silently above the dark glassy surface. During the summer, the pool was resplendent with jade-green water. But cold weather brought a pallor to everything here, and the beautiful pool was not immune.

She and Dane had never ventured past the pool; the oaks were thicker there, intermingled with taller conifers. By all accounts, it seemed the pool was a destination unto itself, and they'd simply never explored anything past the cleared circle. No stream fed the pool; Ari assumed that an underground spring provided the fresh water. Though it was technically noon, no light seemed to reach through the bony grove of trees. She paused, wondering if venturing in would be wise. It would be days until Dane returned, and she wanted to have something to tell him of her search. Ari took a deep breath, traversed the slate pool-rim, and entered the grove at the widest point.

She scuffled her feet so she wouldn't trip on knobby tree roots that seemed to erupt from the ground everywhere. She noticed the ground was harder than the packed dirt she was previously on. Bending down, she brushed aside crisp, paper-thin leaves and dirt. The ground beneath was the same kind of cobblestone that was found everywhere else in the garden. It was so covered by decades of dirt and hidden by brambles that Ari realized she'd need more than her bare hands to uncover it. She picked her way back into the clearing and started jogging toward her house.

Minutes later she returned with hedge trimmers, thick pigskin gloves, and a wide broom. She knew she'd have to work quickly, as the clouds had changed from high and white to low and dark gray: the unmistakable indication of coming rain. Taking the hedge trimmers she lopped away at dead brown blackberry vines and carefully pulled them away and to the side. Every now and then, she'd sweep the cobbles clear of dirt, and continue on. Eventually the rain began, but she noticed the cover of trees protected her from most drops. Ari went on like this for an hour; cutting, clearing, and sweeping. The path appeared unlike the meandering ones in her backyard; this one was straight, purposeful.

Never had she roamed so deeply into the grove; she'd begun to travel down the hill, away from her house. Soon she came to a bramble thicket that seemed impenetrable. Vines climbed high over something Ari couldn't see. She clipped away and tore down the barbwire-like branches. Underneath were wrought-iron supports, which, after much clearing, Ari determined to be a gate. Hefty brick columns, much like those in her own garden, stood at each side, though they formed an elegant arch above the gate. And, like the door in the underground room, this gate presented a swirled leaf motif with vines and bees, and a keyhole with the ever-familiar bee symbol.

Ari tried the gate, which was locked solidly. She stepped back and figured the iron fence ran in a circular path, forming a fairly large enclosure. Inside the gate she could see more brambles and trees. Nothing else on the hilltop was fenced like this. Not even the brass circle had such security. But for what?

176

By now, rain was falling in large plops, and Ari was soaked through. She packed her tools back along the newly-cleared cobblestone path, all the way back to her house. More hands were needed to clear the outside; a new key had to be found to get inside the mysterious iron gate.

*   *   *

Christmas came and went, and Ari's aunts, uncles, and a few cousins descended upon them with joyful noise and celebration. Ari's mom had done the old house justice with the Christmas decorations. This year, they'd room enough for two trees in the house. Despite the ever-present grayness outside, it was warm and cozy inside, with candles and cinnamon and hot chocolate. Riley had even spent the night a few times, and Ari was grateful for her company. Despite all the activity going on around her, Ari's mind would hourly drift to wondering where Dane was, and what he was doing. By New Years' day, she was brimming with anticipation, and trying her hardest not to let it show.

It wasn't until her last class of the day, on the first day back to school, that she got to see Dane. Somehow they always ended up with the same elective together. Last term it had been art; this term it was Spanish class. She was relieved when he found a seat in front of her.

"How was your trip?" she leaned forward, hoping to get as much information before class started.

Dane looked back. All he could manage before the bell rang was, "It was okay. Let's go to coffee after school."

chapter four

Their drinks had been ordered, but it was as busy as lunch hour when they arrived at Cinema Coffee, and every table was full. They waited for a table to open up, and Dane grabbed one as soon as it did.

"How was your Christmas?" he asked casually, almost taunting Ari because he could see the questions in her eyes.

"It was fine. Boring, almost. Tell me about your trip!"

"Well, it was fine. At first it was awkward," he said, honestly. "Then we started talking about all the things we used to do before he went away, before I lived with Rhoda." He took a breath and flipped subjects. "Where is home, Ari? I mean, for you?"

Ari was caught off guard by the question at first, but she understood what he was asking. Mentally she sorted through her versions of home, but only one qualified. "It was in San Francisco, when my grandma was still alive, and we lived in our apartment overlooking the bay. On weekends Lily and I went to Nana and Pop's house and spent the night, and sometimes my friend Alyssa would come with us. I had friends that I'd grown up with since kindergarten, Dane." She met his eyes, but drifted past them. Suddenly all she could see were the images of her childhood: comfortable, warm memories. She reconnected with Dane's eyes. "But it's different now. Nana and Pop passed. I don't even talk to Alyssa anymore." Ari's thought drifted off, caught between past and present.

"But you still have your family," Dane reminded her.

"Yeah, I do. I know you're supposed to say that home is wherever your family is, and that's true. I just miss the place I grew up, and my grandparents." She finally settled back on Dane's eyes. "Where is home for *you*, Dane?"

He shifted a bit and nodded confidently. "I would have to say that this, right now, is the best version of home I've ever had: with

178

Mom, and Lily, and even with Dad being nearby. I was actually really excited to get back home to Hadley Hill."

Ari smiled. "And I'm glad you're back. I forgot to mention that I found something while you were away," she hinted.

"Don't tell me you already found Nadia's grave."

"Actually I don't know what I found," she chuckled. "But I hope you have another key lying around, because we're gonna need it."

*   *   *

They tossed their bikes against a tree next to the pool. It was already getting dark, helped along by heavy cloud cover. Dane didn't say a word as he examined the gate, pulling hollow dried vines from the iron bars. He looked at the bee plaques on both brick columns, and then tried walking to one side or the other to follow the fence, but the briars were too thick. "We're going to have to work on this tomorrow," he said, looking up at the arch. "Saturday work party, Ari."

"Did you know about this? You don't seem surprised by it." Ari said.

"No. I've never been back this far. I guess after finding the underground room, I'm no longer surprised by all the weird things we find on this hill," he chuckled. Ari nodded in agreement.

He took off his coat and threw it over the top of the fence. "What are you doing?" Ari questioned.

"Well, unless you want to hoist *me* over the fence, I'm going to give you a lift over." He grinned and knelt to the ground, taking her hand, but she tried pulling away.

"Are you crazy? What if I can't get out? I'll be stuck in there forever. And," she glanced at the sky, "it's getting dark."

"Don't worry. I have a plan." He pulled her back and she

reluctantly stepped on his knee. She wasn't quite level enough to straighten her arms and jump over, so he lifted her until she could make it. She landed on her hands and feet and rolled to the side, coming to a stop in a thick pile of crunchy leaves. Dane fit his feet between the vine swirls in the gate, carefully making his way to the top of the brick arch. He placed his foot between spikes, then swung his legs over the arch so he could sit on it. Ari wondered what his plan was; the arch had to be at least seven feet at the apex. He paused for a moment and then dropped and rolled onto another deep pile of leaves. He came up with a nest of leaves stuck in his hair.

"So what do you think this is?" Ari got up and made her way along the fence line. Inside, there weren't as many blackberry briars, though there were a good number of trees. She thought they looked different from the oak trees, but couldn't be sure, as they all looked similar without leaves. The entire fenced enclosure was about one hundred and fifty feet across, and Ari assumed it was circular, though the tree trunks obstructed her view across.

"No clue." Dane took the opposite route, shuffling his feet along the ground, kicking aside leaves. They met at the back end of the circular area. From this angle, a large fountain could be seen in the middle of the circle. From the gate, it had been hidden by a large tree trunk. They stepped closer to see. Lines of bricks encircled the fountain, but age and tree roots had encroached and broken many of them. The fountain itself looked to be stone; a large low dish was the bottom pool, with a center column supporting a smaller top dish. Ari imagined water would stream from the top and collect in the bottom pool, but years of rainwater and detritus had blackened the inside of the fountain.

Dusk had settled, and Ari was getting uneasy. "Don't you think we should come back tomorrow when it's light out? It's kind of creepy in here. I don't like being locked in." She headed toward the gate and tried climbing over the way Dane had. Using the ironwork decorations as footholds, she tried hoisting herself over. Just as she thought she had it, she realized the last step to the top of the gate was inches too far. Her extended leg slipped on the wet iron and, missing the bars, she fell straight off. She landed on packed dirt, flat on her back, with a hard, hollow *whump*.

"Oh my gosh! Ari! Are you ok?" Dane appeared above her and then knelt beside. She was gasping; she'd completely knocked the air from her lungs. He tried to carefully pull her to a sitting position, but she waved him off. Lying flat was less painful. After a few moments, Ari could finally breathe.

"Just give me a sec here," she groaned. It was getting colder and she could start to feel the damp ground soak through her sweatshirt. She finally was able to prop herself up on an arm. "I'm going to feel that tomorrow," she said ruefully. With Dane's arm around her back, she finally was able to stand up.

"Are you going to be able to make it over the fence?" Dane knelt once more and she stepped up and took hold of the bars.

"I'm going to have to." Slowly Ari made it to the top of the fence, where she sat, unsure of what to do next. There were no soft piles of leaves on the other side; only cleared cobblestone and briars. Dane went his way over the arch, only this time he climbed down the front side of the gate instead of jumping. Then he came over below where Ari was still sitting on the fence, and lifted up his arms to her.

"Here, I'll catch you," he said, motioning for her to jump. She hesitated, worrying she'd knock him over, but as soon as she eased off the top rail, he caught her under the arms, and placed her gently on the ground. She suddenly realized his close proximity had caused her normal reflexes to slow; however, he wasn't moving away from her, either. Neither one said anything, though it wasn't an awkward silence. It was comfortable, she thought, like when they danced. Darkness prevented her from seeing his face clearly, though she knew with certainty he was looking at her. He finally broke the silence, still not moving away.

"Are you ok to walk back? Or do you need to be carried?" she could hear him smiling, almost teasing her.

"Yes!" she said, laughing, knowing it wasn't necessary. He knelt down and she hopped on, piggyback-style. He made his way carefully over the narrow path, and she was amazed at how easily he carried her.

Finally they connected with the more familiar path of the pool. "Tomorrow," Dane said, "we're going to need a ladder. I'm not letting you jump over the fence again." She could hear him smiling. She tightened her grip on his shoulders, resting her chin on his head.

*   *   *

A brief sun break in the morning brought Dane to Ari's back deck, where he rapped on the screen door. Ari grabbed her jacket, and from the deck, she collected a small painting ladder, the hedge clippers, a rake, and gloves. She'd hinted to her parents that she and Dane were working on a new secret project, and told them not to wait up for her for meals; she had no idea how long it would take to clear the fenced area.

They made their way to the gate. Ari unfolded the ladder and secured it against the fence. Tools were thrown over, then Ari climbed over first, and Dane followed. Ari was silently thankful for the ladder.

They each took tools and began clearing the ground. Ari started raking away the masses of dead leaves. They worked quietly for a bit; Dane eliminating the briars and piling them in a heap, and Ari joining her leaves to the pile. When she reached the far edge of the fence, there were so many trees that she could barely see Dane. Every few minutes, she'd see him walk to the pile.

After raking crackling leaves and brown, skeletal brambles for an hour, Ari decided it was time to take a break. She shuffled in Dane's direction through a deep bed of undisturbed leaves as a shortcut. Suddenly, her foot caught hard against something, and Ari swiftly tumbled into the leaves.

chapter five

"Ow!" Ari felt around in the leaves, trying to determine what she was lying on.

"Ari, are you ok?" Dane found her deep in the pile, and started scooping out around her. "Are you hurt?"

Ari rolled over and took Dane's extended hand. Once again, she was soaked from the wet ground. "No, I'm fine," she grumped. "What did I trip on?"

Dane left to retrieve his rake and Ari felt the ground. Whatever was beneath was cold, solid. Suddenly Ari gasped and flew to her feet, backing away.

"Dane!" Ari's voice resonated with panic.

He appeared instantly at her side. "I think I found it," she breathed.

"Found what?" he asked, and she took his rake. Its metal tines scraped painfully across whatever was beneath. A slightly curved concrete surface was slowly revealed. Dane moved to either side, and started clearing leaves as well. After fifteen minutes, two graves and their headstones were finally visible.

"Here they are," Dane said quietly, touching Nadia's headstone, which was a marble plaque set into the ground at the head of the plot. "Nadia Varishnikov Hadley, 1880-1940. Loving wife and mother, may you dance in heaven," he read. He moved to the next headstone. "Grekov Petrova Hadley. 1876-1942." Dane looked at Ari. "He died just two years after Nadia."

"Your great-great grandparents are buried in our backyard," Ari said, absorbing the thought. "This doesn't seem like a place that would be her favorite spot. Why do you think she was buried all the way out here?"

"I don't know. It doesn't really seem to make sense, does it?

Maybe we'll never know," he said, almost wistful. "Why do you think they're fenced in?"

Ari shrugged. "We might not ever know that either. Let's finish cleaning up in here and leave them in peace."

*   *   *

They'd just finished putting the gardening tools away when Ari's mom poked her head out the back door. "Clam chowder's on the stove if you guys want any. Goodness, what have you two been doing? You're a mess!"

Ari grimaced. "We found Dane's great-great grandparents. Turns out they're—"

"Wait! I told you I didn't want to know!" her mom waved them off, then started laughing. "You guys really found their graves?"

"Yes, ma'am. They aren't near our houses," he added.

"Well, that's all I need to know. Come on in and get dried off."

The briny aroma of the chowder made Ari smile. It reminded her of chilly winter days in San Francisco; it was top on her list of comfort foods. By the time two steaming bowls were on the table, she'd already replaced her leaf-encrusted sweatshirt with a warm sweater. They both started dunking oyster crackers into their respective bowls.

"You've looked through every one of the photo albums at your house?" Ari asked Dane.

"I did last summer, when we found them. Not since then. Why? What are you looking for?" He looked at her quizzically, a hint of suspicion in his jade-and-chocolate eyes.

"I honestly don't know, Dane. Something just feels odd about where we found them, you know?"

He shrugged. "Well, after we eat, let's go over to my house and we can go through them."

As they rounded the corner to Dane's house, they were both surprised to see Dane's dad's truck in the driveway. "Were you expecting your dad?" Ari lowered her voice. Dane shook his head, but rerouted to the kitchen, where he said hello to his dad. Ari hung back, behind Dane. Seeing the weathered and somewhat gruff face of his father always frightened her a little. She didn't know why; she had no real reason to fear him. The atmosphere was amicable enough; two coffee cups sat in front of his mom and dad at the kitchen table. Mrs. Hadley saw Ari and nodded hello, as did his dad, though unsmiling.

The attic was just as Ari had remembered it from the summer before; soft filtered light streamed through the little window, with bits of dust hovering in the air. Boxes and items covered in sheets silently stood sentinel in the musky air. It was cold enough that Ari could see her breath escape in little puffs. In the corner was the trunk with all the photos. They sat in silence; with Ari very carefully examining every album, and Dane sorting each one into family groups: old ones in one pile, and more recent ones in another.

"Look at this photo," Ari handed one to Dane. "Here's a lady tending a beehive," she pointed. The lady's thinness was accentuated by a huge straw hat that was draped with netting. She was wearing gloves, and pulling a honeycomb from a white box, which Ari assumed was the hive. Her face was obscured by the net, but one could tell she was smiling. He turned it over; there was a name written in Russian, but no other clues.

She kept turning pages. Most photos in this oldest album were of pictures of Ari's house and gardens from long ago. The same lady was in several others; in one, she was planting some flowers, in another, she was next to a fountain, which seemed acutely familiar to Ari. "Dane! Look at this!"

"Wow, that's the fountain in the fenced area, I'm sure of it. Do you think that's Nadia in all the garden photos, when she was older?"

Ari nodded. "It's totally possible. Find a picture of when she was younger, and we can compare."

Dane sorted through another of the older albums. "Here's a ballerina photo, I think."

They both looked at the photo Dane was holding. Perhaps it was after a performance, as Nadia was in full costume, holding an enormous bouquet of roses, standing next to a playbill poster. "The Premiere Theater presents world-class ballerina Nadia Varishnikov in Swan Lake," Ari read. Wait, what was Cinema Coffee called when it was first built?"

"I'm pretty sure it was the Premiere. You know how it says that on the front top of the building, with the year it was built?" Dane sounded almost excited.

"Nadia performed there! Wow..." She took that photo from Dane and compared it with the photo of the older lady at the fountain.

"Same smile, Dane. This has to be Nadia when she was older," she concluded, of the older photo. The same Russian name was scripted on the back. "I'm sure I've seen all these before, but I never really looked closely at them. Let's organize these loose photos into groups, like you did with the albums," she started making piles, but kept out the photo of Nadia at the theater.

"I wish I could translate what's written on these," Ari mused, examining the Cyrillic letterforms. "Can we take these photos to the underground room and keep them there so I can go through them again?" Dane nodded, and they both took an armful of albums. As they were coming to the second-floor stairs, they slowed. A heated conversation was occurring in the kitchen, and Dane paused to listen. Most of it was muffled, but a few words could be caught:

"You know that he was in my custody when I left him with Rhoda. Any court will tell you the same," Dane's dad said, loudly and gruffly. His mom's reply couldn't be heard, but his dad's quick response was cutting. "Well, why don't we let the judge decide that, Olivia."

Ari looked at Dane. "What's going on?" she mouthed, nearly silent. He shook his head, clearly unsure. Heavy footsteps indicated his dad was heading for the front door, and Ari and Dane simultaneously backed up against the wall, staying out of sight. Dane was barely breathing; Ari was holding her breath and didn't realize it until they heard the truck start up and back up out of the driveway. "What was that about?" she whispered in his ear, trying to read his expression. He didn't answer; instead, he pounded down the stairs and turned toward the kitchen. Ari followed hesitantly, hanging back a bit, but made it to the kitchen in time for her to hear Dane questioning his mom.

"What's going on, mom?"

Ari's stomach twisted when she saw Mrs. Hadley's tear-filled eyes, which she wiped at almost immediately upon seeing them both. Clearing her throat, she looked at Dane, and then Ari. "I'll go, Dane. Meet you at the circle?" Ari started to back out of the kitchen.

"No," he said, resolutely. "Stay... please."

Mrs. Hadley dabbed her eyes again. "Your father would like to have custody of you again," she said. "I reminded him that last time you were in his care, he left you with Rhoda and moved away."

"Why now? I don't understand. What's the difference if you have custody, or if he does? He lives five minutes from here." Dane sounded on the edge of frustration.

"Because, he's planning on moving away...and taking you with him."

It was so silent for that endless moment, Ari thought her heartbeat was certainly audible by all in the room.

"What?" Dane stammered.

"Your father wants to resume custody because he's decided to move to northern California. Unfortunately," her voice wavered, "he may still have a right to take you. It sounds like we'll be going to family court to sort it out, Dane. The judge may ask you what your preference would be; to stay with us or go with him, although it may not have an effect on the ruling." Mrs. Hadley looked weary, and sad.

Dane said nothing, turned, and strode out the front door. Ari stood like a statue, unsure of what to do. She finally nodded an apology to Mrs. Hadley, and followed Dane to the brass circle. Fortunately, he'd left it unlocked.

She descended into darkness. It wasn't unlike certain situations before, when Ari had come to comfort Dane, and the only consolation she could muster was that he wasn't in physical danger anymore. At least this time, it would be a civil, mediated decision, not coercion by brute force.

A candle wasn't needed for Ari to find Dane; she moved along the wall until she found him sitting in his usual spot. Wordlessly she lit one, then sat right next to him, shoulder to shoulder, and waited. An eternity passed before he said anything.

"I don't want to move away with my dad," he said quietly. Ari looked at him in the light of the single candle. His face was stoic, for the moment.

"I don't want you to either. Did he tell you about this on your trip?"

"Not at all." He turned to Ari, his eyes flashed with something she couldn't identify. She could feel intensity seeping from him, boiling beneath his ever-cool exterior, like a long-dormant volcano about to erupt. She didn't know whether to back away before he became angry, or if she could temper the force of his emotion. The very air snapped with his tension.

"Can you talk to him about it?" she reasoned, figuring a neutral question might diffuse him, but his bitter expression was the quick reply.

"You heard the man. Did you catch the anger in his voice? I don't think this is a debatable topic."

"He'd really want you to move with him even if he knew you didn't want to——"

"Ari," he cut her off. "I never wanted to stay with Rhoda, not for a day, not a week, *not for four years*," he growled. "And he knew that. And where did he leave me? With *her*." There was no softness to his voice, no respite from the acrid pain of abandonment that still lingered in him. But Ari didn't recoil, though she had no words of comfort. Minutes passed as they sat in heavy silence.

Suddenly, Dane got up. "I'm going over there to talk to him," he said, literally jumping up and out of the brass circle before Ari could say a word. She leaped up and jogged after him, trying to close the distance.

"Dane, wait!"

He slowed and looked back, finally stopping. "Please let me know what happens," she asked.

A fraction of softness came over Dane's face. He reached out and cupped her head with his hand, pulling her into a strong and unexpected hug. For the seconds that it lasted, Ari was overwhelmed by his warmth and scent and how his arms could wrap completely around her. She could feel his head bowed next to hers, resting on her shoulder. His fingers were intermingled with her hair, his hand on her neck. As he pulled away, his cheek brushed hers; his hand grazed her other cheek, and then... he was gone, jogging down the path, swallowed by the gray haze.

She stood there, tingling hot; rooted like one of the ancient oaks of the grove, until the piercing cold forced her to move.

*   *   *

Waiting to hear from Dane was agonizing. She went back to her house and placed herself in the window seat; half expecting him to appear in her backyard from the trail that connected their houses. Eventually she picked up a book and tried her hardest to concentrate, but when darkness fell, she dozed away.

Sometime in the night she must've awoken and made her way to bed, but the when and how were fuzzy. Ari noticed she was in her clothes from yesterday, then realized Dane had never come over to tell her how his conversation had gone with his father. She checked her cell phone; there were no messages.

She debated whether or not to go over to his house. She shook her head. Yesterday had been a rollercoaster of emotion for him, and she wanted to respect his space. Still, she ached from not knowing how he was. During breakfast with her family, Ari was unusually silent.

"Honey, you're so quiet, and a million miles away. What's going on?" Her mom's soft demeanor could coax out almost any secret Ari had.

"Dane's dad is trying to get custody of him again and move to northern California," she explained simply. Her crestfallen expression said the rest. Her parents were sympathetic, and her dad asked if there was anything they could do. Ari appreciated their willingness to help.

After breakfast, she meandered to the brass circle, where they'd placed the old family photo albums. She turned on the camping lantern and started sorting photos again. One pile consisted of photos

190

of Nadia, or at least ones Ari assumed were her. The next pile had photos of the houses, or gardens. The rest were of other family members; unidentified children, adults, posed and candid, that could probably only be loosely dated by the clothes they were wearing.

She focused on the ballerina photos. Some looked like they were professionally taken, with the artist's imprint in the corner. Some of the tutus Ari recognized immediately as ones she had in the trunk in her room. There were several more photos of Nadia, backstage after her Swan Lake performance at the Premiere. Ari looked closely at the date: March 17, 1907. She wrote down the date on her hand, and made a mental note to check the microfiche at the library for newspapers around then.

Suddenly the air in the little room *whooshed* upwards as the brass lid was opened. Dane jumped down; Ari noticed he had on the same clothes as yesterday. She smiled, happy he'd returned, but then she noticed his blank expression. It scared her; it was the same hollow look she'd seen when they first met.

"What happened?"

Dane sat silently next to Ari. "I went to his house. He wasn't there, so I figured I'd wait on his front porch till he got home. By eleven-thirty, he was still gone. So I rode my bike around town until I found him." His voice was low, disgusted.

Ari propped herself sideways so she could look at him. "Where was he?"

Finally Dane turned to look at her, and connected with her eyes. "His truck was at the bar."

She didn't know how to respond. He continued. "So I went back to his house and was going to wait until he got home. I fell asleep at some point, and when I woke up this morning, he still hadn't come back."

"I'm so sorry, Dane," she whispered. What could she say to

comfort him? What could she do to erase the depth of disappointment his dad had caused? She tried to block out the image of Dane living far away and alone on nights his dad went to the bar. Then memories of Rhoda came flooding back; hadn't Dane suffered enough? A strange sort of tingling ache started in her stomach.

"Did he have a drinking problem before he left you with Rhoda?" she managed.

"It started after the divorce. It didn't seem like that big of a deal then. I think it probably had something to do with why he was gone for four years, though," Dane looked away, regressing. "Last week when we were traveling he seemed fine. I think I only saw him drink a beer or two, so I assumed he was past all that."

Ari was grasping for a shred of hope. "But at least he wants to be your father again...he came back for you, and he wants to be in your life..." She trailed off. Her hope sounded forced, and she winced.

Dane shook his head, and his eyes drifted away. Silence filled the small room, and his eyes finally rested on the piles of photos Ari had been working on. "What are you working on?"

"I've been sorting out the photos that I think are of Nadia. I'm going to the library sometime to see if they have articles about her performances at the theater. You can see the date on the playbill." She handed him a photo. "I guess I'm just trying to get insight on her life...." Ari trailed off, thinking that nothing seemed as important as Dane's custody battle at the moment.

"I'll go with you tomorrow after school," Dane offered, and Ari smiled in surprise.

chapter seven

School seemed to crawl along that day. It didn't help that Ari glanced at the clock ever fifteen minutes; it was even worse when Riley noticed during history class. Ari was pleasantly surprised to see Dane waiting outside the doorway of her last class after the final bell.

"Hey," he said, slinging his bag over a shoulder. "Ready?"

At the library, Ari's first stop was the microfiche. She accessed archives of the Rivers newspaper, and focused on finding issues from March of 1907. Dane was hovering next to her, also scanning the pages. He pointed at the date as she neared the correct month. "The playbill says the ballet opened on the seventeenth," he whispered. "Check the week before. Maybe they had an announcement in the paper or something."

She slowed her scan. She arrived at March thirteenth. Fortunately, each edition was only a few pages long. On the fifteenth, she found what she was looking for.

"Look! Here's something!" She squinted to read the text. "The Premiere Theater proudly presents Russia's prima ballerina, Nadia Varishnikov, in our production of Swan Lake, beginning the eve of March 17. Three shows will follow over the next week.

"Ms. Varishnikov moved from St. Petersburg four years ago, where she attended the Vaganova St. Petersburg Academy from the age of nine. At seventeen years of age, she debuted on stage at the Bolshoi Theatre as one of the school's top graduating students.

After moving to Rivers, Ms. Varishnikov supplemented her study with the principal ballerina of Allendale's Acadamy of Dance and Theatre, and has also been teaching primary ballet lessons at her in-home ballet studio."

Ari looked over at Dane. "That was at your house!" she exclaimed,.

"There's not too much there we didn't already know," Dane sighed.

"Except it sounded like she was a fantastic ballerina," Ari said, wistfully.

"Try searching for her obituary," he offered.

Ari gave him an odd look, but nodded anyway. "When did she die?"

Dane got on the internet computer next to her, and searched under her name. Little substantial information on her was available, except for a genealogy site with partial family information. "Here," he pointed. "Nadia Alena Hadley (Varishnikov), May of 1880 to December of 1940."

Ari flipped forward to the month of her death. After nearly a half-hour of reading, her search proved fruitful. "Let's see...it starts out with all the information about her as a ballerina. It sounds like she did many different performances at the Premiere. It says she stopped performing in 1914, before the birth of her third child, but continued to teach up until her death."

"What did she die from? She was only sixty," Dane calculated.

"It doesn't say. 'Nadia was involved in many things during her lifetime, including several gardening clubs in the valley, and establishing the first beekeeping society in the area. She is survived by her husband, Grekov Petrova Hadley, and her three children: Eva and Sergei, of Rivers, and Katia, of Woodward.'

Dane and Ari paused for a silent moment. "The bees," Dane mused.

"What?"

"That's why there are little bee sculptures everywhere, Ari. She was a beekeeper." He sounded so sure of himself, Ari couldn't disagree. He turned back to his computer, and typed for several minutes before saying anything more.

"Go to issues from April of 1921 and look for anything about The Golden Hive Society," Dane said, still scanning his computer screen.

"What's that?"

"It sounds like it was the name of her beekeeping group. There's an article on the internet about a lady that turned one-hundred. In her interview, she mentioned she was one of the first members of The Golden Hive Society, founded by Nadia Hadley. She says they held their meetings in the basement of the Premiere Theater, of which Nadia was a board member at the time."

"That makes sense," Ari thought, as she dialed through paper after paper. "I don't see anything here."

"How about a movie Friday night?" Dane asked, a sly smile across his face.

Ari smiled. "I'm assuming we're not going to actually be watching the movie."

*　　　*　　　*

Math books were opened across the small lacquered table at Cinema Coffee. Riley was madly punching in numbers on her calculator with a pencil eraser, while Ari pretended to be reading her math assignment. She glanced above her paper, scanning every visible doorway in the lobby of the theater. Where the ticket counter/coffee bar was, there was a door to a supply closet. Two double doors on either side swung into the auditorium. Matching spiral staircases wound their way to balcony seating, and beneath were doors leading to the men's and women's bathrooms. One door on the far side of the lobby was unmarked. She made a mental note to try that door at some point.

"Hey, spacecase. How's your math coming?" Riley giggled and looked at Ari over the top of her glasses. "You don't seem to be focusing on your...what are you working on there? Ah, equations..."

"I'm doing just fine. But, out of curiosity, where would I go in here if I wanted to see the basement?" Ari ventured.

"The basement?" Riley looked perplexed. "I wasn't aware there was one. Why?"

Ari shrugged, and went for the simple explanation. "Dane's great-great grandma held meetings there."

Riley raised her eyebrows. "Interesting. Well, I'd check under the stage first," she said. "Down around the orchestra pit or in the wings."

"Good idea," Ari agreed, then went back to scribbling a list on her math homework. *Flashlight, camera...*

"Are you going to ask him to the Sadie Hawkins dance?" Riley smiled slyly.

"I didn't even know about it." Ari rolled the thought around in her mind, considering.

"It happens next month. They'll have posters up soon. I'm going to ask Jace, maybe."

Ari just shook her head. "I really don't think Dane would come with me," she finally concluded.

"Oh come on. He showed up at the Winter Formal, didn't he?" Riley reminded her. "How could he possibly say 'no'?"

She had to smile, but just thinking about asking him made Ari nervous. "Naw, I don't want to make him uncomfortable," she lied.

Riley shrugged and went back to her homework. "You guys would make a great couple."

*　　*　　*

Friday night couldn't come soon enough. The low, cold sun had finally made an appearance during the day, and after a swift and early sunset, shimmering stars were visible. Heady wisps of wood smoke perfumed the atmosphere, drifting and collecting in pockets of still air.

Dane had suggested riding their bikes to the theater, which was an experience in itself. Ari had her heaviest black wool peacoat buttoned all the way to her chin, with a knit beanie covering her hair, which, in turn, was covering her freezing ears. Thankfully she'd remembered gloves; riding in the cold, dry night air was shocking. Dane was more bundled up than she'd ever seen him; he'd pulled the collar of his coat up around his ears, and she thought he looked quite imposing. Unobtrusively she smiled, as she saw he was rubbing his hands together madly to keep them warm.

After buying tickets, they briefly sat in the back row. Dane leaned over, impossibly close.

"Where are we going first? Any ideas?"

Ari nodded. "Riley thought there would be a basement entrance near the wings of the stage, or by the orchestra pit. What do you say? Should we make a run for it?"

Dane's eyes gleamed with daring excitement. "Whatever we do, we have to act like we're supposed to be there—no sneaking around— if we get caught, just say we're looking for the restrooms. Can you do it?" he asked, with mock seriousness. Ari nodded. "Follow me," he whispered.

They sidled down the empty back row and casually strolled down the leftmost side aisle. Ari felt like every eye in the darkened theater was on her, but she tried her best to act natural. Dane played up his naturally aloof personality, seeming confident and purposeful. As they neared the side of the stage and rounded the corner of the orchestra pit, she spied a part in the curtain along the wall. Taking Dane's arm, she reached past the gap and slipped behind it; hoping she wouldn't run into a wall. There was just enough space behind the curtain for Dane to squeeze in behind her; quickly he tugged the curtain closed.

Inky darkness blinded them, but by sound and feel they knew they were in a very small and enclosed space. Instantly they began feeling at the walls about them. Dane's hand rested on a doorknob, which thankfully turned easily and silently in his grip. His still-freezing hand found Ari's, and they moved together through the doorway. Once that door was shut, a new kind of darkness surrounded them.

This time, the space felt larger. Her pulse quickened as cold and musty air moved across her face. It felt like a small amount of fresh outdoor breeze had circulated through thick, stagnant air. Muffled audio from the movie echoed across the room. Ari hadn't yet dropped Dane's hand; she feared being separated in the blackness. He took a few steps forward, then started to stumble downwards. Ari suppressed a yelp and tried anchoring him against whatever was pulling him down. He stopped after a step or two, and Ari remembered her flashlight was in her pocket.

The small cone of light revealed that Dane was two steps below her, on a steep flight of wide stairs. "Thanks for holding me up," he said gratefully. They both carefully descended, gripping the large banister that led the way down. Ari kept a hand on Dane's shoulder and the beam pointed ahead. He then motioned for the flashlight, and, at the bottom of the stairs, he swept it across the area.

The basement was huge; so big, the light of the flashlight couldn't illuminate from one side to the other. What they could see, nearby, were stacks and stacks of chairs, huge objects covered with sheets, and old trunks and closets lining the walls.

"Where do we start?" Ari said under her breath. "What are we even looking for, Dane?"

He shrugged and whispered back, "I'm not even really sure, Ari."

They moved slowly across the room. It seemed as wide as the

entire building, and Ari estimated it to run from the edge of the orchestra pit to the back wall of the theater. Dane was shining the flashlight on the ceiling, which seemed unusually high for a basement. Ornate crown molding bordered the top, and the decor seemed generally the same as the rest of the theater.

"Why's it so fancy down here?" she mused. "Basements usually are small, low, and not ornately decorated."

"No clue," Dane said, and started peering behind a sheet that was draped over a large object. "Whoa!"

Ari looked. A huge tree was underneath! Under closer examination, she saw it was a tree made out of twisted paper and glue. "These are props for plays, Dane." She smiled, and went to the next object. It was a giant nutcracker, made portable with a hidden wheeled base. "For *The Nutcracker* ballet, I'm sure." There were more trees, giant blossoms, animals, and walls, doors, and pieces of sets. Along the back wall, there were huge rolls of fabric. "Dane, I bet these are backgrounds for the stage." Ari tugged on the edge of one. It looked like a sky background.

They moved to the closets, which opened with resistant creaks. Ari gasped a little bit, as thousands of sequined costumes glinted in the pale flashlight beam. One particular dress had a giant skirt; she pulled it out and discovered the most ornate Elizabethan dress. Dane chuckled. "Remember, we have to be outta here right after the movie is over, or we're locked in all night." Ari sighed and put the dress back.

Dane started opening various trunks. A few were labeled. "A Midsummer Night's Dream," said one. Appropriate props filled the trunk, plus scripts, photos of performances, and guest lists. Several others corresponded to their labeled production. They split up and started searching others. Ari came across one that said "Valley Soroptimist," then another next to it, called "B.P.O.E., Chapter 112."

"Dane!" she hissed. "I think I found something!"

He was at her side in a second. "I bet these are trunks that belonged to groups that met down here. Maybe this served as a meeting hall for lots of groups. Look for a Golden Hive Society trunk!"

They were just about to start lifting trunks off one another when they both heard the staircase door open. Instinctively, they dodged behind the closest sheet-draped prop, and Ari snapped off the flashlight. She felt Dane shift her to the side and pull her to a crouch with him, so they were entirely concealed. Her heart was fluttering from the fear of being discovered, and possibly because Dane was holding her. Not intentionally, she assumed, but his hands were still resting on her waist, keeping her low.

Just then, the lights popped on, illuminating the entire room. It was even bigger than imagined. Large bowl-shaped fixtures, diffused by amber glass shades, hung from the ceiling. They watched an apron-clad barista carry a large box of paper cups down the stairs. Dane and Ari were holding their breath, statuesque. The barista deposited the cups in an empty closet, then whirled around, scanning the room. Dane ducked his head quickly, resting it against Ari's back. The barista didn't seem to be aware of their presence, and she headed back up the stairs, unknowing. At the top of the stairs, she clicked the lights off again, and the room fell back into darkness, made deeper by their unadjusted eyes.

The darkness created a strange tension between them. Ari felt Dane exhale in relief; his head was now right next to hers, and his scent filled her senses, to the point where she was dizzy with it. She must have swayed; suddenly Dane was pulling her to her feet. She felt hot again; and gasped for breath. "Ari...are you ok?" He tried to steady her as she stumbled slightly. Dane turned her around and was supporting her with a hand under her shoulder blade, and one still on her waist. Was it the darkness and lack of depth perception that caused her to sway? Or the sudden rush of adrenaline from almost being discovered?

Dizziness completely overcame her and she slumped against the prop, still in his arms. If Dane was talking to her, she couldn't hear it now. A faint buzzing in her ears was all she could focus on. After a long-lasting second, she felt something warm on her cheek. Dane's hand was cradling her jaw, then he softly felt her forehead with his hand, brushing up under her hair. Finally the buzzing subsided.

"Ari, are you okay?" she thought she could hear him ask. It sounded far away at first, even though she could feel his breath on her face, he was so close. "Ari?"

After endless moments Ari's eyes had finally adjusted, helping to alleviate dizziness. She found his neck with her hand, and moved to his face, feeling his cheek. It was soft but prickled with faint whiskers. Time seemed to move thickly, fractionally. She could see that Dane was now the one completely frozen, watching her as she touched his face. *What am I doing?* her mind frantically shouted.

At that moment, a muffled crescendo from the movie could be heard booming through the basement. "Ari, are you feeling ok?" Dane asked again in a whispered voice, not looking away. She wanted to stay there, like gravity was pulling her to him. Suddenly she realized the movie could be coming to an end. She'd lost all track of time. Ari pulled her hand back and took a deep breath.

"I feel a little dizzy, that's all," she managed, then, "we need to keep looking for the box." She shook off the spell he'd cast on her and tried to focus. "Keep searching."

With the flashlight on, they moved deftly around the stored boxes and trunks, placing some on the ground. "Here it is!" Dane found a trunk with "GHS" written in white chalk. They opened it swiftly. Inside were stacks of notebooks, beekeeping hats, books, and all sorts of tools they couldn't identify. "Look at all this stuff," he mused.

"Look for photos!" Ari piled through quickly, opening each notebook, and closing it if she couldn't identify any photos inside. There were log books of each meeting, none of which contained any photos. She was flipping through a log from 1922 when something heavy fell out and made a loud *clunk* on the hardwood floor. Dane jolted at the sound and Ari gasped, desperately hoping nobody heard. She reached down and picked up the object: a heavy, black, wrought-iron key with an ornate bee on the handle.

chapter eight

The audio from the movie ceased and shuffling movements could be heard in the auditorium. Ari took hold of the key and looked with wide eyes at Dane, but he was too busy putting things away. "We need to get this stuff back in the trunk!" Dane finished arranging everything back into the Society box, and Ari began stacking the other boxes back into place. They quickly looked over the space, making sure everything was in the same place as before.

"What about the key?" Ari asked, holding it in her hand.

"It goes to the iron gate, I'm sure of it," he said, breathlessly. "Put it in your pocket."

"What?" She shook her head. "Take it?"

"If it doesn't work, we'll bring it back. But if it does, it belongs to the family," he reasoned. Ari understood and stuffed it in her coat pocket.

"Hurry, let's go!" Dane pulled her by the hand around the obstacles in the room, and at the curtain, he paused. Waiting until the last patrons were turned away and heading up the aisle, Dane then slipped through the curtain with Ari still in hand. He was walking faster than usual, trying to catch up with the exiting patrons. Once they'd made it into the lobby, he failed to drop her hand. Ari was half concentrating on looking nonchalant, and half concentrating on her hand that was fully enclosed in his.

Once they got to their bikes, Dane let out a breath. "Wow, we made it," he said finally, flashing one of his beautiful smiles. Ari beamed back.

*　　*　　*

The next morning, Ari awoke burning up, with a terrible sore throat and deep aches. *So I was getting sick after all,* she figured. At least it might explain last night's dizziness, or at least, part of it. She was trying hard to remember if she'd given Dane the key, or if it was still in her coat pocket. Then she recalled touching his face, and wondered if she'd really done that, too. Before she could decide clearly what had happened, she fell back into a fitful sleep. She was vaguely aware of her mom coming into her room a few times, once to bring water with a bendy straw dangling off to the side, and then another time, when she brought some medicine for Ari's fever.

Strange dreams wove in and out of her slumber, like uninvited visions. Physical discomfort from the fever seemed to seep into her dreams, tainting them as nightmares. She thrashed her covers off in a subconscious effort to get comfortable. In one dream, she was back in the basement of the theater, only something in the darkness was chasing her. Dodging obstacles, she was running desperately away from whatever it was. And then, it had her arm. She yelled and tugged away, and then awoke with a horrible start. Dane's face was above hers, and it was *his* hand on her arm. He was propped on the edge of her bed, looking down at her.

"That was quite the dream you were having," he smiled sadly at Ari. "I tried waking you but I think I made it worse." Now that she was safely awake, he took hold of her closest hand with both of his. This time, Ari felt more than fever burning at her, but for once, she knew she could veil it as sickness.

The sunlight in her room reflected off the walls and pierced through the green in his eyes like seawater on a sunny day, and for the first time in a long while, she could see the hazel splashes that only appeared in bright light. Wordlessly he held her in his gaze; and she had no desire to shy away. "I thought you seemed really warm last night. How are you feeling?" She shrugged, and again he reached to her forehead and brushed away her hair. She closed her eyes as his hand skimmed her face, gauging her temperature. "Wow, you've got a pretty good fever. Can I get anything for you?"

She smiled in appreciation, but shook her head. "I can't think of anything," she said, her voice strained and rasping. Pain made words difficult. She swallowed hard. "Can you stay here a while, though?"

204

She didn't want to sound needy, but appreciated his company.

He looked pleased, which, to Ari, was an uncommon expression. "Of course."

"Did I give you the key last night?" She asked, still unsure.

He dug into his pocket and procured the key, smiling slyly. "It's the right one, Ari. I tried it this morning. It turns all the way around, just like the key for the brass circle. It was a little rusty, but it belongs to our iron gate. We won't have to climb over anymore."

"Thank goodness. But it's not like I really want to get in there, anyway. Most people have just trees and plants and nice things in their backyard. We have graves." She rolled her eyes and Dane chuckled.

"But we also had treasure..." he reminded, and Ari nodded in agreement.

"Why was the key in with the beekeeping things?" she wondered out loud. "That wasn't exactly what I expected to find down there. I was hoping for more photos of Nadia and your family, or something to do with her ballet performances." She swallowed painfully. "We need to spend more time digging around in the basement, I think. I feel like there's more to find."

Dane looked sad. "I don't know how much time we have..." his voice wavered. "I found out last night that a date has been set for family court. We have about three weeks until then."

Ari didn't know what to say; her only reaction was the horrible, twisting, tingling feeling that made her stomach drop. This time, she tried to stay level, tempering her worry with questions.

"What does that mean, exactly?"

"Well, I think the judge will decide who gets custody and stuff like that. To be honest, the last time we went, I was too young and don't remember the process exactly." His voice was gravelly, tough.

"What are you going to tell the judge? Are you going to say anything about your dad's drinking?"

He furrowed his brow and supported his head with his hands. "I don't know, Ari. That could've been a one-time thing, or he could have a problem like Rhoda did. I don't know how to figure it out. Will they believe a sixteen year-old kid against his father?"

She reached out to his arm and rested her hand on it. "I can help you. We'll figure it out like we've figured out other stuff. We still have a few weeks, right?"

"You're always so hopeful," he said, locking eyes with her. She tightened her grip on his arm, and he rested his hand on top of hers.

Ari tried blocking out even the possibility of Dane moving away with his dad. She had more than just selfish reasons for him to stay; in her heart, she wanted to believe the very best place for him was here, with his mom and sister, in a stable home. She was afraid of what would happen if things didn't go well with his dad. She didn't want to see Dane retreat behind the wall of caution that had taken so long for her to push past; for him to let her in, inch by inch.

chapter nine

Days went by, and even into the week, Ari couldn't shake the sickness that had kept her bedridden. Every winter she suffered from at least one case of illness. But this time seemed longer, harsher, than most. Every day after school, Dane would come by and stay until dinner. He'd usually have her Spanish homework with him, and they'd mostly focus on finishing assignments and speculating on Dane's family history. By the time she felt well enough to get dressed and move around the house, the week was nearly over. *One week down, two to go,* echoed in her mind. So far, Dane didn't seem more worried or affected than usual. Or, if he did, he didn't show it.

When Ari finally returned to school, she noticed the posters announcing the upcoming Sadie Hawkins dance, just as Riley had warned. The dance happened to fall two days before Dane's family court date. *How could he care about something like a stupid dance when he's worried about something so much more important?* She shook her head, knowing now it would be almost insensitive to ask him to go.

*   *   *

Ari's stomach was churning inside, and it only got worse as the day went on. Two weeks had passed too quickly and on Dane's court date, Ari was anxiously awaiting news from him. She'd searched for him at lunch, with no luck. She was worried something had happened. Even in passing between classes, there was no sign of him. Ari hoped he'd be in Spanish class; otherwise she'd have to wait even longer to hear the judge's ruling.

Finally, Spanish class arrived. Just as the first bell rang, Dane strode through the door and, without looking at Ari, sat in his seat in front of her. With scrutiny she examined Dane's countenance from behind. He didn't look at her at all during class; and even after the bell rang, he gathered his things and exited the class without acknowledging her. It was only when she caught up with him as he was heading to his locker that he looked at her.

She was afraid to say or ask anything. She simply walked alongside until she reached her locker, where she had to stop to drop off her books before heading home. Dane stopped with her, which eased her worry a bit. The halls were already almost cleared, and the din of slamming lockers had lessened. He leaned against the closed locker to the side of hers, his head ducked.

"Can you tell me what happened in court?" Ari finally broke the silence.

Dane sniffed, defiantly, like he was almost laughing at something unknown to Ari. It made her uncomfortable, almost like she didn't want to know now.

"The judge asked me questions, and also asked mom a lot of questions about our living situation, mom's job, and stuff like that. He also asked about my dad, and I told the judge everything that's happened since he came back. It was decided that I have to live with Dad here in town for the next four weeks, so the advocate and a social worker can observe our living situation and Dad's ability to parent and provide for me. After a month, we all go back to court and the judge will give us his ruling. He said my case will take longer than normal because Dad wants to move out of state and take me with him. The judge said if my dad wasn't planning on moving, it would be a much quicker process."

Ari was speechless. She hadn't been expecting this outcome. *Four weeks away from Hadley Hill.* Four weeks and possibly forever.

"When do you start at his house?" She pretended to believe it was only temporary, and feigned hope in her voice.

"It starts tomorrow. The advocate and social worker will be making unannounced visits after that." He almost sounded disgusted, Ari thought. Then a lighter expression eased across his eyes, and he pulled something from his pocket, and took her hand.

"Ari, this is yours now." He placed the wrought-iron key in her palm. She shook her head, to refuse, but he'd already turned and started walking away.

Sharp memories of the last key he'd given her, the one to the brass circle, pierced her thoughts. He had been leaving that time, too. *He only gives me keys when he thinks he won't be back.*

"No," she said resolutely. "Wait!"

Dane slowed but didn't turn around. She whirled around him, and he was forced to stop. She saw lines of water edging his eyes, and witnessing a fraction of his emotion caused her thinly-stretched visage of hope to vaporize. She felt hot tears welling in her own eyes, and she immediately wiped them away so Dane wouldn't see them.

"What does this mean?" She held the key out to him. "Are you giving up? Do you really have no hope that the judge will see what's best for you?" Her voice strained with anguish.

"I'm not thinking about it now," Dane said simply. "There's not much I can do, Ari." He didn't sound angry, just exasperated, hopeless.

Wordlessly they unlocked their bikes. The late February sun hinted at warmer days to come, and the sunlight helped raise Ari's spirits on the ride home. When they reached Hadley Lane, Dane pulled up next to her.

"We can still hang out while I'm at my dad's. His house is right by the school."

"I know."

"How about we go dig around in the basement of the theater on Friday again? We didn't have time to get all the way through the Golden Hive trunk."

Ari tried to smile. "Ok. The nine o'clock showing?"

"Sounds good," he said, turning up the driveway to his house.

*　　*　　*

During the rest of the week, a soaking rain permeated everything, and Ari didn't venture outside at all, except for riding to and from school. That was probably the worst part; riding to school alone. She had grown so accustomed to going almost everywhere with Dane that she felt nearly lost without him. Both Ari's mom and Riley noticed a shift in Ari's mood; while Ari tried desperately to smile, there was a sadness that came through her eyes that everybody noticed.

On Friday night, Ari slipped on her rain boots in preparation for the soggy bike ride to Dane's father's house. Her mom noticed her preparations and offered to drive her into town. Ari hoped her mom wouldn't notice the bulge of an empty backpack under her raincoat.

"I don't want you to get sick again, from the cold," her mom said, and Ari gratefully accepted.

The car door slammed shut, and Ari stood in front of 3683 Archer Drive. Ari had only ridden past the house with Dane; she'd never been inside. Something about the house felt eerily similar to Dane's house when Rhoda lived there, but Ari didn't know exactly why. She rang the dimly-lit doorbell. Heavy footsteps approached and she could hear locks being undone. Dane's dad appeared in the door; cigarette smoke rolled off him in vapid wisps. He turned on the porch light when he saw it was Ari; beyond that, there was little recognition of her. He stepped back, hollered for Dane, and disappeared back into the darkness of the house.

She stood shivering on the porch, in front of the empty doorway for a moment. She wasn't sure if she was supposed to go inside, but it didn't seem inviting at all, so she stayed there. Finally she could hear lighter, quicker footsteps coming near. Dane appeared in the doorway, and she could instantly smell the scent of shampoo and detergent. She couldn't help but smile at him; his hair was barely dry, and in a spikey, towel-dried mess, and he was trying to button up his shirt and pull on his coat all at the same time.

210

"You'll be freezing if you don't put a hat on or something," Ari giggled. "It's already soaking out here."

"Ok, mom. I'll grab a hat. Where's your bike?" Dane questioned, running his hands through his shaggy hair. Ari breathed in his scent for just a second, subconsciously.

"Mom dropped me off. I didn't want to ride in the rain."

"How are you going to get back? You aren't going to walk all the way, are you?"

She shrugged. "I'm not sure yet. Will your dad be awake when we get back?"

"I don't know. So far, he's been pretty good about sticking at home while I've been here." He'd pulled a knit beanie from his jacket pocket and pulled it tight over his head. It almost made him unrecognizable; only his curved nose and strong profile identified him.

"I'm totally prepared for tonight," she said, turning her back to him. "I have an empty backpack for whatever treasures we find," Ari smiled proudly.

"From historical researcher to petty thief," Dane said, smiling, as they walked the rain-washed sidewalks into the main area of town. The Cinema Coffee marquis lights created orbed reflections on the street; Dane bought their tickets at the booth and, like before, they settled in the back row before moving down the aisle to the door behind the curtain. There seemed to be fewer people in the theater than the last time. This time, they both had flashlights, and they carefully picked their way down the large staircase.

Dane crossed the room and found the trunk, exactly where they're replaced it. "Do you think people come down here very often?" Ari whispered, helping him lift other trunks off the top.

"Probably not. Maybe only when they hold plays here, and that's only a few times a year. I'm sure nobody has looked in the Golden

211

Hive Society trunk since the last meeting was held."

"So nobody's going to notice if things might be mysteriously missing from the trunk, right? She lifted the lid and held the flashlight under her chin. They'd hidden themselves behind a large, sheet-covered prop.

"I doubt it." Dane lifted a layer of notebooks and Ari dug through the files she'd already seen before. Out came the beekeeping supplies, books, and meeting logs. Ari was a little disappointed when they reached the bottom of the trunk. Everything else had just been papers in files, notebooks, or journals. She sighed in the dark; the sound was swallowed by the enormity of the room. Adjusting the flashlight, she unwound a red thread that secured a manila folder. Black and white photographs slipped from the folder. Dane's flashlight beam settled on the photo that had fallen to the floor. It was a grainy image of an anguish-stricken woman, lying on the street, blood pouring from a wound on her chest. Ari gasped.

chapter ten

"What *is* this?" Ari breathed, horrified. She dared pick up the old photo, which was curled at the edges and browned, like it had been soaked in coffee. The expression on the woman's face was so pained that it hurt to look at it. It was an older woman, wearing a kerchief on over her hair, and a heavy winter coat. The woman's gloved hand was balled in a fist near the wound. Blurred images of people's running feet could be seen around her. Nobody was helping the dying woman.

Dane seemed as shocked as Ari. "It looks like she's been shot."

Quickly Ari grabbed other photos: more injured, fleeing, terrified people. A portrait of a mother and a daughter, strangely out of context. A blurry panoramic; a line of people with guns, and across the way, a mass of people, running. Ari flipped this one over. "Still from news reel, 1905," was scribed in familiar, delicate handwriting.

"Start looking through the other folders," Ari commanded urgently. The folder Dane had contained newspapers. Some were in Russian; others in English. They all were photos from the same event; different views of a single moment in time. The Russian editions didn't seem like a normal newspaper; they were small, with crease lines that, when folded, reduced the missive to a hand-sized piece. The papers in English cried out, "Massacre in Russia!", "Demonstrators Executed!", and, "Bloody Sunday Claims Hundreds."

Swinging her backpack to the front, Ari started shoving folders into it. "What are you doing?" Dane asked, bewildered.

"This has something to do with your family, I'm sure of it. The Russian papers, the photos...please, help me get stuff in here."

Without further hesitation, Dane complied. A cursory inventory of the journals and folders revealed that some regarded the same subject, and others were related to the Golden Hive Society. The latter were left in the trunk; the former were stuffed into Ari's backpack. Even the items completely scribed in Russian were important, Ari figured.

"Take this one too," Dane handed Ari a notebook full of the same, delicate handwriting. It was in English, and she examined a page in the middle of the journal. Ari started reading aloud:

"Olga Tischenko welcomed me into her home. She was also at the Winter Palace on that day; her mother, father, and two younger brothers were all marching. Her father was a factory worker and her mother worked at a corner market. Her father and one younger brother were killed; the father was shot and the brother was trampled in the stampede. Olga gave me reproductions of the photographs and records she had; she even kept a list of the murdered, compiled by an underground group. My mother's name was not on that list. It seems that, despite her good records and information, I have come to another end.

"I should have begun my search much sooner; however, after Grekov insisted I leave immediately, I was unable to do much research from the States. I never knew if my mother had been looking for me, as I should have been searching for her. I know the chance of her survival was small; I was lucky to have survived myself. I often wondered what would have happened if I had not fallen and been injured; perhaps we would have never been separated. I think about her every day, and the choice I made between my mother and my new husband." Ari looked up at Dane, her eyes sad.

"It sounds like something horrible happened to her," Dane said softly. "Maybe our family has always had it hard. Maybe that's just how life is for us."

Ari was determined. "I'm going to look on the internet to see if I can figure out what Nadia was writing about, when we get home...uh, when *I* get home, I guess," Ari sighed. "I hate that you don't live next door anymore," she suddenly confessed, almost before she knew what she was saying, and Dane turned from the photos to look at her, searchingly. She couldn't get past the benign innocence of his eyes, so wickedly magnetic and calm. He smiled sweetly, and Ari knew she hadn't said something that he didn't already know.

The longer the silence stretched out, the more electric the space between them became. Ari's awareness settled solely on his proximity to her; she'd long given up trying to think of something to say. Thankfully, Dane filled the silence.

"You've got a beautiful soul, you know that, Ari? Don't ever change," Dane whispered, then looked away quickly.

Ari blushed and smiled; a warmth washed all over her. Nobody but her mom had ever called her *beautiful*. She saw it wasn't easy for Dane to confess, and she didn't even know what to say in return. Before she had to think much longer, Dane stood up and offered a hand to help her up. She realized that, once again, time had slipped by and they had to replace the Society trunk where it belonged. Taking his hand, she pulled herself up, with her now-heavy backpack nearly pulling her backward.

They carefully replaced all trunks to original positions, waited behind the curtain, and carefully exited behind the moviegoers. Outside, a light mist was rewetting the pavement.

"Do you want me to walk home with you?" Dane asked, shifting her backpack to his other shoulder.

"I already texted my mom and asked her to pick me up at your house," she said, closing her phone.

"How are you going to explain the backpack?" A sly grin slipped across Dane's face.

*   *   *

It didn't take much searching for Ari to find out what Nadia had written about in her journal. What Ari found was so shocking, she decided to wait until Dane could join her before digging any deeper. Now that he lived in town, though, she wasn't sure if she should call his house or just appear at the door. She didn't want his dad to dislike her any more than it seemed he already did. She paused at her computer, and looked at her cell phone. She had to retrieve Dane's number from her backpack; she hadn't even stored it in her phone yet.

Ari dialed the number and silently hoped Dane would pick up instead of his father. She sighed with relief when Dane answered.

"You have to come over right away!" Ari said, then took a breath. "Can you?"

There was such a long pause Ari didn't know if he was still on the line. Finally his voice returned. "Um, I dunno, Ari. Can you come over here?"

There was no pickup truck in the driveway of Dane's dad's house when Ari arrived. The lightly sunny day promised a break from the rain and grayness, but the absence of darkness in the weather had instead settled in Dane's eyes. He didn't say a word as she climbed the stairs in the unfamiliar house; she just followed him upwards.

"Are you ok?" Ari asked.

"I'm fine," he said, turning into the dormer-style top floor. "But my dad got upset at me when we came back last night." Dane settled on the edge of a tiny bed, which happened to be the only furniture in the entire room. Ari perched herself against the wall.

"I *know* I told him where we'd be, and when I'd be home, Ari. But when I got in, he didn't remember any of it. He'd been sleeping on the couch and woke up when I came in."

"Had he been drinking?"

"Well, yeah, there were some bottles around the couch. I don't think he was drunk...but honestly, Ari, I don't even know him well enough to know when he is, and when he isn't." Dane was disgusted, almost angry. "He left after that and hasn't been back."

"And you wanted me to come over in case he comes back?"

Dane considered her question. "I'm not afraid of him," he said, slowly. "But I don't know why I asked you to come over. I don't know if I'm waiting for him to come back, or hoping he won't." He flopped backwards onto the bed, his knees hanging over the side. "This is so messed up," he breathed. "I shouldn't even be here." Suddenly he propped himself up again. "I should be at home, on our hill," he said, looking straight at Ari. "Come on," he said, pulling her up. "Let's go."

It was almost the same kind of apprehension she had when Rhoda had been around. During the sunny ride back up the hill, Ari was tense with concern. She sidled up to Dane as they walked their bikes up the gravel lane.

"Is he going to come looking for you up here? Will you get in trouble by the court-appointed advocate? What if this causes you to be placed in his care *forever*?" She couldn't stop the flow of worried outcomes, and she felt like things were spiraling out of control.

He slowed a bit and hooked his arm around Ari's shoulders, but didn't say a word. They walked together all the way to her driveway, her fears still leaping against her heart. He seemed confident and comforting, in his silent way. She looped her own arm around his waist, and it surprised her how skinny he was. He pulled her head to his. "Don't worry about what's going to happen," he assured her.

"Why?" she asked back, swiveling her head towards Dane, at an angle that caused him to smile.

"Because I don't want you to worry. You've done more for me in the last year than anyone has in my entire life, Ari."

She had nothing to respond with; she was as transparent to him as the secret pool they shared in the oak grove. Just then, they both heard car tires crunching up the drive. Ari jumped back to her bike and Dane quickly darted to the side of Ari's house, and she followed, pushing her bike into the backyard. They waited around the side of the house to see who it was.

"Why are we hiding?" Ari whispered.

"I dunno," Dane said back. "Maybe because if it's my dad, I don't want to talk to him right now."

"What if he calls the police?"

The car passed, and they both let out a sigh. It was only Ari's mom, pulling into the driveway.

"He won't because of the note I left. I told him where I was going and why."

Ari shrugged, hoping the note would be a sufficient explanation for his father. She then remembered why Dane was with her in the first place.

*   *   *

"On January 22, 1905, in St. Petersburg, Russia, citizens marched in a peaceful demonstration to the Winter Palace, to present a petition to Tsar Nicholas II regarding working conditions of the lower classes. The march was organized by Father Gapon, who believed the Tsar would hear the pleas of the overworked and underpaid. 200,000 workers, along with their families and children, converged near the Winter Palace without resistance, until, unexplainably, police began firing shots into the crowd. Panic ensued, with an estimated 1,000 people being shot or injured in the resulting stampede." Ari briefly stopped reading the newspaper article and looked at Dane. "This incident sparked immediate rioting around the city, and is thought to have been a major factor in the Revolution of 1905."

Ari picked up the journal full of Nadia's notes. "Remember when she wrote about being injured? I wonder if she was caught in the crowd, somehow got hurt, and then was separated from her mother. She must've kept searching for her mother after she moved here, and these were probably all her notes..." She sifted through the crumbling newspapers. "Do you think she ever found her?"

"I don't know," he said, quietly. "I can't believe one of my relatives was a part of something so important and historic. I bet I'm the first person in my family to know this much about our history." He smiled in appreciation. "After reading this about Nadia, I guess I should be thankful I have both parents."

"And I think you are," Ari said, firmly. "But I'm sorry things aren't going well with your dad." She paused, gauging how far she could be honest with Dane. "I feel like he's almost being selfish with you. He shouldn't think he gets to move away and take you with him, after he left you with Rhoda." It was uncomfortable for Ari to speak against his father; but Dane nodded. Suddenly they were both aware of footsteps coming up the stairs.

Ari's mom poked her head in the room. "Hi hon," she nodded at Ari. "Dane, nice to see you around again." She smiled warmly. "Your dad is at the door, wanting to know where you are. I figured you'd be wherever Ari was. I'll let him know you're here."

Before Dane could protest, Ari's mom was gone. With wide eyes, Ari stared at Dane. "Are you going down there?"

She could see he was quickly weighing his decision. A tension burned in his eyes; something halfway between hard indifference and anger. His jaw was set, his muscles were tense. *The wall is up*, Ari thought. The shield that shrouded emotion, the barrier that he'd worked hard to perfect through four years of hurt, was back. Ari admired Dane's strength and independence, but not when it was borne in defense of pain.

"I should probably go see what he has to say."

Ari rose to go with him, but Dane immediately held her back. "No," he shook his head, but Ari held onto his arms, unflinching.

"If I'm with you, maybe he'll be reasonable," she pleaded. He looked at her, searching.

"I'm sorry," he said quickly. "I can't tell you what to do in your own house." He sounded a little embarrassed.

They slipped down the stairs. His father was standing in the entryway, waiting. He looked at Dane.

"Time to go, son." His voice, as always, was gravelly and rough.

Dane bristled. "Ari and I were doing some research—"

"I said, it's time to *go*." The emphasis on *go* indicated there was no room for debate. Dane turned and looked at Ari, an apology in his eyes, then followed his father out the door. They left without saying anything. Ari stood there, holding the banister, wondering why she felt like she'd done something wrong.

*   *   *

"I don't want to call his house, and he doesn't have a cell phone." Ari carefully unwrapped her sandwich. She and Riley were sitting on the lawn of the high school; three days of sun had warmed everything just enough so it was comfortable to be outside. "And I haven't seen him in passing at all today; and he's been gone four days. I'm a little worried." She tried to mask the sadness in her voice.

"Why are you worried? Do you think his dad has taken off with him?" Riley asked, concerned.

"I don't know. I don't think Dane would go along with that."

"Have you gone past his house?"

Ari wrinkled her nose. "I don't want to stalk him."

Riley giggled. "What if he needs you right now?"

Ari looked at Riley, considering. *Does he really need me?* She'd never thought about it like that; it had always been *her* needing *him*. Every time she thought about Dane moving away, it sent her into spasms of panic and twisted her insides. It almost scared her, how much she required his presence, his friendship, his smile. But Dane? He was too strong, too independent to ask much from her, she figured.

"I don't know that he does. Maybe I should just let him be for a while."

Riley gave her an askance glance. "That doesn't sound like you, Ari. He's your best friend. Everyone knows that. If I had a dollar for every time someone asked me if you two were going out, I'd be fabulously well off," her blue eyes smiled behind her glasses.

221

"Whaaat?" Ari shook her head, disbelieving.

Riley just smiled. "It's your call, hon." Riley threw away her empty lunch bag.

*   *   *

The curtains were all drawn, except for the window on the top floor. The old truck was in the driveway. Ari paused for a good thirty seconds before moving. Finally, she set her bike down and marched to the front door, gathering her courage about her.

The old front door whooshed open and startled Ari enough that she imperceptibly jolted back. Dane's father stood at the door, gazing down at her.

"Hi, Mr. Hadley. I was wondering if Dane was around?" Her voice was strong, masking her fear.

"He's sick. You'll have to come back another time," was the gruff reply, and the door began to close.

"I have his homework," she quickly lied, stepping into the doorway, determined. His father stopped, sighed.

"Fine. He's upstairs." The door floated open, and once again, Dane's dad disappeared into the eerily dark house, despite it being full daylight. Ari crept through the entryway and up the creaky stairs.

Once at the doorway to the dormer floor, she knocked lightly. There was no reply, so she gently opened the door. The room was stuffy, the air stagnant. Dane lay sleeping on the lone bed, which Ari could now see was much too small for him. He was shirtless with a pair of shorts; beads of sweat covered his brow, and his dark hair was matted and slicked with perspiration. She carefully sat on the edge of the bed, as close to him as possible, without disturbing him.

His breathing sounded raspy and labored. His chest heaved with each breath. One hand was over his head, and though it seemed he was deeply asleep, he would twitch or jolt every few moments. His cheeks burned bright red, and his expression was pained, even in his slumber.

At the end of the dormer was a small half bathroom; Ari found a washcloth and soaked it in cold water. Again she carefully sat, and as slowly as possible lowered the cold compress to his forehead. For a moment, she thought she'd succeeded in doing so without waking him, but his breathing changed and he slowly opened his eyes. He put a hand over the compress, yet didn't focus on Ari. His eyes were clouded and drowsy. She felt badly he'd awoken. Holding her breath, she waited to see if he'd drift back to sleep. Instead, he slowly propped himself up on an arm, taking the compress off.

"Hey," he said, his voice barely audible.

"Are you alright?" Ari whispered, hoping his dad wouldn't hear. She scooted closer to the head of the bed and took the compress, wiping away perspiration from his forehead and face. He started to say something, but was caught in a spasm of coughing which doubled him over. Ari noticed a faint rash blooming across his chest.

"Don't move," she said, examining closer. Tiny dots of red were everywhere. "You have some sort of rash," she mentioned, and he laid back on his pillow, while trying to see what she was looking at. She brushed the rash with her hands and Dane recoiled.

"Your hands are freezing, Ari," he said, trying to smile. "Those little bumps? I've had them a day or two." He gave the rash a scratch, but Ari caught his hand.

"Don't, you could make it worse," she reprimanded. She could tell he didn't feel well enough to talk anymore; she refolded the cold compress and once again placed it on his forehead, then sat in silence on his bedside as he lay there. She didn't know what more she could do to help; she figured she'd stay with him as long as she could. Ari didn't have to wait for that, as Dane quickly fell back in a deep, feverish sleep.

She watched his face for a moment. She'd long before

memorized every feature, every expression. *Does he need me?* she wondered, watching beads of sweat run into his dark, curled lashes. Ari grabbed her backpack and quietly crept down the narrow stairs and slipped out the front door.

*　　*　　*

Two more days of sun-filled skies almost distracted Ari from Dane's continued absence. It was almost as if spring was desperately trying to break through the ever-present grayness, and everybody was flocking outside to feel the precious rays of sun.

Ari had accompanied Riley home after school to finish homework before the weekend. Riley's house happened to be only two blocks behind Dane's father's house, and Ari glanced at it as they walked past.

"So where's he been? I've noticed you've been looking awful lonely lately," Riley chuckled.

"He's really sick. I went to see him on Wednesday," she said, kicking a rock along the road. She then tried to explain about his father and the custody situation, most of which Riley had already heard bits and pieces about. Ari noticed the pickup truck seemed was missing from Dane's house. *Maybe his dad will still be gone later,* she hoped.

Homework was the last thing on Ari's mind, but she tried to focus, sitting there, in Riley's window seat. It was always her favorite place in the old Victorian house, which seemed to rise far above the other houses on the block. The biology book in Ari's lap was turned to the chapter on anatomy, but Ari was lost watching the sunset; blue and pink clouds with striations and the last reaching rays of a late winter sun. She nearly jumped out of the seat when her cell phone began to vibrate in her pocket. An unfamiliar number showed up on the screen.

"Hello?"

"Ari? Can you come over?" Dane sounded worse than before; more than just his voice was weak; how he sounded frightened Ari.

"I'll be right there," she promised. She looked apologetically at Riley. "That was Dane; he sounds bad. I need to go help him," she said, hoping there would be a way she actually could help.

The pickup was still missing as Ari walked up to the house. Even so, she knocked on the front door and waited for seconds to pass before she tried the doorknob. Thankfully, it was open. The house was as still and dark as it had been the last time; she pounded up the stairs and through the half-open doorway to the dormer room. Dane was lying listlessly to one side; the next thing Ari noticed was his rash: it had spread across the rest of his chest and was bright red and welted. She gasped.

"It looks pretty bad, huh?" was all he could say. It sounded like his throat was badly swollen. She sat on his bed and carefully felt around his neck, under his jaw. Her brow furrowed as she pushed slightly; Dane gave her a pained, puzzled look.

"Your neck is really swollen, and it sounds like you can barely talk," she said quietly. He just nodded. "I think you need to go see a doctor," she continued. "Where is your dad?"

Dane shrugged, and quickly pulled the only blanket on the bed up towards his chin. Goosebumps covered his arms. "He's been gone for awhile," he managed. Fever had passed to chills; Ari quickly went downstairs to find another blanket.

It was hard to navigate the unfamiliar, dark house. In a space that appeared to be the living room, a single couch faced a small, antennaed TV, and a woven throw was rumpled in a corner. *It will have to do*, Ari figured, as she raced back up the stairs.

Dane had rolled to the other side, and Ari firmly tucked the throw around him. "I'm going to go find your dad," she declared quickly, but Dane reached out and grabbed her arm.

225

"I'm fine," he insisted.

Ari turned and looked at him, sure of herself. "You need a doctor."

*   *   *

The only thing Ari knew for certain was that Dane's dad had recently started working at the lumber mill during the day. In the evening, there weren't too many venues that he would likely frequent. She rode past one of the three bars in town; no pickup truck was in sight. The movie theater parking lot was full, but there was no sign of his dad there, either.

Darkness was covering the little town of Rivers, but there seemed to be more activity on this particular Friday night; Ari figured the drier weather and teases of spring were drawing people out. She furiously pedaled past the next two bars; half of her was relieved that he didn't seem to be at either one. The other half was worried she wouldn't be able to find him at all. She was about to get her cell phone out of her pocket to call Dane's mom when a familiar old truck caught the corner of her eye, parked askew in a spot behind the bowling alley. A buzzing neon sign declared the back door as the entrance to the "Back Alley."

She leaned her bike against the outer wall of the building. Inside she could hear the thunderous clunk of bowling balls hitting the floor, the muffled crashes of pins, and thumping music from the lounge. Ari took hold of the bowling-pin handles and glanced at the eye-level sign with red letters, which screamed *NO MINORS*. She took a breath and pulled the door open.

chapter twelve

Her eyes had to adjust to the darkness; only arcade games, TV's, and buzzing beer signs lit the space. Cigarette smoke stung her eyes and she struggled to pick out Dane's dad from the crowd of overall-clad mill workers. Finally, she spotted him, seated at the bar and watching a basketball game on a wall-mounted flat screen.

"Hey! Girl! You're not supposed to be in here!" The bartender had spotted her. Her heart started to jackhammer, but she pushed past a group of grizzled men that smelled like sweat, sawdust, and dirt. Before the bartender could reach her, she was beside Dane's father.

"Mr. Hadley!" She had a hand on his arm; he couldn't ignore her. She had startled him; for a moment he stared, like he was trying to decide if she were real or not. Finally, he shook his head.

"What are you doing here?" He mashed his cigarette in an already-full, glass ashtray.

"Mr. Hadley, Dane needs you, right now. He needs to see a doctor. You have to go home," she said. Ari had never been good at confrontation, especially with adults, but at that moment, her voice was steel. She was pulling strength from somewhere unknown; standing firm in front of someone who frightened her, ignoring even the bartender as he addressed them.

"Mark, you gotta get the girl outta here. No minors," he pointed at another sign.

Dane's dad sighed and the stool he was on scraped against the floor as he stood. Ari wordlessly followed him through the throng of silent, staring men. Most of them looked as surprised as Dane's dad.

The cool air of the night filled Ari's lungs, flushing out the cigarette smoke. His dad started to get in the truck. "Well?" He motioned at the passenger door. "Get in."

227

She quickly hefted her bike into the bed of the truck, and lifted herself into the cab. The truck started with a growl, and they drove the four blocks to his house in silence. Ari dared even look at him; he looked neither concerned nor angry. As soon as they rolled into the driveway, he got out without looking at Ari, and entered the house. She slowly pulled her bike from the truck; waiting to hear or see something from the inside. Moments passed; nothing happened except for the light in Dane's window turning on. Ari pedaled away; hoping Dane wouldn't be in trouble for what she'd just done.

*　　*　　*

"You went in the *lounge*?" Ari's mom was half-amused, and half astounded. "Hon, you could've called me. I would have dropped everything to help." She wasn't mad, Ari knew, just surprised. Ari was in her bathrobe, sitting over a cup of tea. Her mom was across the table, waiting for German pancakes to finish cooking. The new morning had brought a thick blanket of clouds and drizzle, and Ari mourned the sun's disappearance.

"Did you notice the crocuses are coming up in the backyard?" Her mom pointed to some deep purple, white, and yellow spears in the middle of the rose bed. "I had no idea you'd planted bulbs last summer; I love them."

Ari shook her head. "I didn't," she said, thinking back to everything she'd planted.

"They must've been here before us, then. I love them just the same. I can't wait until the tulip trees and cherries start to bloom. Just a few more weeks," her mom smiled.

Just a few more weeks, Ari repeated. Just a few more until Dane's placement would be decided. Ari's mom pulled the tall pancake from the oven just as the doorbell rang. Lily ran to the door and opened it a crack as Ari watched. Lily hollered back at her, "Arrrii! It's for yooooou!"

Mrs. Hadley was standing nervously at the front door. Ari smiled and motioned her inside, but she shook her head. "Ari, dear, I just wanted to stop by and see if you wanted to come with me to the hospital to see Dane."

"What happened?" Ari's mom had overheard and come to the door, pulling her bathrobe tighter. "Why, Olivia, is Dane alright?"

Mrs. Hadley smiled sadly. "Thankfully the doctor believes they began treating him just in time. He was diagnosed with scarlet fever last night, and they began running tests this morning. He hasn't responded to the medication yet, but they said it may take some time. If he hadn't gotten to the hospital in time, things could've gotten much worse."

Ari was already grabbing her coat and zipping it over her pajamas.

*   *   *

Hospitals made Ari uneasy. Not enough to keep her away from Dane, but enough to increase her heartbeat an uncomfortable measure. She was following Mrs. Hadley, who was following a white-clad nurse wearing squeaky rubber shoes. The nurse stopped at a room, glanced at the chart, and affirmed it was the correct patient.

"He's right in here, ladies. Looks like he's scheduled to be released tonight." She smiled sweetly, then turned and left.

Ari hung back as Mrs. Hadley settled at Dane's side. Dane smiled weakly, but looked considerably better than he had the day prior. They exchanged a few muffled words, and Mrs. Hadley motioned for Ari to take her place. "I'm going to go find Mark," she mentioned as she headed to the hallway.

There were no tubes or scary machines on Dane, save the IV drip in his arm, which was carefully taped over. Ari hesitantly approached the bed. A knot was slowly twisting into an uncomfortable gnarl of nerves in her stomach. Strong, independent, aloof Dane, now stretched thin on a reclining hospital bed. *It's just a*

229

fever, she reassured herself. *He's not dying. He'll be fine...*

"Ari." His eyes settled on her, and she could see he was comfortable, rested. She let out a breath she'd been unknowingly holding, and finally approached him. He patted the bedside next to him, and she sat down as he reached out to her.

"Where did you find my dad last night?" Dane's voice was stronger than before.

"He didn't tell you?"

Dane shook his head.

"At the bowling alley lounge." She stared at the IV in his arm.

"But how did you get him to come home?"

"I went in and got him." She met his eyes, and he smiled, incredulous.

Ari just raised an eyebrow and shrugged. "What?"

Suddenly he reached his long arms around and pulled her to his chest. She was fully engulfed; she knew he was holding her as tight as his lessened strength would allow. His heartbeat was too fast, he was still unusually warm, and she could hear his labored breathing. She dug her own arms around and settled against him; here, everything was safe. Anything he couldn't, or didn't, say with words was perfectly translated through the way he was gently pulling her hair across her neck and holding her. It astounded her how much his contact translated; every touch sent a shock of tingles through her. She would have stayed there forever, except Dane's chest began to rock with spasms. Ari sat up suddenly, worried, until she realized he was chuckling.

"I can just see you, little Ari, pushing past the big, husky mill workers, demanding to see my father." His smile lit up the room like sunlight, warming Ari right through. His face then turned serious. "You have guts, Ari."

230

"You didn't get in trouble with your dad for what I did?"

He shook his head. "He just came up and got me. I think I fell asleep in the emergency room right after we got here."

"The nurse said you get to go home tonight," Ari smiled, but Dane scowled.

"Dad's house feels like home just about as much as this hospital room does..." his voice drifted; his eyes were heavy. Ari watched as he rolled to his side, facing her; he smiled and closed his eyes. It was becoming easy to recognize when Dane was in a deep sleep; his breathing lengthened out and he'd twitch every now and then. Once she knew he was asleep, she scooted closer to him and took his hand; both of her small hands were needed to cover one of his. She felt the slight roughness of his grip; examined how blue veins cris-crossed the tight skin of the back of his hand.

The sharp *snap* of the divider curtain being pulled back suddenly startled her, and Dane's dad appeared from behind. Ari dropped Dane's hand faster than if it had scalded her. His father's face looked weathered, gray; like salty sun-bleached driftwood. She shifted uncomfortably; it was time to leave Dane's side, but she'd have to make her way past his dad first. He eyed her as she excused herself past him; she didn't like his penetrating glare. Quickly passing him, she found Mrs. Hadley near the nurses' station.

*   *   *

The school hallway was eerily silent. Weak sunlight was streaming through the windows between locker groups. Ari dumped her Spanish book into the bottom of her locker, and it landed with a louder *thud* than she intended. She looked up and down the hallway. Nobody appeared; she was safe. Minutes into Spanish class, Ari had feigned illness and asked to be excused to the office. After a cursory review by the less-than-interested school nurse, Ari had been written a pass. It wasn't exactly that she was ill. The best she could figure was that she was tired, or lonely, or just *down*. Whatever it was, it had lingered since her visit with Dane two days prior. Even the impatient sun, trying so hard to push away winter, did little to lift her melancholy.

The night before was the first time she'd had a dream about Dane. It had been so real and so strange that the images tainted the entire next day. It began with Dane in the hospital bed, just as he had really been, only his rash was bleeding, like the Russian woman in the photo they'd found. His skin was peeling away, and he was entangled in tubes and electrodes. Ari was next to him, helpless to do anything. His eyes were blank; not deathlike, but emotionless. Despite her pleading, he wouldn't look at her, or react. She'd awoken stunned, confused, and reminding herself that it was only a dream.

Riding home from school that day was a chore. She still wasn't used to riding alone; all she could think about was how she hadn't meant to take it for granted when Dane used to ride to school and back with her, every single day. She was worried that he hadn't called her; worried that his father wasn't taking care of him, and even more concerned that the weeks were closing in on a decision she had no control over.

Despite being lonely, Ari breathed with relief when she reached her home and it was quiet and still. No cars in the driveway meant she had the house to herself for the next few hours; no need to explain why she was home early or why she wasn't herself. Trying to verbalize her emptiness that day would be like trying to reassemble a dandelion weed after it had been blown to the wind on a wish.

The iron key in her pocket had been digging into her leg all day. She hadn't ventured to the fenced burial plot since she and Dane had left it after cleaning, almost two months ago. But today, she guessed the venue would befit her mood. Once inside the oak grove, however, it was much changed since she'd last seen it. The cobblestone path to the pool was sprouting with light green grass blades, and the dim evening sunlight revealed tiny lily pads under the mud-black water. Newly-sprouted vines with heart-shaped leaves encircled wrought-iron bars, clamoring for height. Ari had to tear some away from the lock when used the key.

Inside the fenced enclosure, she could also see subtle hints of life beginning to return to the once-pallid landscape. With chagrin she noticed lively green blackberry vines were growing with vigor in places they'd been cut away. Every tree that was once a tangle of gray sticks now promised growth, with buds at each joint. Little purple and yellow violas crawled along the ground, their faces turned to the sky for light. Purple and white crocuses, like in Ari's backyard, were also making an abundant appearance.

It's not fair he doesn't get to see this, Ari reasoned. She wandered to the center of the enclosure, looking west toward the gate and path. Waning strands of sunlight wove through the trees, casting a warm orange glow. She thought back to the photo-like images she had of Dane, and how utterly empty it was without him. His presence on the hill was permeating and definite. She walked to the graves, so silent and cold, and re-read the names aloud. *Hadley*. It was a stately name, she thought. *Ari Hadley*, she said to herself jokingly, then shook her head.

A crunching sound caught her breath and she whirled, horrified, hoping nobody had overheard her.

Adrenaline stung through her body, from her feet to her heart, but when she saw what had stepped through the open gate, she relaxed.

A fawn had strayed into the enclosure, and was statuesque, looking right at Ari, ears forward. Dappled white spots flanked his tawny back. Ari held her breath, freezing every molecule in her body. She'd never been so close to a deer before; she couldn't even remember seeing one that wasn't along the side of the road, alive or not. The deer slowly picked his way along the cobblestones; not taking his eyes off Ari. She had never held eye contact with an animal like this; but with a flick of an ear, the fawn bounded away with speed that caused Ari to start.

Even after the deer had disappeared, Ari stood motionless. The deer's quick retreat had stirred up fluffy seeds that floated in the waning sunlight, like heaven-bound snowflakes. Ari had to smile, though her heart pulled hard at the joy she had momentarily felt. She had expected the fenced-in grave garden to nurture her lonely sadness, but the slow transformation beginning there, in the late winter's orange sun, infused her with hope.

*   *   *

There were just too many bags of soil. There were compost mixes, seedling soils, peat moss, manure-infused soil, African violet mix, and cactus medium. A big bag labeled "general purpose topsoil," almost too big for Ari to handle, seemed to be the right choice. She hollered for her dad, who was carefully comparing two types of bare root roses. He had mentioned the garden was in desperate need of preparation for spring, and Ari eagerly accepted the task, hoping it would allow her to think of anything but Dane, if only for a while.

"I'll bring the cart around." Her dad shook his head at the roses and finally placed both in the garden cart. "But first, come over here and pick out some roses. How about making a new bed on the south side of the garden?"

Thorny rose crowns, devoid of leaves, were loosely planted in buckets of sawdust on the floor. Ari examined the plastic tags, each with color photos of the blossom the rose was to produce. Unusual colors drew her in, and she quickly picked three different varieties.

"Last thing we need to get are some bypass pruners for all the trimming we'll need to do once things start growing." While her father was comparing pruners, Ari browsed the garden gear. She picked out new gloves and tried them on, then threw them in the basket, which was nearly overfilled with plants and bags of soil.

*   *   *

"So, from what we could tell, Dane's great-great grandma was separated from her mother during the Bloody Sunday massacre in St. Petersburg. From the notebook we found, it seemed she searched and searched after moving to the United States, but there was no mention, or photos, of them ever being reunited. Isn't that sad?" Ari turned to her dad, who was digging a hole with a hand spade. She hadn't spoken to anyone about what she and Dane had found at all, but the longing inside her for anything to do with Dane was pushing it all out. It had been over a week since she'd last seen him, and she had given up trying not to think about him.

"That's amazing, Ari. Nadia was a part of history. What's really incredible are all the things you've found of hers; that after all these decades, evidence is still intact." Whenever they were working on a project, it was always hard for Ari not to spill everything on her mind—or *almost* everything—to her dad, who always thoughtfully listened.

Ari was digging her own spot for one of the roses she'd picked. She watched as her dad placed the rose's root ball into the hole, then filled around it with earth. He noticed her watching. "When you plant yours, make sure the soil doesn't go above this big knot here." He pointed to the joint where the stems sprouted out. Ari nodded, then placed her own rose in the soil. "How is Dane doing, anyway?" Her

235

dad moved to the next rosebush. At the mention of his name, a twinge shuddered through Ari.

"I don't know. I haven't gone to see him since the hospital." She suppressed any inflection in her voice, but it was her dad who sounded surprised.

"That was some time ago. I take it he's at his dad's house now?"

She nodded, scooping soil over a root ball. Ari wanted to tell her dad how selfish Mr. Hadley was for wanting to move away with Dane. She wanted to tell him how much she wished to see Dane, but was afraid. Of what, she wasn't sure, but it was enough to keep her from calling or visiting. Maybe it was the image of Dane's dad, glaring right through her, in the hospital room. She thought back on his cold stare, and shuddered. So deep in thought, Ari had stopped working on the roses and sat there, trowel in hand.

"Would you like me to go over there with you, to visit him?" her dad offered. Ari just shook her head *no*; she really wanted to say yes, but a lump was forming in her throat. She quickly turned away and started scooping bark mulch onto the rose bed, trying to think of anything but Dane.

After dinner that night, Ari ventured into the backyard, where the pleasant smell of heady bark dust lingered. She had extinguished the porch lights; only light from the kitchen windows partially spilled into the yard. Past the rose bed she walked, following the cobblestone path away from errant light. The pasture before the oak grove was the darkest place; she laid a heavy blanket on the grass and faced the stars. As she closed her eyes, sounds reached her ears: dishes clinking in the kitchen sink, as her mom and Lily washed. Somewhere in the house, her dad was listening to jazz. Miles Davis, she guessed. An early cricket was calling a mate from inside the oak grove.

Her eyes opened and adjusted to the depth of darkness. She pulled the top half of the blanket tight around her; though on the cusp of spring, the chill bite of winter hadn't retreated. The stars pulsed in the cold air; shining and sharp like illuminated ice crystals. Ari breathed in deep, the cold air stinging her nose and head like an instant ice cream headache. She wished it would freeze her thoughts, too, but they went right back to Dane. She thought about him, just down the hill and into town a little ways; they were separated by a bike-ride's length but it felt so much farther. The only hope she could conjure was that the next day was Monday; perhaps he'd be well enough to be back at school.

*   *   *

"Hon, you haven't said a word all lunch," Riley pushed a bag of chips at Ari, startling her.

"I just don't know why he isn't back yet. Doesn't that seem weird?" Ari munched a chip slowly, scanning the yard full of eating students.

"What's weird is that you haven't gone to visit him in a week," she gently reminded, without accusation, though Ari still flinched a bit.

"His dad hates me, I think," Ari mustered. "I don't want to be over there all the time, bugging them. I just wonder why he hasn't even called, you know?"

Riley nodded. "I'm sure his dad doesn't hate you. Is he *really* that scary?"

"There's just something about him. It's the way he looks at me, with eyes just like Dane's, but older, more tired, wary. He never speaks to me. He's so gruff."

They watched the last of the lunch crowd begin to flow back inside the school as heavy clouds blotted out the sunlight. A bitter wind began to whip away lunch bags, and students scurried after them. Ari and Riley retreated to the warmth of the building, though Ari felt just as cold as the starting rain.

*   *   *

Nothing that some coffee can't fix, Ari thought, looking down at her frothy drink. The buzz of chattering voices in the coffee shop helped soothe her loneliness, though now she wondered if it wasn't self-imposed. She scooted down the bench to be next to the window. Outside, rain pelted everything, and washed the world a shade of gray. The good weather they'd had was only a tease, and it made the rain that much harder to bear.

She got out her math book and folder, determined not to focus on anything but the numbers in front of her. A few minutes passed in silent concentration. Suddenly the table bumped as someone sat down right next to her. Without even looking, she knew who it was, and beamed.

"Hey, you. I was beginning to wonder if you'd left me for dead," Dane said, smiling slightly, and threw his arm around her shoulders. He looked mostly normal again, thought his face looked thinner, and his eyes a little tired, but his smile covered it all. Ari smiled back, relief washing over her in a warm wave. She side-hugged him back, secretly enjoying his closeness.

"I'm sorry. I didn't want to bother you, or your dad." Her words hung there, unsure, uncomfortable.

Dane pulled back and looked at her, closely. "It never bothers me when you're around." He sounded confused.

Ari didn't know what to say, sitting there, under his arm, not wanting to move. "I think your dad hates me. It made him mad when I came and got him at the bowling alley. I didn't want him to be more upset that I was coming over all the time." She looked down at her coffee, avoiding his eyes; he was turned and looking right at her. Her face burned a bit, but after telling him, she felt a little better, though embarrassed.

"That's why you didn't come around?"

"Yeah." She finally turned and looked at him.

"He doesn't hate you, Ari. He treats everybody like that."

She considered this, but it didn't exactly make her feel any better. He scanned her face, like he was reading her, then asked, "So... why didn't you ask me to the Sadie Hawkins Dance?"

His question caught her so off-guard that she froze, her mouth open a little. "What?"

"You never asked me to the dance. I was surprised." He didn't sound hurt, just curious.

"It was right around the time when you had your first court date, and I thought there were way more important things going on than just going to a stupid dance."

He nodded, understanding. "I would have gone."

Ari shrugged. "I'm sorry."

Dane just shook his head. "No apologies needed, Ari. I was just wondering." Inwardly she chided herself for not having the courage to ask him in the first place. Her thoughts froze when he reached out and smoothed her hair a little.

"We go for our court date in three days," he mumbled, looking away and out the window. Ari knew that already, but didn't say anything about how she'd been counting away the days until he either came back to Hadley Hill or moved away for good.

"Has your social worker stopped by yet?"

"Yeah, she did after I got back from the hospital. She asked a few questions, looked over the house, and asked dad some questions. I was still recovering in bed for the most part, so I'm not really sure how it went."

He paused and took a deep breath.

"My dad is clueless about what to do with me." He turned back to Ari. "I think maybe he seemed upset at you because he was embarrassed that you saw I needed help when I was sick, and he was oblivious to it." He sat back and smiled. "I asked him if I could spend my last days at mom's house. He said it was fine."

A slow smile spread across Ari's face. "Starting when?"

Dane smiled and stole Ari's cup of coffee for a quick sip. "Starting now."

chapter fourteen

Three extra blankets were barely stuffed under Ari's arm. One flashlight and two cups of cocoa were in the other hand as she backed out of the screen door and onto her porch. Somewhere past the backyard, Dane was already out near the edge of the oak grove. The night sky was still caught in the azure in-between, when dusky red hues seamlessly blended to a pure and crisp blue. The brightest stars in the sky were becoming visible.

She marched through the grass, finally seeing Dane's shadowy silhouette. The blankets went down on the ground, and she sipped her cocoa as Dane spun around, facing the stars in every direction. "This was a good idea, Ari. It's great the weather is getting better finally." He spoke in a hushed voice, and it was nearly lost in the vastness of the sky. Even the oak grove seemed small and low compared to the open stars.

Ari laid on one blanket and pulled her coat around her, securing the hood. She quickly realized the cold ground beneath was quickly seeping through her; and before Dane could claim the other blanket, she had the second throw wrapped firmly around her.

"Hey, where'd the other one go?" Dane nudged Ari with his toe, then realized her trickery. "You'd have me freeze out here, Ari. Scoot over."

She made just enough room on the edge of the blanket for Dane to lay out, stick straight. She automatically scooted closer to him, trying to glean whatever heat from him she could get. A flash of light dropped silently across the sky; before she could point to it, it was over.

"I saw it," Dane whispered, and she smiled. Somehow the enormity of the sky pulled her closer to him. By the time the edges of the horizon had lost the dusky redness of sundown, a bright swath of stellar lights banded from north to south. Though the silence between them was comfortable, Ari was half-tempted to try and verbalize what she felt for Dane. She thought it would be easy, since he was only lying next to her and not conjuring her very soul with his inescapable gaze. However, every time she tried to think of a way to start, it dissolved into a jumble of words in her head. Knowing she might not get another chance only added pressure and made speaking impossible. She started to say something; at that exact moment Dane also began to speak.

She giggled. "Sorry. You first." Any tension she'd been feeling dissipated with her laughter, but Dane's voice was low and serious.

"I just wanted you to know, if things don't go well at court, I appreciate everything you've done for me." He sounded dissatisfied and switched to his side, leaning on his elbow. His face was close to hers, and she could feel warm puffs of air as he breathed. She could also feel him looking intensely at her, so she turned his direction. His features were obscured by lack of light; all she could really see were glints of light reflecting off his eyes. His voice softened. "Ari..."

She waited an eternity for him to continue. It looked like he was trying to figure out what to say, just as she'd been doing.

"What?" she pleaded.

After minutes of silence, he smiled slightly, caught her head in the crook of his elbow, and settled back to gazing at the stars. She rolled over and sighed, resting on his folded arm. Her head was just touching his, and she wished that through osmosis his thoughts would float into hers so she wouldn't have to guess anymore.

Something about the night was electric and vibrant; the air no longer had the crisp dryness of winter, but smelled sweetly of new life and growth. Being so close to Dane, she was awash in his scent too, which was familiar and intoxicating, all at the same time. A ground-hugging breeze suddenly chilled them both, and Dane sat up suddenly. Before she realized her top blanket was gone, Dane had it wrapped around his shoulders.

"Hey!" Ari scolded. Dane held open the blanket.

"You're gonna to have to come here. This one's mine now." Even in the dark, she could see he was grinning. Ari got up and sat inside Dane's open arms, which he folded around her, then propped his chin on her shoulder. His cheek brushed against hers. She tried to ignore her flip-flopping stomach, or the chills that involuntarily ripped through her. "Still cold?" Dane asked, incredulously.

"No, I'm fine," she said quietly, realizing at his close proximity, she didn't have to speak above a whisper for him to hear. He held her just a little tighter, and she couldn't help but smile. She dropped her head back onto his shoulder, looking straight up at the stars. Strands of jazz drifted past whenever the breeze would shift. Ari closed her eyes and inhaled deeply. She wanted to root herself to this moment forever; without thinking, she snuggled in closer, until there was no space between them. She was so close, she could feel every breath that Dane took.

A white-hot streak burned across the sky, so bright that Ari startled. She felt Dane chuckle.

"I hope we get more nights like this," he breathed.

Ari wondered if he meant more crystal-clear, starry nights—or just nights when he'd be one house away.

"Hey, I have an idea," he said suddenly. He got up quickly and motioned for Ari to grab a blanket. "Follow me." He took her hand and started jogging through the oak grove. Normally Ari wasn't a fan of running through the oak grove at night, but with her hand in Dane's, it wasn't so intimidating. She glanced up at the sky through the tree crowns, then pulled on Dane's hand to slow him.

"Dane, look up," she whispered.

Away from the lights of either house, the stars pierced the surrounding darkness like hot blue pinpricks of light. She could hear Dane smiling. "I've got something better to show you," he said, and resumed jogging toward his house.

Once at his home, Dane bounded up the stairs. Ari had to take them two at a time to keep up. They rounded the corner at the top, and passed into his bedroom. He went to his wood-framed window and raised the bottom sash.

"You first," he grinned, motioning out the window.

"Wait, what?"

"I sit out on the roof once in sometimes. There's a nice little ledge outside. Once you get out there you'll see why," he explained.

"Uh—ok," Ari stammered, hesitating. "But you go first."

Dane shrugged and disappeared through the open window. Like in her own room, his alcove windows had a seat that made it fairly easy to get out. Ari followed, ignoring her debilitating fear of heights. She carefully picked her legs up and over the wooden windowsill. *This is nuts*, she thought as she stepped onto the steeply angled roof.

Dane caught one of her hands and helped her out. Ari caught her breath as she suddenly realized she was the highest point for miles—standing there, one hand held by Dane and one hand on the alcove roof—she could see forever. She grinned as she looked over the treetops and down Hadley Hill. To the southeast, she could see the hazy glow of lights above Rivers. To the south, she could see the roofline of her home. Beyond that, it was a three-hundred and sixty degree view of stars, rolling hills, and the glittering Elgin River in the distance.

"Dane, this is incredible!" she whispered. He was sitting below the window, and she glanced down at him, grinning. Then she gasped when she once again noticed the steep pitch of the roof.

"Hey, you'll be fine," Dane reassured her. "Look, if you rolled off this roof, you'd just land above our front porch," he said, pointing below them. Sure enough, the roof covering the porch came out below them at a low angle. Ari gave a small sigh of relief.

"Just enjoy the view. I won't let you fall," he whispered, and she detected a mischievous grin.

Carefully, she sat down on the sandpaper-y roof shingles. At least they had a lot of grip to them, she thought. Dane sidled up to her and threw the blanket over her shoulders.

"Before I discovered the underground circle, I would come up here a lot to get away from Rhoda," he said quietly. "It was great because I'd get on top of the window alcove and she wouldn't even think to look out the window for me. It was like I'd disappeared. Some nights I'd stay up here for hours, but I didn't mind. Sometimes I still come up here. I can see your roofline—" he stopped short.

Ari waited for him to finish his thought, but he simply turned to face her. "I'm glad I'm not alone on this hill anymore, Ari. You came along and changed everything."

She beamed and reached around him with her arms. It was an awkwardly-angled hug, as she was literally gripping the roof with her feet, but he pulled her in close and stayed that way. Her heart flip-flopped again. She listened as breezes rustled the oak grove; a lone owl started hooting in a faraway tree. She could feel Dane's warmth, and she wanted to say something to return his affection, but words wouldn't form. The comfortable, electric silence between them was perfect.

*   *   *

Four more days stood between Ari and spring break; but it wasn't until Riley mentioned it that Ari realized how close it was. The day of Dane's court date loomed before all else; and past that, her thoughts hadn't reached.

She knew Dane wouldn't be at school after lunch, since the hearing was right in the middle of the day, though it didn't keep her from looking for him between classes, out of sheer habit. By Spanish class, her gaze kept drifting to his seat, which seemed to have been empty more often than not in the past term. Her hand was over the cell phone in her pocket, waiting for the telltale vibration of an incoming call. She assumed he would let her know what had happened, though fearful thoughts of an undesirable outcome had been swirling in her mind all day.

Riley saw her distant detachment as Ari sorted through the books in her locker after school. "When will he know?" Riley asked.

"I assume today," she mumbled, zipping up her bag.

"Well, come over and wait at my house," Riley offered, and Ari was grateful. The nervousness she'd felt throughout the day had begun to wear on her stomach, and she was weary from concern.

Riley's stately Victorian house was still and quiet upon their arrival. She surveyed the contents of the refrigerator as Ari lounged on a barstool at counter divider. "Anything good in there?"

Riley pulled out a jar of pickles, some bread, and chips. "How about a pickle sandwich?"

Ari giggled and waved her hand to pass, though she wasn't above sneaking some chips as Riley assembled her odd snack creation.

"So what are we doing for spring break?" Riley said, between bites. "I'm sticking around and I'll be sad if there isn't anything to do for a whole week."

"I'm not doing anything, as far as I know. I don't even think my parents realize it's next week," Ari assumed. She wondered if it would be her first week without Dane, then quickly shut away the thought. *There's no way the judge would rule in his dad's favor*, she considered. *He has to know Dane's better off with his mom—who couldn't see that?*

"You're worried about Dane leaving," Riley assessed, jolting Ari from her reasoning.

"Am I that transparent?" she sighed. "Yeah, I am. I guess I don't want to admit how much I need him." Even as she said it, Ari was shocked at her admission.

"Have you told him that?"

"No! Of course not," Ari countered, a little horrified. "I don't want him to know how...*dependent* on him I am. It's silly. I don't want him to think I'm needy." She pulled her silent cell phone from her pocket, checking for the hundredth time, only to see no calls had been received. "It wouldn't make a difference anyway. I'm sure I'll find out soon enough what happened."

Two hours passed, with otherwise light conversation over homework. The afternoon was waning when Ari rode away from Riley's, headed toward Dane's father's house, on the way to her own. When she rounded the corner of his street, her mind did a double take. She slowed to a stop. The next image unfolded in slow motion.

Mr. Hadley's old truck wasn't in its usual place in the driveway. Instead, it was parked alongside the sidewalk, the bed filled to the top and covered with a tarp, which was lashed to the sides. In the driveway was a U-haul, its ramp down. Everything was still for a moment, and Ari counted the houses. Two-story, blue, peeling paint. Not a neighbor's house. *Dane's dad's house.* And Dane, who had appeared from inside the house, was hauling a dolly stacked with boxes.

Ari's stomach dropped; she could feel herself tingling down to her feet. Her balance wavered and she only stayed upright because of the bicycle propped underneath her. She watched Dane reappear from the truck without boxes; his father then appeared from the house with more boxes. Suddenly breathing became difficult and Ari struggled, trying to stay silent despite an involuntary gasp.

chapter fifteen

She wheeled the bike around and pedaled furiously, across town and out the country road, up the gravel hill. She dumped her bike next to the house and sprinted through the backyard, taking the path to the pool. Newly sprouted blackberry vines ripped at her as she twisted and dodged down the cobbles. Streams of tears ran unhindered down her cheeks, burning hot, then turning cold in the evening air. At the black iron gate, she stopped, but only long enough to pull its key from her pocket. She jammed it into the lock and pushed the gate open so hard that the gate clanked against the fence, reverberating along its length.

Refusal swept through Ari's mind. The cold, curved concrete top of Nadia's grave was the first place Ari found to stop herself. *Why didn't he tell me?* New tears welled in Ari's eyes as hurt mixed with sadness as she imagined a new reality. Several gasps brought new oxygen to her lungs, and she laid back on the rough grave. She closed her eyes, breathed in the sweet air, and tried to still her mind from the racing thoughts.

When her eyes opened, she realized the sky was darkening to an azure-blue, and the only feeling stronger than her sadness was an aversion to being in the gated graveyard. Slowly she made her way back to the safety of her backyard.

The comforting glow of orange-lit windows beckoned her inside the house, though she thoroughly wiped at her wet face with a sweatshirt sleeve before entering. Her mom was stirring away at dinner, facing away from Ari. Withholding sniffles, Ari slipped through the kitchen. She made it to her room before dissolving into tears again.

Not bothering to turn on the lights, Ari found the window seat. Stars were beginning to pierce through a layer of haze in the early spring sky. Just as her face was beginning to dry, there was a gentle knock on her door.

"Come in," she said, as even-toned as possible.

Her mom poked her head in the dark room. "Dinner's ready. Why's it so dark in here?"

"Watching the stars."

Something in Ari's voice must've cracked, because her mom stepped inside. "What's wrong?"

Her lip trembled, and a cascade of emotion overwhelmed her before she could put up a strong front. *I wish I was more like him,* she thought quickly. Between sniffs, she tried explaining.

"Dane's moving away. I saw him loading things into a U-haul after school." She again wiped her face with sleeve-covered hands. Her mom reached out and engulfed her in a hug.

"I'm so sorry, honey. Did he say when they're leaving?"

Ari shook her buried head. "He didn't say anything at all. I just saw him loading the truck..." Her voice trailed. "I'm not hungry for dinner."

Her mom nodded, and sympathetically patted Ari's back. "Come down when you're ready." Her mom apologized again, then left, closing the door behind her. In the dark, quiet room, Ari found the picture Riley had taken at the dance, and her stomach started to twist all over again.

*   *   *

The plate was unsteady in Ari's hands, balancing precariously on the rim of her drinking glass. It was pitch black as she made her way through the pasture and into the oak grove, but she didn't care. She had stayed in her room until the tears had stopped; when her eyes were no longer puffy and red, she'd descended to the dining room. Her mom had lovingly reserved a cellophane-wrapped plate in the refrigerator; it was still slightly warm when Ari hit the reheat button on the microwave. The underground room was her destination, despite the cold, dark night, and the relative lateness of the hour.

The lid opened silently; the inky darkness of the room below gave Ari pause, even after scanning the room with her flashlight. The emptiness brought a fresh flood of tears. She slipped down the steps and quickly closed the circle, sinking into the iciness. A single candle sputtered to life at the touch of a match, illuminating only the corner where Ari sat.

She slowly picked at dinner; the lasagna her mom had made looked as wonderful as always, but after only a few bites, unceasing tears interfered with eating. She pushed the plate to the side and pulled her arms about her, slouching into the wall of the earthen room.

The cold was welcome, numbing. Ari wished the sharp chill would seep into her tears and freeze them, but nothing could stop the sobs. Whooshing air caused her to startle. She realized all at once that in her sadness, she'd forgotten to lock the hatch behind her. Her heart surged with adrenaline until a familiar face appeared in the gaping black void.

"Ari?"

Dane furrowed his brow upon seeing her wet cheeks and puffy eyes, and a look of sorrow and compassion both washed over his face, and he descended into the dimly lit corner. Ari didn't know what to say or do; a single swipe to her tears with her sleeve didn't erase the telltale signs of hours of crying. It took every ounce of willpower for Ari to withhold more sobs that were building, all at the sight of Dane.

"What are you doing here?" she rasped, completely surprised. Dane started to say something, but Ari cut him off. "I know you don't need me, Dane, not with how strong and independent you are." The words were coming out faster than she wanted, but it was too late to stop. "But you need to know that no matter where you go, or what happens from now on, I won't give up hope that things will turn out okay for you and your dad. I just want the best for you. And...I can't imagine what it will be like without you." The words stung as they came out. She took a deep breath, but to her horror, she started crying again.

He pulled her to him and used his sweatshirt sleeve to wipe away at her face. "Ari, what do you mean, 'without me?' "

"The moving truck. I saw you today, moving things from your dad's house. Were you going to tell me goodbye, even?"

Dane's face was intense; processing. Suddenly he gasped. "Oh, no, Ari...no...you thought we were moving away?"

This time Ari shook her head. "What, you're not?"

A wide smile replaced Dane's confusion. "I guess I should've called you right after court. It was a complete surprise—Dad withdrew his custody challenge. He told the judge that after I was hospitalized, he realized a few things: he thought I was better off with my mom and sister. He realized he'd rather live nearby with the whole family in the same town than just him and I far away. He saw I wasn't happy about moving away. So..." Dane smoothed out Ari's hair, and gently touched her cheek, "... you saw me moving his things into a van, because he's going to live in a two-bedroom apartment in town, instead of that big house that he won't need."

Ari was stunned and overwhelmed; her mind was still processing the sudden change of events. Dane looked apologetically at her. "I was going to surprise you by being all moved back into mom's house by tomorrow morning," he explained, "but I guess my plan kind of backfired. I had no idea you'd see the moving truck."

Finally Ari sighed, releasing all tension that had knotted her stomach and muscles. A small smile appeared. "You're not moving away..." was all she could manage, and Dane shook his head, a reaffirming *no*.

*   *   *

The U-haul *beep beep beeped*, backing away from Dane's mom's house, and a brown haze of dust followed it down Hadley Lane.

Sunshine streamed through tree branches, creating rays of light along the sun-warmed gravel. Dane's dad waved a hand out of the window as the truck disappeared around the corner; Ari hefted one of three boxes into her arms.

"You didn't take that much stuff over there to begin with," she observed, as he piled the other two boxes into his own arms.

"I hoped I wouldn't be over there for very long."

Ari watched her footing as she ascended the porch steps. "Me too," she smiled.

Mrs. Hadley passed them, with Molly close behind. Mrs. Hadley was carrying a bag of soil; Molly was holding an oversized floppy straw hat on her head while toting a bucket full of garden tools.

"You two have fun unpacking," his mother mused. "Your sis and I are going to start sprucing up the garden, for our first spring here." Mrs. Hadley paused and gave Dane a kiss on the cheek, which caused Ari to giggle and Dane to blush.

Once in his room, Dane's way of unpacking was methodical. Ari watched, amused, as he pulled each item from the box, neatly smoothed it, and hung it in the proper area of his closet. Dane turned to see Ari observing with rapt attention.

"What?" he demanded.

"Oh, nothing," Ari smiled, looking around the rest of his room, which was a typical boy room. An unmade bed was the focal point to an unorganized disarray of objects. But his closet, as she'd never noticed before, was immaculate. "Why are you so tidy when it comes to your clothes? See, this is my method—" she proceeded to upturn the box she'd carried, spilling its contents on his bed. "Much easier." She picked up a shirt and flung it to Dane, and something fluttered violently from the folds of the shirt and landed on the floor. She bent down to retrieve it.

A white business-size envelope was lying next to her foot. *Ari* was scribed in Dane's neat all-caps handwriting. She picked it up, about to open it, when Dane bounded across the room in a single leap, trying to snatch the envelope.

Ari deftly jumped to the side and flattened against the wall. "Whoa! What's this? It's got my name on it."

Dane looked at her, pleading with his eyes. She held the envelope behind her back, pinned out of reach.

"I, uh, need that back." He was asking, but not begging. A slow, wicked smile played on Ari's lips.

"Why?"

"Because..." He was grasping for an answer, a good one. His eyes were gleaming, almost up for Ari's game. Whatever was in the envelope wasn't *that* important, his eyes revealed. He was inches from Ari, his hand on the wall next to her. Ari ducked under his arm and bounded down the stairs. She could hear him hiss her name under his breath, and she laughed, bolting through the front door.

The trail through the oak grove was guarded by new, green briars, but Ari twisted, giggling, through them. She could hear him sprinting after her, but rounding the earthen pool, she switched trails to the gated graveyard. His footfalls were softer, farther now, but he was still hollering her name, somewhere between the trees. With a fast twist, the iron key popped the gate open, and for the second time in two days, she found herself bounding into the middle of the gated trees. But what she had failed to see in the darkness of the prior night caused her to stop, gasp, and completely forget about the envelope with her name on it.

chapter sixteen

Dane came to a sudden stop beside Ari.

The trees, once thought by Ari and Dane to be oak trees in the naked bareness of winter, were alive with delicate pink blossoms. Three trees deep, they were arranged in a crown-like encirclement around the fountain. It was the sound—a palpable hum—which brought Ari and Dane to respective halts.

Thousands of honeybees hovered feet above Ari's and Dane's heads. A slow, steady drone penetrated the earth, the trees, the air, as the little creatures alighted on a blossom, did their work, and flew a short jump to the next blossom. Oblivious to anything aside from pollen-gathering, the bees filled every branch. Sunlight streamed through the heavy-laden trees, leafless in pink splendor.

"Don't move," Dane whispered, and barely nodded towards one particular tree trunk. "I think that's a hive right there."

Ari glanced at a nearby trunk. Streams of bees, like lanes of traffic, were coming and going from an open knot. A sudden conclusion dawned on Ari instantly, and she felt her eyes welling.

"Dane, this is it. This *was* her favorite spot."

Dane looked at Ari, his jade-and-hazel eyes questioning.

"Nadia. This was where she kept her beehives. The cherry trees here probably were pollinated by her bees, just like this. It's amazing." She was almost whispering. *I should be terrified*, she thought. The memory of the hot sharpness of single bee sting when she was a child was enough to cause her to wear shoes outside when most children went barefoot all summer long. But the stunning beauty of it all overpowered any fear. A wide smile of wonderment spread across her face. "Unbelievable."

They both gazed straight up, through the cotton-candy branches that were moving alive, to the sunlit-bright sky of early spring. Not only were the trees in fervent bloom; life on the ground had taken over. Even Nadia's and Grekov's graves were overtaken by heart-shaped morning glory leaves. With blackberry vines removed, wild roses had begun to reclaim the iron bars, transforming it into a living fence.

"She probably had the gate and fence put around the trees and hives to keep her kids from getting stung." Dane said quietly while turning in a slow circle. "I bet her beekeeping society came here sometimes, too. That's why the key was in the Golden Hive Society box." He smiled. "I can see why this was her favorite spot."

Ari squinted in the sun and looked back at Dane. "Me too."

She realized she was still holding the envelope she'd spirited away from his room. She turned to him and pleaded. "Can I read this now? Unless it's for someone else named Ari…"

Dane sighed nervously. "Sure, go ahead. I wrote it before the court date, and I was going to give it to you before I moved, if that's how things had ended up." He looked away shyly.

Ari perched herself on the end of Nadia's grave, and Dane sat back-to-back with her. Ari silently opened the carefully creased letter:

Ari,

If you're reading this, I have to apologize. I wish things had gone differently in court, and you know I never wanted to move away. I'm mostly sorry, though, that we won't be able to have another summer together, or another dance, or evenings doing homework together in the underground room.

Ari, I'll never understand why you cared for me so much, especially last summer, when you barely even knew me, but went out of your way to help me find my family. You're fearless, and tough, and I love that about you. I'll never forget it.

Ari blushed; she was glad Dane wasn't watching her read.

I can't promise I'll be back anytime soon, but I can promise that it will be hard to find a friend like you. You're uncomplicated, and adventurous, and we had so much fun together. Never change, beautiful Ari. You're perfect just as you are.

-Dane

She read it again, and then once more, making sure that what she read was really on the page. Her cheeks burned to the tips of her ears. She was quiet for so long that Dane turned around to make sure she was still there.

"Are you ok?" he asked.

"Yes, of course." She finally turned around and looked at him deeply, trying to reconcile the words on the page with the person they came from. "This—what you wrote—thank you," she stammered, trying to come up with words that could reveal the depth of her feelings for Dane. Nothing she thought of could come close, but she managed, "This is the kindest thing anyone has ever said to me."

A sudden gust of wind shook a million cherry petals loose, and they floated like confetti through the air. Ari couldn't stop smiling, and Dane reached out and brushed the petals from her hair.

*   *   *

It was like a block party, except the Hadleys and the Cartwrights were the only families celebrating, and instead of having a city block, they had an entire hill to themselves. On the first day of spring break, the weather hadn't disappointed. Dinner was served at the picnic table just as the sun hid behind the trees to the west.

White globe lights intermingled with a newly-blooming wisteria on Mrs. Hadley's front porch. The picnic table, in the Hadley's front yard, was stacked with food from both houses, and white tealights in canning jars cast a warm glow over the families. Lily and Molly giggled at the end of the table, picking out watermelon seeds and collecting them between their plates; Ari and Dane were next to them, passing around a dish of corn. Mrs. Hadley was discussing gardening with Ari's mom, and her dad flipped the last of the burger patties on the grill.

Dane's father was the only person not in attendance, though Dane assured Ari that it was because of moving, not avoidance, that he wasn't there.

After dessert, Ari's dad lit up a pipe and sat with the mothers on the Hadley's front porch. The girls had gone inside to play in Molly's room, and Ari and Dane started off into the oak grove, with no particular destination in mind.

"We could play hide and seek in the woods," Dane teased, and Ari made a face.

"That sounds safe," she smirked. "Nothing like running through low-hanging branches and blackberry bushes. How about having a cup of coffee at your house?"

"No way. Mom's coffee is too strong. I pass. How about we go climb some cherry trees?"

She couldn't tell if he was joking or not, but they made their way to the fenced cherry orchard anyway. Darkness hid the branches, but a rising full moon in the east reflected off the blossoms, creating an eerily beautiful, pale glow. No bees could be heard now; only an occasional cricket sounded off.

"Be sure we don't climb the one with the beehive," Ari reminded, assuming they would indeed try climbing one of the trees.

"Good call." Dane pointed to the tree with the knot. "I think it was that one." He found another tree with low, thick branches. "How about this one?"

Ari nodded, and jumped up, easily reaching the lowest branch. She tried swinging her legs up, but the awkward angle of the next highest branch made it nearly impossible to reach with her legs. Dane stood with his arms crossed, watching her progression, smiling slightly.

"You're not going to help me, are you?" Ari laughed, realizing her struggle made for good entertainment. Dane finally walked over, caught Ari's legs, and hoisted her to the higher branch. Once she was able to stand securely, Dane easily swung himself up as well.

Ari proceeded to climb two more branches higher. The low angle made it fairly easy to remain standing. Dane followed. Eventually they were both on the same branch, nearly in the center of the tree. Blossoms obscured their view of almost anything, save other branches with blossoms.

"It's like being in a huge cloud," Ari observed, looking back at Dane. He was standing next to her, his arm behind her back, spanning the distance between two supporting branches with his reach. Ari wobbled a bit as the darkness and uneven angle of the branches made for tricky footing.

"Need some help balancing?" Dane chuckled, and wrapped his arm around her shoulder, still grasping the supporting branch. *It doesn't get any better than this*, Ari thought. She noticed Dane was grinning wide; without thinking, she suddenly found herself moving toward him. She saw her hand pull his face downward toward her own. Dane froze and she felt his entire body tense. *What are you doing?* her thoughts raced. Even in the darkness, she could feel the intensity of his gaze. His face was an inch from her own. She could feel his breath on her lips. Ari ignored the tremors in her hands and the inability to pull in a full breath; she was well-practiced at being lightheaded in his presence. She couldn't take her eyes off of his.

"Ari!" A voice hollered, echoing in the distance. "Dane! Dessert is ready!" Her dad's voice carried across the hill, diffused by the oak grove. Ari gasped audibly, as if she had been awoken from a spell. Dane hadn't backed away from her, and she hadn't moved either. She could still feel him, tensed, his arm around her neck and shoulder. She was still struggling to pull in a full breath without shaking.

"We should go," she finally whispered, unmoving. Dane was still looking at her with a kind of intensity she'd never seen before. After an eternal moment, Dane nodded.

"Yeah, they're waiting for us," he said softly. He deftly jumped down from the tree and waited for Ari at the bottom, holding out his hands for her. She accepted his help and he easily caught her as she shimmied down from the lowest branch. It always amazed her that, despite his leanness, he had incredible strength. When her feet reached the ground, she noticed he paused for a second longer than she expected, his hands still around her waist...then he took her hand.

They jogged through the iron gate, around the silent earthen pool, joined the path by the underground room, and then burst out into the open clearing of pasture behind Ari's house.

The strands of garden lights that Ari's mom had hung were gently swaying in the evening breeze. The moon was now high in the sky, and the last wisps of sunset light were fading. Lily and Molly were gathering cupcakes from the dessert table, and the adults were pouring drinks.

Ari chose a spot at the table next to Lily, and to Ari's surprise, Dane sat next to her. Once everyone was seated, Dane cleared his throat and stood up.

"I, um, I'd like to say something real quick," he started. Ari looked up at him, surprised. The adults quieted their conversation.

"I want to thank the Cartwrights for all your help in, well, changing my situation. Last year at this time, I was in a really bad place. Ari," he smiled and glanced downward at her, "you came here, with your family, and changed what I thought to be an impossible situation. I owe everything to you guys." He cleared his throat again and sat down.

"Dane, we were more than happy to help," her dad replied. "Getting to know you and your family has made a world of difference for our family, too," he said. "This move wasn't easy for any of us, especially for Ari, but now we have a beautiful place to call home and we know some of its amazing history." The other adults nodded in agreement, and easy conversation started up again. The parents started discussing the underground treasure, when Dane leaned over and spoke in Ari's ear.

"You made all the difference, Ari. You're fearless and brave and I love you for that," he whispered.

Ari stopped chewing her cupcake and, wide-eyed, looked straight at Dane. His gaze was steady and unwavering. He had absolutely meant every word that he had just said.

Read on for an exclusive excerpt from the compelling follow-up to The Incredible Secrets of Hadley Hill:

chapter one

Ari Cartwright rubbed her eyes as sunlight streamed into her room. She wasn't ready to get up, but a singular thought caused her to open her eyes.

I almost kissed him last night.

In a half-awake daze she recalled the past night: being high among the frothy moonlit cherry blossoms, standing on a tree branch, with Dane's arm around her. Unexpectedly, she'd reached up and almost kissed him. She started getting butterflies in her stomach as she replayed it in her head. Ari certainly hadn't planned to try and kiss him that night. Although she'd daydreamed about it plenty, she had never actually intended to act on it. Soon their parents could be heard calling for them through the night: dessert was ready, and they'd jogged out of the cherry orchard, past the silent earthen pool, and through the darkened oak grove back to the backyard potluck the families were having together.

Just as unexpectedly, in the warm glow of the garden lights, Dane had leaned over and whispered to her: *you're fearless and brave and I love you for that.*

His words had sent electricity and warmth through her body; she could barely believe what he had confessed. Yet the look in his eyes showed that he had meant every word.

She loved his smile and his honesty. He was easily one of her best friends and the person she enjoyed spending time with the most. What he had said to her seemed to suggest that he cared for her as well. Ari smiled at the thought, but now just thinking of him tied her up in nervous knots.

Ari sat up in bed. She thought she heard her seven-year old little sister Lily giggling outside her bedroom door. It wasn't unusual for Lily to jump in bed with Ari in the wee hours of the morning, either to snuggle or to tickle Ari. But this morning, she thought other voices were with Lily's. To her surprise, there was a quiet knock on the door before her entire family peeked into her room.

chapter two

"Happy birthday, Aribelle!" Lily was carefully holding a single cupcake, and Ari's mom and dad were carrying a small but beautifully wrapped box.

Ari smiled in total surprise. It had completely escaped her that today was her sixteenth birthday.

"Open it! Open it!" On Ari's lap, Lily placed the cupcake and a box. Ari unwrapped the box to find some nail polish, sugar scrub, and lotions.

"Lily, you're so sweet! You know just what I like," she said, squeezing her little sister hard enough to make Lily squeal. The younger Cartwright giggled and pulled on her mom's hand.

"Now *you* guys! Give her the box!"

Ari's mom handed the golden-glittered box to Ari, and she carefully untied the ribbon and opened the box. Inside was a gift card to the only spa in Rivers.

"We thought you might like to take Riley to have a spa day, you know, have some girl time," her mom said, smiling. "My first baby girl is growing up," she added quietly.

Ari blushed. "Thank you, guys—this is awesome! I'll give Riley a call and see if she can go."

"Oh, and Aribelle, we need to schedule some driving lessons," her dad reminded her. "We probably should've started that a year ago, but…"

Technically, Ari could've gotten her permit a year ago, but it was almost exactly a year prior that her family had learned they would be moving. Her dad's change in employment had uprooted them all from San Francisco, the home they had known and loved for Ari's entire life, and had brought them here: to a small rural town hundreds of miles away, and so completely opposite everything she had ever known.

Against all odds, this place, with its history and beauty, had grown on Ari. And it was perhaps because of Dane that she had been able to make the transition in the first place.

Ari thanked her family again and reached for her phone. She had more than a spa day to tell Riley about.

* * *

Ari and Riley walked their bikes along the sidewalk. The early May afternoon was sunny, but had no heat in it. Signs of spring's arrival were evident everywhere: tulip trees planted in downtown Rivers were bursting open, bright green grass was growing thin and tall, and there was a change in the air.

"Alright, hon, what's going on?" Riley pushed her glasses back up onto her nose and stared her friend down. "You said on the phone you had something crazy to tell me. Well...spill it!" Riley smiled her fantastic grin.

Ari pulled her bike over to the edge of the sidewalk and stopped. "I almost kissed him in the cherry orchard last night!" she whispered.

"Dane?" Riley whispered back. "You *almost* kissed him?"

Ari nodded.

"But what happened? Why didn't you?"

"Dad started calling for us because dessert was ready. We went back to my backyard and Dane got up and thanked my parents—and me—for helping him change his situation. Then—"Ari lowered her voice, "—once the parents were having dessert and chatting with each other, he

263

leaned over and told me that the loved me for being fearless and brave." She paused and looked at Riley.

Riley smiled. "Whoa, Ari. That's just about the best compliment I have ever heard. He's serious about how much he cares for you," she grinned madly.

"I think he was being sincere, Riley. I think he might really, actually like me as much as I like him," Ari concluded. Riley shook her head in amazement.

"Well, of course he does. You guys are attached at the hip—like best friends. I don't know him that well, but I've never seen him spend as much time with anyone as he does with you!"

Riley pushed her beach cruiser next to Ari's, and continued. "You guys have had some incredible adventures together in the last ten months. You're closer than most best friends or couples I know, but in a different way. You guys work together really well," she concluded.

They'd reached the spa and parked their bikes. After checking in, they were guided to the pedicure chairs. Ari leaned back in hers and closed her eyes.

"We *do* work together well. When we had a problem to solve, or history to figure out, we got it done." She opened her eyes and turned to Riley. "I just wish I knew if he likes me as much as I like him," Ari sighed.

* * *

The makeover during their spa day had been Ari's favorite part. She wasn't confident in her own abilities with makeup, at least, not compared with Riley's level of skill, so any help she could get was appreciated. The stylist who had done Ari's makeup had guessed correctly that Ari was an unfussy, active girl who liked a natural look. Ari took the hand mirror and liked what she saw: her barely-there freckles were still visible, but her brown eyes had been emphasized with a hint of black eyeliner, her brows had been cleaned up, and a natural lip stain had been applied. Her long, straight brown hair had grown past her shoulders since her last haircut at the beginning of the school year, and she'd had it trimmed up, with long straight bangs added in.

"Happy birthday, by the way," Riley leaned over, looking into the mirror with Ari. "You look fantastic. Not that you don't all the time," she smiled, "but you look carefree today. This past ten months has had some rough spots for you, and for once, you don't have anything to worry about," Riley concluded. Ari had to agree: she had no worries at the moment, and it felt fantastic.

Watch for the 2018 sequel release by following our Facebook page: https://www.facebook.com/OwlRoomPress/